FORBIDDEN FRUIT

Diane L. Kowalyshyn

Forbidden Fruit

Copyright © 2025 by Diane L. Kowalyshyn

Book Cover by *Christine d'Abo*

First edition June 2025

Trade Paperback ISBN 978-1-7779747-4-9

Digital ISBN 978-1-7779747-5-6

Dedication

I would like to thank my wonderful husband who is forever promoting me and my books.
I love you.

Chapter 1

Dr. Aliesa Atworth's day went from bad to deplorable.

At the end of the street, emergency vehicles cocooned the entrance of the Arts and Sciences building. Lights flashed. Barricades kept a crowd of spectators at a safe distance. The police re-routed traffic. Emergency personnel rushed in and out of the Kern building.

Shit.

Not again.

Earlier this month, a minor explosion occurred in the lab adjacent to hers and required emergency intervention. A volatile substance ignited and noxious fumes had to be dispelled. A nuisance. It meant she would be shut out of her building for the rest of the day.

There were protocols in these situations. And since she didn't want to annoy the people in charge, she approached a junior officer directing the traffic. "Excuse me," she said. "My lab is on the second floor. I'm wondering when I might be able to go and retrieve some of my files."

"The entire building is closed," the officer said.

"I understand, but surely exceptions can be made."

The young recruit's eyes glazed over. "What's your name?"

"It's Dr. Aliesa Atworth."

The expression on the young female officer's face registered shock, then confusion. She must be fresh out of the academy and this disaster her first emergency situation. Aliesa smiled and went to side step her.

"Hold on, you can't go in there." The policewoman placed her hand on Aliesa's shoulder.

"But I need to get inside. I have important files in there."

"Wait here," the cop said. She walked over to an unmarked car and the officer sitting in the front seat.

This woman was as green as new grass. She would learn her lesson the hard way. Badgering her boss wouldn't earn her any brownie points. Aliesa didn't care one way or the other, she wanted her damned files. Any second the detective would rip a strip off the junior officer—tell the woman to handle it, but to Aliesa's utter surprise he leaned around the woman to see her.

He strode over to where she stood. "Are you Dr. Aliesa Atworth?" he asked.

"Yes," she said, reading his badge and ID. "Is there something wrong, Detective Lowry?"

"May I see your identification?"

Aliesa didn't have her purse with her. She'd left it in her locker in the faculty lounge. "Sure thing. If you'd escort me to my locker, I'll be happy to confirm my identity."

The detective stepped aside and waved her through the barricade. The two of them entered the deserted building and headed for the stairs.

"Did Dr. Tennaka set fire to his test sample again?"

The detective took two stairs at a time. She hurried to keep the same pace. She paused on the landing to catch her breath. "I'm guessing, no. The air would be more acrid."

Detective Lowry stood at the top of the staircase and waited for her. "What do you do here?"

"Who me?" she asked. She hated telling people about her work. Eyes glazed over in a matter of moments.

"Everyone in this building is working on one kind of project or another."

Aliesa nodded. "I'm doing stem cell research." The limited explanation generally satisfied the layman.

"Oh. I see. Stem cell research is pretty controversial right now, isn't it?"

"There is a moral issue when it comes to using fetal stem cells. I chose to avoid the ethical debate by utilizing stem cells derived from an alternative source."

The detective's eyes widened. "Do you have any enemies, Dr. Atworth?"

"What?" He'd caught her off guard with such an ominous question. Across the hall, yellow police tape cordoned off her lab and security stood outside the door.

"That's my room," Aliesa said. A sick feeling settled in the pit of her stomach. Her precious study may have been compromised. Great. Just great. Grayson would whine even louder if she needed to re-run the entire sample. She launched herself toward the door.

Lowry grabbed her arm and brought her to a halt. "Your identification?"

"Right," she said. A few more minutes wouldn't make

any difference. A contaminated sample would still be contaminated in another ten minutes. She led the detective across the hall in the other direction and into the staff room. He followed her, even when she walked inside the female bathroom. "Guess it's a good thing I don't have to...you know...go."

"Feel free," he said. "I can wait."

Yeah, right. Aliesa couldn't bring herself to make eye contact with the dark-haired detective. She sure as hell wasn't about to let him listen to her urinate. "I'm fine, thanks." She walked over to the lockers and opened the combination lock. She withdrew her purse, wallet, and ID.

Lowry examined the BU photo card.

"Now, will you please tell me what's going on?"

"Did anyone else have access to your lab?" the detective asked.

"Only my lab assistant," Aliesa said. "But she went home earlier today."

Something flashed in the detective's eyes—a sliver of regret? He led her back out into the hall. At the opposite end of the corridor, she noticed a student, wearing earbuds, exiting another classroom.

"What the hell?" The detective turned and hurried to intercept the oblivious student.

She saw her opportunity and dashed toward the guard standing sentinel at her door. When she approached, the man did the oddest thing—he stepped aside. She tore through the tape and barreled inside.

Time shattered.

Shards of glass, beakers, and test tubes, glistened on the floor like quartz crystals crunching beneath her feet. Every drawer had been pulled and overturned, the contents scattered. Her entire body shook with the cold vengeance surrounding her. Liquid preservatives and lab chemicals flooded the floor, assailing her nostrils with an ammonia-like smell. The pungent odors made her eyes water. A metallic tang hung in the air from the sticky dark liquid on the floor.

She turned and noticed a man standing between the workstations. He wore a black jacket with the word coroner stamped across the back. When he leaned to reach for something, she saw what he'd been examining.

Her knees buckled and bile lurched into her throat.

"No," she swallowed and wailed like a wounded animal.

"God dammit." Detective Lowry grabbed her arm.

"The guard," she stammered.

"What guard? Dr. Atworth, you're contaminating an active crime scene." He guided her through the wreckage and into the vacant hall.

Lowry was right, there was no guard. He snapped his fingers in her face, which momentarily broke her trance. "Do you know the identity of the victim?"

Torn, mangled flesh—lifeless, tortured eyes—an authentic kabuki death mask. "She left early...how? She was my best friend. It's my lab assistant, Evelyne Mathews." Aliesa leaned over and hurled into the nearest trash bin.

She steadied herself against the cool painted brick wall and slid onto the tiled floor in a black haze.

Chapter 2

E lliot Vance barely made it inside the faculty lounge before he heard Lowry running from the far end of the hall toward the lab. Van deliberately stepped aside so Dr. Atworth could see the consequences of trying to slice a piece of the cartel's pie—he wanted her to see up close and personal how they handled their competition.

He'd been the first to arrive on the scene. He called it in. Based on his years of experience, this crime wasn't even cold—the perps had been gone a half-hour tops. He'd swiped a jacket out of the backseat of one of the cruisers on the street and went to stand at the lab door. He knew she'd come and when she did he wanted to be there to figure out his next move.

He'd done his research. A huge mistake had been made. All of which really pissed him off. Distributing drugs to college students constituted a huge conflict of interest for him. A vision of his kid sister flashed into his head when he'd stalked across the hall and into the faculty lounge.

In the men's room, he splashed cold water on his face—his tired eyes had seen too much death. He'd been riding an emotional tidal wave for the past forty-eight hours on route from Trujillo, Peru. But this wave, in the whole scheme of things, was nothing more than another aftershock, a by-product of the tsunami which seized control of his life not quite a year ago. Trauma so great it shattered his career with the DEA and forced him into this more personal and private war—shit that happened when God looked the wrong way.

The outer door to the lounge swung open and hit the doorstop with a thud. He crept to the door and cracked it so he could see and hear the commotion in the lounge.

Aliesa roused as the detective placed her on the couch. She winced when the ME waved the broken ampoule of smelling salts beneath her nose. Ammonia. Her first coherent thought came in the form of a wish. She prayed she'd been horribly mistaken. Only the coppery stench of blood from the soles of her shoes brought reality crashing back.

Her stomach revolted again.

What was up with that? She'd been working with blood samples for years, but, suddenly, the very sight and smell had her repeatedly running to upchuck, this time in the bathroom sink.

And she made it just in time.

She cupped her hand and slurped water, swished it around her mouth, and spit it out in the sink. She spied her reflection and noticed Detective Lowry standing right behind her.

"Are you okay?" he asked.

She nodded. "Where's the ME?"

"He went back to the lab to finish."

Aliesa thought about what the coroner would be doing. First he'd take the liver temperature and then he'd search for ligature marks. "Who would do such a thing?" Aliesa's mind numbed and her eyes burned. "Evelyne was a good person. She always treated me as if the world was out of step and I was normal."

Aliesa remembered the scene inside her lab. Smashed glass, test tubes, pipettes, and beakers were strewn across the counters and floor. The supply cupboards had been emptied. The entire sample of cultured stem cells had been dumped on the floor creating another biohazard. There was nothing left.

As much as she wanted to, she couldn't bring herself to cry. Not for her best friend, and not for her precious test samples.

Hell, she still hadn't shed a tear over her father's murder or her mother's passing. There was something really wrong with her. Some flaw prohibiting her from crying for the people she'd loved and lost.

"You need to come to the station. I have some questions."

Mutely, Aliesa nodded and walked toward the door. She barely had the energy to put one foot in front of the other.

Then she remembered. "I need my meds."

"If it was inside the lab I doubt it survived," the detective said. "What kind of medication is it?"

"Heart medication." A stretch. The injection would impact many different organs—heart, liver, muscle, nerve, and skin. "It's not in the lab. I keep it in my office at the back of the room."

"Where?"

"In an insulated lunch bag, inside the mini-fridge."

The detective told her to stay put and he crossed the hall and disappeared behind the crime scene tape. Moments later, he returned.

Before he handed over the sac, he unzipped it and sifted through the contents. Aliesa collected her purse and jacket from her locker and they drove to police headquarters where he deposited her in one of the station's interrogation rooms and began a litany of questions.

"Where were you when your lab was being destroyed?" the detective asked.

"I had an administrative meeting with Grayson Everet across campus."

"How long was your meeting?"

"Half an hour." She thought it had been the worst half hour of her life. She'd been wrong.

"How long were you out of the lab?"

"About two hours. I had a shower in the faculty lounge before the meeting." Aliesa continued to rub her hands in her lap. She might have been right across the hall when Ev was attacked.

The detective didn't respond. He began another line of questions. "How many people knew you were doing stem cell research?"

Aliesa felt lightheaded.

She sat across from Lowry at a rectangular, simulated-wood grain table. The cold metal of the chair caused shivers to spider down her back. "Only a few. I posted a notice a few weeks ago for volunteers. Only certain blood types were accepted."

"Did your volunteers know they were participating in a stem cell research study?"

"Not exactly."

"What do you mean? Either they did or they didn't?"

Aliesa recoiled with his accusatory tone. The detective knew how to intimidate people. "I'm working on a vitamin study, I've noted some interesting side effects I plan to publish."

"Not divulging all of the facts to your subjects is unethical and might even be considered a motive."

"I withdrew blood, targeted their stem cells, and then treated those cells with mega doses of vitamins," she said, evenly.

"Do you think your subjects would have agreed to participate if you'd been completely honest with them?"

Aliesa had danced around the side effects of her study. At this point, considering the fact her lab had been destroyed, telling the detective she'd been working on anti-aging injections would have confused the issue even more. The third party ethics committee would kill the project entirely. Then she thought about Evelyne and her situation seemed trivial indeed. "If I'd been completely honest with my test sample, I would've had more volunteers than I could handle," she whispered.

A desk sergeant poked his head inside the interrogation room. "Telephone call, Lowry."

Aliesa was happy for the break. The detective insinuated this whole thing had somehow been her fault.

She felt awful enough. Her best friend, scratch that, her only friend was dead and, once again, she found herself entirely alone.

Chapter 3

Aliesa sat in the interrogation room and scrubbed her temples with cold, bloodless fingers. Her mind wandered and she dropped into a discussion she had with Evelyne a few short weeks ago.

Ev walked into the lab and hung her coat on one of the wall hooks behind the door. "So what's next?"

"Clinical trials," Aliesa said, placing another slide beneath the microscope, she soon lost herself among the electrons.

"Yo," Evelyne said, heaving her bag on the shelf. "I'm tired of trying to pry bits and bites of information out of you. I've been on this project from the onset, and I feel like an outsider. It's time you started to share. I know you're not being deliberately aloof, but being oblivious doesn't make it any less wrong."

Evelyne's desperate tone finally struck home. "Have I offended you?" Aliesa asked.

"Hell, yes," Evelyne said.

"Well, I never intended..."

"I know," Evelyne sighed. "I don't want your apology. I want you to talk to me. We've been working together for the last year. I've opened up to you. I thought we'd connected. I thought we were friends."

Aliesa blinked. "We are. This isn't your fault, it's mine. I'm socially inept. To be honest, I'm not sure I even know how to be a friend."

"Do you trust me?"

"I trust you, Evelyne. If I didn't I wouldn't have given you your own key to the lab."

Evelyne smiled and her brow creased. "In that case I need to be kept in the loop. I know I'll never have your brain-power but I'm not an idiot."

"You're a gifted chemist and I'd be lost without you," Aliesa said. "Again, it's not you. I've been holding my cards tight to my chest because I don't want this to turn into clinical trials. Not yet. Those will attract the attention of the FDA."

"What's wrong with that?"

"There are too many restrictions. Grayson approved the funds for a vitamin study nothing more. But there's a bigger picture. I'm confident I can improve cellular health in general."

"Meaning?"

"Down the road? Stem-cell supplements—an apple a day theory on steroids. And I'm not talking a daily regime. One dose every month for a few consecutive months should eliminate the threat of illness completely."

Evelyne's mouth curled into a smile. "Holy shit. A modern-day fountain of youth formula." She waited for Aliesa to crack a smile. "Are you serious?"

"Yep." Aliesa scooped her paperwork from the desk.

"Tell me you're going to bring in some lab techs to help isolate the stem cells from the blood samples."

Aliesa shook her head.

"You've got to be kidding. How the hell are we going to manage this experiment all by ourselves? We've been putting in eighteen hour days and we've only been dealing with one test sample."

"Now don't get your bra in a knot. The fewer people familiar with this project, the better. We'll only be managing a very small test sample in the beginning."

"How small?"

"A hundred tops."

Evelyne put her head on the desk. She drew several steady breaths. "About fifty more than we can possibly handle."

"We don't have a choice. A hundred is the minimum test number we can run. Anything less and we'll forfeit credibility."

"And I suppose you have a plan of attack or you wouldn't still be sitting here so calm and collected."

Aliesa went over to the computer terminal to refer to some archived research articles on stem cell therapy. "I've been giving the stem-cell vitamin dose my full attention."

"And?"

"In all of the research studies, heart muscle stem cells were injected into the damaged heart muscle after an angioplasty."

"How many heart muscle stem cells were injected?" Evelyne asked.

"Ten thousand," Aliesa said. "And the heart repaired itself in less than half the time."

"The heart study used a completely different protocol."

"True. And this is just speculation at this point."

"Okay, but if we were ready for clinical trials what would you consider a normal dose?"

"Our therapy needs to be a gradual but consistent change."

"How much and how many?" Evelyne asked.

"Leave it to you to boil it down to the basics. If fifty thousand cells is an acceptable benchmark, and we've cultured five different types of stem cells..."

"Ten thousand heart muscle, ten liver, ten skeletal muscle, ten nerve, and ten skin."

Aliesa nodded. "No more though. Injecting too many cells too quickly could be problematic. It makes sense to spread the therapy across three injections, one month apart."

"With what kind of follow up?"

"Basic tests should provide the data we need; heart rate, blood pressure, urine sample. Problem solving, for nerve and brain function. A simple photograph to track dermis changes."

"How often?"

"Twice a week."

"As usual," Evelyne said. "You've done your homework. But nothing like this would happen for at least a year maybe more."

"Hopefully we'll have a full staff by then."

"What have you told Grayson? He isn't what I would call patient about these things."

"You're right. But he didn't ask as many questions as you."

"Meaning?"

"He has no clue about the time frame. I'm sure he thinks we'll have a viable working model for our anti-aging booster after a few months of trials."

"When are you going to tell him?"

"There's only one way to handle Grayson and it's on a need-to-know basis. I'll tell him not one second before."

Evelyne nodded. "So where do we get our blood samples?"

"I posted a notice on the board an hour ago. People should start trickling in tomorrow morning. Of course we'll have to screen the candidates, make sure they're healthy and get them to sign a waiver."

"And what exactly do we call this study?"

"We call it what it is—vitamin injection therapy. If we called it anti-aging research, we'd have a stampede. "

"Well, technically it's not a lie," Evelyne said.

"Okay. Here's the plan. Since this is the proverbial calm before the storm, I want you to go home and get a good night's sleep. From here on out, things are going to be pretty busy."

"Are you going home, too?"

"Right after I finish this report." Aliesa continued to jot notes in her log.

"All right then," Evelyne said. "I accept your offer. A good night's sleep sounds positively orgasmic." She took off her lab coat and hung it on the hook. She collected her bag and jacket. "As long as I can trust you."

"To get lucky or have a good night's sleep?" Aliesa smiled.

"I'm serious," Evelyne said.

"I know. I promise."

Evelyne opened the lab door and left. Aliesa perched on the stool. She filled a hypodermic with a cocktail of her vitamin-boosted stem cells then placed a tourniquet on her upper arm. Lightly she tapped the vein in the crease of her arm.

"What are you doing?" Evelyne blurted, standing in the opened door.

Aliesa sprang to her feet. She placed her hand over her heart. "You scared me," she said. "Did you forget something?"

"No. I figured you'd left something out. Talk about gullible. I believed you."

"I never lied," Aliesa said. She released the tourniquet on her arm and went to Evelyne.

"Really? 'Cause from this angle it appears like you did." Evelyne's eyes had turned to glass.

"Ev. Sit. Let me explain."

Evelyne let Aliesa lead her over to a stool.

"I didn't think you'd understand," she said.

"Well you really didn't give me a chance one way or the other. You shut me out. Again."

"What I'm doing goes against every researcher's rule. I didn't want to compromise your ethics."

"So why are *you* doing it?"

Aliesa sat beside her. "For a lot of reasons."

"I'm listening."

"For one, the stem cells are mine. They've reached confluence and if I don't use them they will die. And if I've miscalculated with the dose, the only person to suffer will be me."

"Not good enough," Evelyne said, her arms crossed tightly.

Aliesa knew her only friend meant well. "My mother and my mother's mother died of breast cancer. I know what's in store for me. I need to do something to interrupt the genetic predisposition." She sighed. "Yes, I shut you out but for all the right reasons. The less you know about what I'm doing the better. This is the stupidest thing I've ever done."

"You're not stupid," Evelyne whispered. "You're brilliant. Sooner or later you'll get this friend thing. And just so you know, I totally wondered when you were going to give yourself the first injection."

"You were? You don't think it's risky?"

"I would question anyone else, but knowing you, it's in the bag."

"Are you mad at me?"

"Not as long as you make one more promise."

"What?"

"You don't think I'm going to stand still and let you reap all the rewards of this protocol do you?"

"We're a team. You'll get equal recognition."

"I'm not talking annotation. I want to be a guinea pig, too, and drink from the fountain of youth."

The door of the interrogation room swung open and instantly she was pulled out of her recollection when Detective Lowry barged inside.

"Now where were we?" he asked. "Oh, yes. How long *had* Evelyne Mathews been working for you?"

Aliesa swallowed the lump in her throat with the detective's reference to Evelyne in the past tense. She turned her hands over in her lap. "For about a year. We'd become very close," Aliesa whispered. "I interviewed several candidates for the position and spoke with her professors. Everyone loved her. Why would anyone want to hurt her?"

Lowry shrugged. "If it's any consolation I don't think

she was the intended target. Forensics is still going over the lab, but, right now, I have two schools of thought."

"Care to share them?" Aliesa glared at Lowry who watched her every move.

"The assailant trashed the lab to make a statement. Maybe they were protesting your work, or trying to find something."

"It's all so senseless," Aliesa said.

"Hardly."

"I beg your pardon?" A searing headache pulsed pain between her eyes.

"Listen," Lowry explained. "Your lab assistant was strangled and her throat was slashed. It was personal. The murderer wanted something. Information Evelyne couldn't provide."

"Then why her?"

The detective's wide and sturdy stance told her he believed whole-heartedly in his answer. "They made a huge mistake. They didn't want her. They were after you."

Chapter 4

L owry's words clanged in Aliesa's ears.

"Me?" Nothing made any sense anymore.

"I'm afraid so," Lowry said. "Evelyne was wearing your lab coat and nametag."

Aliesa's ears began to ring and her vision tunneled. Her throat scorched with the remnants of bile she forced herself to keep swallowing.

Up until a moment ago, Aliesa didn't think there could be anything worse than losing a good friend. But she'd been wrong. Her best friend lay dead on a stainless steel slab in the morgue because of her.

Who would have done such a thing and why? Had someone found out about her research? Three people in the entire world knew about her work—besides herself, Grayson, and Evelyne. Now there were only two.

If someone had mistaken Evelyne for her, they really weren't very smart. Why would they kill anyone before they had a working vaccine and could claim the spoils for themselves?

Grayson wouldn't have been so stupid. He threatened to cut her funding at their meeting and she never really trusted him, but she ruled him out because they'd been together at the time of the murder. Besides, he was too weak-willed to kill anyone.

Soon Aliesa couldn't swallow the growing knob in her throat and she charged to the ladies bathroom at police headquarters. Only this time, she suffered a fate worse than retching, the dry heaves. By the time she returned to the interrogation room she felt like a martini, shaken not stirred.

When the detective spotted her he helped her over to the chair. "Are you all right?" he asked. "You're a weird shade of green."

"As far as days go, I've had better," Aliesa said.

Lowry went out in the hall. She heard coins drop into a machine and the detective popped the top of a soda and placed it in front of her. "Drink it. It'll make you feel better." Ginger ale. It would settle her stomach.

Aliesa almost refused on the grounds she preferred diet soda, and then she thought better of it. The sugar boost would do her a world of good right now. "Thanks," she said.

"I'm sorry about blurting out the truth like I did," the detective said. "It was cruel and uncalled for."

Her color must have been bad because the detective was actually being nice to her. She studied his face for any outward signs of his compassion. His eyes were void of any and the way he played her made her wonder about the reason for this game.

"I've arranged for an officer to escort you home."

She closed her mouth because it dropped open.

Lowry's abrupt change toward her didn't make any sense either. She thought she would be here for hours trying to convince him she had nothing to do with Ev's death and now he couldn't wait to cut her loose. Odd about face, to say the least.

"It's not necessary," Aliesa said. "I'll grab a cab home."

"Nonsense. The least I can do is get you safely to your door."

She narrowed her eyes. "Am I no longer a suspect?"

Lowry shook his head. She got the distinct impression orders were being followed. "But don't leave town." He reached into his pocket and pulled out a slip of cardboard. "Call me if you think of anything to help resolve this case."

Aliesa took the business card from the detective and dropped it into her bag.

Like an automaton she let herself be led outside and into a waiting car. The female officer never said a word to her as she wove her way through Boston's downtown core and pulled to the curb of her building—Bayfront Towers. "Did you want me to escort you upstairs?"

Aliesa shook her head. "That's not necessary. My building has a state-of-the-art security system." She reached into her purse and pulled out her key card and her phone. She never turned back as she walked inside the building's vestibule and swiped to open the inside door. In all of the earlier confusion, she hadn't powered on her phone, she always switched it off whenever she met with Grayson.

She watched the officer pull away from the curb, then she switched on her phone and swiped for the elevator.

Her phone beeped indicating she had one new voice mail. Absentmindedly, she retrieved it.

"Hi, it's me, Ev…"

Aliesa gasped and nearly dropped the handset. She wobbled on unsteady legs and jammed the phone back into her bag like a burning ember.

Oh, God, this couldn't be happening.

Her heart raced. She reached out to steady herself—leaned against the wall and took several deep breaths.

Ev called her and since there had been such a limited window, Aliesa wondered if Ev knew she was in trouble and called her for help. No, she finally decided. Evelyne knew better. She'd call nine-one-one, not her. And based on the time stamp, she must have been attacked shortly after. Please, God, let it be before, she didn't think she could bear a call during the attack.

Aliesa had been so preoccupied with her thoughts she boarded the elevator in a trance. She needed to set her fears aside to listen to the message. There might even be a clue to Evelyne's murderer in the message, but the idea of hearing her friend's voice from beyond the grave really freaked her out.

Aliesa slid her card key into the automatic reader and nothing happened. Another first.

Welcome to her day.

She withdrew the key card and tried it again. Suddenly the lift began its ascent. The elevator key went back into her bag and she removed the card for her door.

Bayfront Towers had been designed with two penthouses on the top floor—hers, and a corporate suite, owned by the Largo Bank. The elevator opened and she stepped onto the marble tile in the short hall. When she went to slide the card into the slot, the unlatched door to her suite silently slipped ajar.

Chapter 5

Aliesa stood frozen, struggling to remember if maybe she'd forgotten to lock it. When had she been home last?

Two days ago.

Surely she couldn't have been so absorbed she'd neglected to pull the door closed. Stanger things had happened. She'd forgotten before. The lack of assuredness stung. She'd been juggling too much. With trepidation, Aliesa stuck her nose through the opening and peeked inside. Everything seemed to be in place. The seven-foot gilded mirror leaned against the wall, a collection of pottery crocks squatted on the floor at the end of the hall.

She shrugged off her unease and decided everything remained exactly how she'd left it. She swung her purse to the floor and went to snag a hanger in the closet when a loud crash in the bedroom startled her.

Fear stabbed her.

She turned to bolt and slammed full bore into a solid wall of muscle. A man grabbed her and whispered in her ear. "I'm not going to hurt you. We have to get out of here." Silently, he slid the closet door shut, handed Aliesa her purse. Black piercing eyes stole her breath and kept her quiet. She didn't have a lot of options. Besides, if this bruiser meant to harm her, she'd already be dead.

The precinct detective had been right.

She'd been the intended target after all. Her knees buckled. Strong arms supported her as he maneuvered her back out the door.

Aliesa's phone bleated.

Until this moment, Aliesa never realized how loud cell phone chimes were. The ring tone signified she had one unheard voice mail. The ding pierced the silence like a trumpet.

She could have cried.

The man pulled her out into the hall and stealthily closed the door. Aliesa dug inside her purse, searching for the elevator key. In a flash he sped in front, dragging her along with him. They passed the elevator call button and he flung her inside the other penthouse suite. He swung the door shut and closed it as quietly as possible. Then he braced both hands on the door as he peeked through the peephole.

Déjà vu.

Van watched the same two South American men burst into the hall. One brandished a Glock, the other slid a custom blade out of his pocket about eight inches long. He'd seen both of them in Peru not even a week ago. They were Cartel henchmen who went by the names Jorge and Axel.

Next time Van would make sure his informant gave him exclusive rights to the intel. He'd barely had enough time to find a good place to hide before Jorge and Axel arrived and shit hit the shredder.

Jorge and Axel's orders had been to shut down the small independent manufacturer and they arrived not long after Dr. Marcus Hernandez came to say goodbye to his classroom at the Universidad Nacional de Trijillo, his home during his fellowship for the past five years.

Van ducked inside a storage cabinet and watched as Jorge and Axel did their job.

"May I help you?" Hernandez asked.

"Where is it?" Jorge asked.

"What do you want, señor?" Hernandez asked.

Jorge had six inches on Axel. Both were neatly attired in long pants and short-sleeved shirts. Jorge could have been a professional dancer, lithe and sinewy, with a scar deeply etched on one cheek. Axel—a bar-room bouncer, short and stubby, with a nose flattened flush on his face.

"Are you lost?" Hernandez asked.

Jorge tipped his head toward Axel. The unspoken instruction received loud and clear. Axel retraced his steps to the classroom door and locked it.

Hernandez became quiet and held onto the counter. Then he puffed out his chest. "You're making a big mistake. If you don't leave right this minute I'm going to call security." He stepped over to the telephone on the wall and snatched the receiver.

Jorge smiled and sidled over to the doctor. His toothy grin seemed to put Hernandez at ease, until he reached right around him and tore the phone off the wall. He shoved Hernandez out of his way and began rummaging through the base cabinets.

Glass beakers exploded as they hit the floor. Test tubes shattered and pipettes clattered as they dropped.

Hernandez backed away, inching toward his office, likely an attempt to barricade himself inside.

"Where is it?" Jorge's patience had worn thin. He toppled chairs and desks.

Hernandez continued to slink backward.

Axel leapfrogged over the fallen desks and nabbed Hernandez by the scruff of his neck.

"I swear I don't know what you're talking about," Hernandez whimpered.

That's when Axel hauled off and sucker-punched Hernandez square in the gut. The doctor doubled over and winced as he tried to draw air into his lungs.

Jorge grabbed Hernandez's head by a shock of hair, tilting it back. Hernandez's eyes were pained and unfocused.

Axel folded thick arms across his chest. "We can do this the easy way or hard way. It's your choice."

Hernandez couldn't draw a steady breath and Van doubted he could speak. Somehow he pursed his lips and words came out. "I have money," he rasped.

"Are your ears painted on? We don't want your money." Jorge grabbed Hernandez and threw him against the wall. Then he slid a butterfly knife out of his pocket, flipped it open, and pressed the edge to Marcus's throat.

"But you don't understand. I'm a scientist. I produce an anti-leukemic from periwinkle."

Jorge moved with choreographed precision. Silver

gleamed. There was a whoosh and a sickly scream. When he brought the blade of his knife to eye level, Hernandez's eyes widened as a hunk of flesh dropped onto his shoulder and tumbled to the floor.

Hernandez wailed and covered the mangled remains of his ear with his hand.

"Each time you answer incorrectly I will remove another body part," Jorge said. "Let's try one more time, shall we? Where is it?"

"FedEx collected it this afternoon," Hernandez said. "I forwarded it to my processing contractor in Quincy, Massachusetts."

Jorge shrugged. Once again he nodded to Axel who grabbed Hernandez's hand, pressing it flat to the wall.

"What are you doing? I told you, it's gone," Hernandez said on a whimper.

And with as much effort as slicing a manioc root, Jorge lopped off Hernandez's pinky.

Another shriek. Spittle dripped from the doctor's lips as he regarded the bleeding stump.

"Good thing we know someone who works at FedEx," Jorge said. Axel pulled his phone out of his pocket and dialed a number. "It'll only take a moment to corroborate your story."

Check mate.

Van shook his head.

Hernandez's head bobbed up and down. His cheeks flushed and he began to shake uncontrollably.

"Would you like to change your story?" Jorge asked after listening in on Axel's short telephone conversation.

"I shipped it to a colleague at Boston University."

Jorge held a knife to Hernandez's throat. A puddle, Van guessed was urine, pooled beneath Hernandez's feet.

"What's your colleague's name?" Jorge asked, examining his nails.

"Dr. Atworth," Hernandez said.

"The truth can be very messy." Jorge tossed his knife into the air. In one fluid motion he grabbed the handle and pirouetted, dragging the edge across Hernandez's carotid.

Arterial blood spurted.

Hernandez's lifeless body dropped to the floor like an unstrung marionette.

Jorge and Axel fist pumped each other and grinned.

Hernandez's desk computer pinged.

Incoming email, most likely.

The pair stepped over Hernandez and walked into the adjacent office. Jorge used his handkerchief to mop the blood from his face. He sat at the desk and Axel leered over his shoulder at the computer screen.

"Maybe he was telling the truth," Jorge said, wiping the blood from his knife with his handkerchief before he folded it and put it in his pocket. "Guess there's really only one way to find out."

"Better let the boss know," Axel said.

Van waited until both men left, then he hurried over to the computer and opened the email. Van read the last message from a Dr. Aliesa Atworth.

Interesting to say the least. So much so he decided to export all of the messages onto a flash drive so he could go over them later.

With three minutes left to complete the download the

classroom door thudded open and a female caretaker wheeled her cleaning cart inside the classroom. Van ducked below the edge of the desk to wait for the files to transfer.

Two minutes.

The woman righted the desks by the door and began what Van guessed was her nightly ritual. She dunked the mop into her bucket and backed down the center aisle.

One minute.

Glass crunched under her feet and the mop slowed when the floor became streaked and sticky. "Slobs," the woman said, shaking her head. She crouched and collected the larger shards.

She dunked her mop again, and before she set to work she turned to survey the rest of the aisle. Her eyes drifted to Hernandez's mangled body in a heap a couple of feet away. She let out an ear-drum shattering scream, dropped the mop and flew from the classroom waving her arms.

Download complete.

Van ejected the drive and slipped through the back door to the emergency exit.

Dr. Aliesa Atworth's email emblazoned in his memory

> Marcus,
> Need one more shipment. Promise to go
> through proper channels next time.
> Aliesa

Van had been hot on the heels of Jorge and Axel ever since. The pair had killed two people. They had no way of knowing they'd found the right lab but killed the wrong gal, but it wouldn't take long for them to figure it out if he didn't make some calls. He needed to step on it. Accidents like this didn't happen often, but when they did, time mattered.

First Van got the real identity of the victim suppressed. Once he knew the size of the cocaine shipment and had it in his possession he would arrest Atworth for manufacturing and distributing cocaine.

When Detective Lowry took Atworth to the station, Van set his plan in motion. He called the only person he could trust—a man with enough power to make it happen.

The Admiral.

Van had saved the Admiral's life a couple of years ago and had gotten a few lifelong privileges. Phone calls were made. Rules were bent. Others were broken.

Van had two weeks.

Damn the Admiral worked fast.

Van expected Dr. Atworth to be waylaid in the Boston PD's red tape for at least another hour. He hoped she would arrive after Jorge and Axel finished ransacking her apartment. He'd conducted surveillance in the adjoining penthouse, just in case.

When nature called, he left his post. He couldn't believe his eyes when he glared though the peephole and saw Dr. Atworth entering her apartment.

Sure they'd made it safely back into the other penthouse but Van knew they weren't in the clear yet.

The easiest solution would be throwing the dead bolt, but not if he wanted Aliesa to remain dead for the next two weeks. The door lock of this condo happened to be the noisiest mechanism he'd ever heard. If Jorge and Axel heard a thunk now they'd come running. He wedged the toe of his boot against the door and grabbed the doorknob with both hands. He'd have to manually simulate a locked door.

When he faced the doctor, he noticed her eyes were tightly closed. She stood as stiff as a two-by-four, leaning against the door—purse tightly clutched beneath her chin, knuckles white.

"Pssst." Van's soft barely audible hiss got her attention. Her eyes sprang open and she watched him.

He mouthed, "Move away from the peep hole."

Immediately she tucked into the corner. Both of them glared at the peephole.

Suddenly, the glass in the hole darkened.

Van braced himself. It would play out one of two ways. Jorge and Axel had seen Van and Aliesa dart into the other penthouse and were preparing to attack, or they saw nothing and were simply being thorough. Van centered all of his strength on keeping the doorknob immobile.

The knob wiggled back and forth. Van didn't budge. The peephole remained dark. He held the knob so tightly his hands had gone numb. Then he had a sickening thought. The doctor's cell phone had alarmed minutes ago had already begun its next countdown. The darn thing would beep at regular intervals until she discarded the voice mail. Since the doctor's eyes were still watching his every move he mouthed, "Fix your cell phone."

She caught on right away and rooted around in her bag.

Then came another harrowing thought.

He had visions of the doctor shutting the damn thing off. Some android cells played a parting tune before powering-off. A tune would be ten times worse than a solitary beep. Before he could issue any more instructions, Dr. Aliesa Atworth withdrew her phone from her purse and shucked the battery like a corncob husk.

Chapter 6

Van let out the breath he'd been holding. Aliesa Atworth proved to be as smart as the dossier his IT guy, Drew Nystyshyn, from ABC Inquiries said. Van came across Drew a few months ago when a friend and former Special Forces sniper, Sloan Picard, recommended him. Now Van relied on Drew for all of his intel.

The pressure on the doorknob evaporated.

Van hazarded a peek through the peephole. Both Jorge and Axel had turned and were heading back into Aliesa's penthouse.

As quietly as possible, Van set the dead bolt. Then he squeezed past Aliesa and meandered into the living room.

Another crisis averted.

With his peripheral vision he watched her. She'd thrown her shoulders back and followed him into the condo. He sat on the sofa, thumbing through a coffee-table book on Salvador Dali. When Van arrived at Bayfront Towers and learned Aliesa's apartment was being searched, it took Drew less than ten minutes to learn this penthouse suite had been purchased for corporate use and was currently unoccupied. Without glancing at her he said, "Get comfortable. They'll be searching your place for a while."

She cleared her throat. "I'm Dr. Aliesa Atworth, and you are?"

He continued studying the glossy images in the book. "You can call me Van."

She angled her head. "Wait a minute. Weren't you the guy guarding my lab at BU earlier today? You let me go in there knowing full well what I'd find." Her brow creased and her bottom lip quivered.

One out of ten people would have recognized him under such stressful circumstances. Her powers of observation were quite remarkable.

"Why didn't you stop me?"

"I thought you needed to see what happens to people in your line of work." Her forehead wrinkled—like she had no idea what he meant.

"You're welcome, by the way."

"I beg your pardon?"

"For saving your life."

Aliesa stood at the edge of the sofa, her hands twisting the leather of her purse. "How do I know I haven't compounded my problems by hooking up with you?"

Van stopped turning pages and slapped the book shut. "For someone with a genius IQ you're not very smart. Those men over there came to get the shipment Hernandez sent to you. They don't discriminate. They'll kill whoever stands in their way. Did you think the letters after your name would protect you?" He scrubbed his hand across his whiskered chin. "Now why don't you cut your losses and tell me where it is. I'll go to bat for you. I'll talk to the authorities about your cooperation."

"What are you talking about? Who are they?"

"The Alarcon Cartel. Your competition."

"The cartel wants Camu camu?"

"Is that what you call it?"

Aliesa nodded. "Why would they come to Boston to get something grown in Peru? It doesn't make sense. Are you sure they don't want my anti-aging serum?"

Van hid his surprise with an expression as unmarked as a new deck of cards. This woman didn't seem to know what he was talking about. Camu camu? Anti-aging serum? What the hell was going on here?

"And who are you?" Aliesa asked.

Back at BU when Aliesa pushed past him to go into her lab he noticed something that took his breath away. Soul-searing loneliness. The same kind driving him. "I'm an independent contractor."

"What do you mean?"

"I'm self employed."

"You're a soldier of fortune?"

"No," Van stated emphatically. "I'm a vigilante with a cause."

"I see," Aliesa said, rubbing between her eyes. "To stay alive I need to make a deal with the devil."

Van didn't care what she called him as long as he got the drugs out of circulation. "How did you come to know Dr. Hernandez?"

"Hernandez doesn't have anything to do with any of this." Aliesa said. "I swear he's totally innocent."

Right. Why in the hell would she try to protect him? Unless they were way more than business partners? "Answer the question!"

His sharp tone startled her. "He was my lab partner in

my final year of grad school. We spent the better part of three months with our heads pressed together doing clinical work."

That had to be ten years ago. "And?" For some strange reason he needed to know if they were lovers.

"I contacted him a couple of months ago when my first batch of stem cells euthanized. He had something I needed."

"What did he have?"

She lifted her chin haughtily. "A nicotinamide adenine dinucleotide, or NAD. A coenzyme so my cells remain viable." She obviously noticed his confusion because she tried to explain. "NAD is used extensively in glycolysis."

"Glycolysis?"

"It's one of the most universal metabolic processes common to all types of organisms. The process whereby sugar is converted into energy. The safest sources are found in nature."

"Okay."

"I needed either a Billygoat plum or Camu camu. Since the plum is a flowering plant from Australia, I opted for the Camu camu—a swamp shrub from the Amazonian rainforest. I should have gotten an official Material Transfer Agreement, but the paperwork alone would've set my research back months so I kind of side-stepped the system."

"You got your Camu camu illegally?"

She clamped her mouth shut. Her lips tightened. "No. Dr. Hernandez's been studying another rainforest plant called periwinkle or Vinca minor. Since he has a Material Transfer Agreement, he sent me the Camu

camu under his umbrella."

"I see," Van said. Could this woman be oblivious to Henandez's other interests? Or maybe he merely wished it to be the case. "Sounds almost too simple."

"Nothing is ever easy." Aliesa sat on the edge of the sofa. She thought about those first few days after the fruit first arrived at her lab. Evelyne had been very close to giving up. She'd prepared the growth medium mix—Ham's Medium, a complex combination of ingredients allowing human cells to grow in culture with a cytokine, and Camu camu, as the ascorbic acid source.

And nothing happened. No change in the sample.

"What makes you think vitamin C is the missing link?" Evelyne asked.

Aliesa had never been so tired. So much so she scared herself the last time she caught her reflection in the mirror. Dark circles had taken residence beneath her eyes and her hair hadn't been brushed in days. "Ev, I don't know how to explain it, but I know I'm right. Besides high amounts of vitamin C, Camu camu contains potassium, various mineral and amino acids—all of the necessary ingredients for cell development."

"I don't doubt you're right. All I'm saying is we should have seen positive results already—unless we need a more invasive introduction."

Aliesa sliced a piece of fruit open on the lab table.

There was a large seed embedded in the fleshy pulp. The aroma had a sour bite from the high ascorbic acid content of the fruit. Her mouth went completely dry. "What did you say?"

Evelyne turned toward Aliesa. "The only thing I haven't done is inject the cells directly."

"Of course," Aliesa turned and headed to the computer and did a search. She opened the first article and scanned the content. "Could it really be so simple. I thought I remembered reading an article on ascorbic acid as a chemotherapy agent not too long ago and here it is. Ascorbic acid preferentially killed the neoplastic cells. It's virtually non-toxic at any dosage."

Evelyne put her hands on her hips. "And the ascorbic acid didn't suppress the immune system like most other chemotherapy agents?"

"Here's the best part," Aliesa said. "Ascorbic acid seems to increase the resistance to infectious agents. It strengthens the extracellular matrix, and enhances bactericidal activity."

"Bonus. The cells will live longer." Evelyne said.

Aliesa faced Evelyne and smiled. "Well? What the hell are we waiting for?"

With renewed vigor the two of them set to work.

Aliesa had harvested a new batch of cells from her personal blood stores and once the cells were isolated, she introduced the cytokine and injected the Camu camu serum.

In less than twenty-four hours, a marked difference in the rate of growth had occurred. The cells divided quickly and the numbers expanded exponentially. In less than a week, the cells reached confluence. Not only did the introduction of Camu camu serum hasten the pace of development, it eradicated any weak or inferior cells. And these remaining cells were supercharged. They were stronger, healthier, more resilient, and for the most part, at the beginning of their life cycle.

"Sounds too easy," Van said, snapping her out of her memory. The layman had no idea the hoops science wielded.

"Yes, I got the Camu camu from Dr. Henandez but the responsibility for the wrongdoing is mine. And I don't want this indiscretion to reflect on Dr. Hernandez. I told him I would gladly file my own Transfer Agreement, but he insisted."

"Expensive favor," Van said. "He's dead."

Only then did she falter.

In less than thirty seconds she gasped for air with a full-fledged panic attack.

What had she done? If she hadn't contacted Marcus, he might still be alive. First Evelyne had been murdered, now Marcus. People lived their whole lives without ever causing harm to another living soul. And in the last few hours she'd discovered she'd been solely responsible for two deaths.

Regret, the weight of a cement block crushed her chest. She hyperventilated. The room began to darken.

Once again, Van came to her rescue.

He grabbed her purse and forced her head between her knees. Then he overturned the contents of her bag onto the coffee table and grabbed the empty satchel holding it tight to her mouth. "Breathe," he said.

She concentrated on drawing air in and out of her lungs until the darkness brightened.

"Feeling better?" he asked.

She nodded and sat. Van lowered the purse and sifted through the contents scattered across the table. Keys, wallet, phone parts, lunch bag.

She shook her head. Tears welled in her eyes. "This is all my fault."

"I seriously doubt it," Van said. "Hernandez was murdered because he'd been manufacturing cocaine hydrochloride."

Chapter 7

"Cocaine?" Aliesa said. Not possible. "Dr. Hernandez devoted his life to saving people. He lives in Peru to develop and produce an anti-leukemic."

"In your world, maybe," Van said. "In my world he produced a recreational stimulant notorious for killing people."

Aliesa noticed the stoic expression on Van's face. Something personal made him hold something back. Then she had another thought. Hernandez was a fairly common surname. What if they'd gotten him confused with someone else. "I can't believe it."

"I'm having a little trouble with his so called philanthropic efforts myself."

"Not with his credentials," Aliesa said. "Are you sure the cartel killed the right man?"

"Contrary to what you might think, the Alarcan cartel doesn't go around killing people. They got wind of his operation, the same way I did and got rid of him."

"How senseless." Aliesa shook her head. "Did you know his findings were published in Scientific American. He had the backing of one of the largest pharmaceutical manufacturers out there—a company called Panacealla. Not only did they pay for his

Department of Agriculture's Transfer Agreement, they leased him lab space at the university. Producing his anti-leukemic with Vinca minor is a convoluted process."

"Oh, yeah?" Van said with a taunting lilt.

"The production of vassicine hydrochloride requires a talented chemist. Periwinkle leaves, water, and sulfuric acid are combined and macerated. The paste is washed in kerosene, chilled, dissolved in methyl alcohol, crystallized and dissolved again in sulfuric acid. Then, there's further washing, oxidation, and separation with potassium permanganate, benzol, and sodium carbonate."

"The only difference between making cocaine and vassicine hydrochloride is the raw material you begin with. The vassicine uses periwinkle and cocaine uses coca. Nice recap, by the way, you make it sound like you've manufactured the stuff once or twice yourself."

"Just because I know how it's done doesn't mean I've done it. I've never done anything illegal in my entire life."

"Oh, right. And you obtained the Camu camu through all of the proper channels."

She opened her mouth to counter a response but quickly closed it. Point well taken.

"Just so you know, manufacturing cocaine isn't an art. Natives make this shit in the jungle. Most of these farmers can barely read, let alone write. They use the slash and burn technique when harvesting coca—a technique which leaves no vegetative matter left to replenish the soil. The coca plant extracts every vital mineral from the soil and subsequent crop rotation is not an option."

"What a waste," Aliesa said.

"Did you know over 80 percent of the crops, coffee, potatoes, asparagus, and various other fruits and vegetables grown in Peru are for export?"

Aliesa shook her head.

"I had a friend of mine check all the farmers whose export numbers didn't reflect the national average. For the past few months, I'd been working my way through the list. Found this small plantation whose crops never seemed to leave the country."

"Why are you telling me this?"

"You asked me for proof."

Van sat straight and watched Aliesa very carefully.

"Pedros Santos owned a stake of land on the fringe of Trujillo. I found him in a bar called The Black Cat, on the outskirts of town. He didn't want to talk to me but I can be pretty persuasive when I need to be."

Aliesa watched him. She bit her bottom lip.

Van remembered Pedro rubbing a calloused hand across his upper lip fingering the dark mole at the corner of his mouth before he ordered a couple of beers.

Moments later the waitress set the bottles on the rough-hewn table.

"Are you DEA?" Pedro asked.

"I wouldn't be sitting in here having a beer with you if I was," Van said.

Pedro remained still. "What do you want?"

"I want to know why you don't have an export license

for your crops." Van said.

"I don't need one because I sell my crops locally."

"Not at the market," Van said. "I checked."

"No, not at the market." Pedro's hand shook as he took a sip of his beer. "Señor, I'm a peasant farmer trying to feed my family."

"And I have no quarrel with you, though I think you need to be very careful. If an outsider like me notices the discrepancy, it's a safe bet the Alarcan will too. That is, if they don't already know."

"Have you heard something?" Pedro's eyes scoured the bar for anyone within earshot.

"You seem frightened. Do you have reason to be?" Van asked.

Pedro leaned close. "Once a month I supply a professor at the university with periwinkle."

"Anything else?"

He shook his head. "A portion of every delivery contains...cocoa. It's buried in some of the skids."

"You might want to rethink your decision in the future," Van said.

"Our agreement is complete once I deliver this next shipment."

"Why?"

"He said something about his contract not being renewed."

"When are you supposed to deliver it?"

"Tomorrow."

Van turned toward Aliesa when he finished his story.

"That's not proof," Aliesa said. "That's heresay."

"And that's exactly why I broke into the lab two days later. I collected two unknown powder samples from the surfaces in his lab and ran field tests on them."

"What kind of a field tests?"

"I used Substance Identification Kits from the DEA—leftovers from the agency."

His answer startled her.

"The vial of liquid in the first test sample remained clear and colorless but in the second vial it turned blue—positive for cocaine."

Moments later, Hernandez entered the university lab and then, Jorge and Axel joined him. Van spared Aliesa those gruesome details.

"Why do you believe Dr. Hernandez's death has something to do with me?" Aliesa asked, her breath catching again.

Van gathered the contents of her purse he'd dumped on the coffee table when she started to hyperventilate and began handing everything back to her. "Because of an email you sent to Hernandez."

"Yes. I ran out of Camu camu and I needed him to send me more."

"I see."

"Do you?" Aliesa asked.

Aliesa took her wallet, keys, phone, battery pack, and shoved them into her purse. Before he handed over her lunch bag he tried to feel the contents through the insulated bag.

She snatched it from him.

Her reaction made him wonder what she was hiding in the bag. Ever since he'd gotten her out of the other penthouse she'd been clinging to her damn purse like it was some sort of magic amulet.

"I read your email on Hernandez's computer right

after those two Alarcon Cartel goons in your apartment read it."

"But I wasn't asking him to send me drugs, I needed more Camu camu for my test samples."

"You could have called it 'Pie in the Sky' and they would have thought you meant cocaine."

Chapter 8

Aliesa re-inserted the battery into the back of her phone and pulled a business card out of her wallet. "I'm calling the detective to tell him the two men who killed Evelyne are ransacking my apartment right now." She began pressing numbers.

"Not so fast," Van said. He reached over, plucked the phone from her hand, and pushed end. "Dead people don't make telephone calls."

Aliesa stilled. Her stomach burned with his comment.

"Now don't go and hyperventilate yourself into a stupor again. Evelyne's identity is going to be kept under wraps for the next little while. If those two men next door think you're dead you're relatively safe for the time being. In the meantime, you can try to convince me you're innocent while I search for the cocaine. Of course, if you prefer, I can reverse things, but you'll have to put your trust in the hands of the Boston PD and I'm fairly certain your life expectancy will be nil with them."

If Aliesa had to describe the man sitting across from her in a word, it would be uber-competent. It oozed from him. He seemed dangerous. His rough and woody appearance would rattle any prizefighter.

Aliesa's mind began firing at warp speed. Her brain

flooded with observations and questions. Why didn't he want her to call the police? His connections didn't make him out to be a good guy. In fact, everything he'd told her made her wonder about him being the opposite.

Maybe *he* murdered Evelyne.

Maybe *he* wanted the cocaine.

If so, what would *he* do with her when he discovered she didn't have a clue about the cocaine or its whereabouts?

And her last theory—maybe this entire cocaine story had been fabricated because he wanted to snag her formula.

Her stem-cell serum would be worth millions. Hell. Who was she kidding? Hundreds of millions.

He'd unobtrusively examined the entire contents of her purse. For now, the two remaining stem-cell injections in her lunch bag were undetected, but she would have to guard them closely.

"I think I'll take my chances with you," she said—her voice a mere squeak.

"Thanks for the glowing vote of confidence," Van said.

His syrupy tone made her wince. Out of her element, Aliesa tried to approach this situation from a clinical standpoint. There were too many unknown values to muster any real confidence. "What do we do first?"

"We'll camp in your penthouse as soon as Jorge and Axel finish their search."

"You know them?"

"I know their names. I know they work for the cartel. Nothing more."

Logical thinking. She clutched her purse close to her chest, sat back on the ultrasuede sofa, and tried to relax.

Yeah, right. Like she'd ever be able to calm her racing heart. Someone tried to murder her today. If she started thinking about Evelyne, she'd feel queasy again. So she sat forward and asked the first question which popped into her head. "How are you affiliated with the Largo Bank?"

Van turned toward her with the oddest expression on his face. "What?"

"The Largo Bank. This penthouse is owned by the Largo Bank."

Van raised his eyebrows. "Do you think I'm one of their customers?"

She'd merely assumed he'd gained legitimate access to the penthouse. "Oh. How did you side-step the building's security?"

"The same way Jorge and Axel did. Nothing is ever completely secure."

Then, just as it had before, Aliesa's cell phone beeped. Van pointed to the phone in her hand.

"Are you going to answer the call you missed?"

She squeezed the phone. "It's Evelyne. She must have called and left a message right before she..."

"Do you want me to listen to it first?"

Aliesa shook her head. She'd force herself to listen to the message. What if Evelyne made the call after being stabbed? No. Stop. Aliesa didn't recall seeing a phone at the crime scene so she wouldn't hear her friend take her last breath. What if Evelyne relayed a detailed description of her assailant and the man turned out to be Van? "I'll do it," Aliesa said, swallowing hard. She dialed the voice mail number and put the phone to her ear.

"Hi, it's me." Evelyne's voice singsonged. "Thought

you could use a little pep talk. You can handle Grayson. Stand your ground. He'll want you to race through the stages, but don't do it. Don't let him bully you into something not right. He'll get over it. Hope everything goes well. See you tomorrow."

Typical Evelyne. She'd always been there for her. Until Evelyne, Aliesa never knew what it felt like to have someone in her corner—someone she could confide and depend on. Tears welled in her eyes. She'd only just found her and now she was gone.

"Well? What did she say?"

Fatigue lowered her eyelids to half-mast. She rubbed her forehead and wiped the tears from her eyes throughout the interrogation. "Evelyne called to bolster my confidence. She knew I didn't want to go to my administrative meeting. I'm not very good at politics."

"You were schmoozing while they ransacked your lab and killed your best friend?"

"I had a meeting to try to extend my funding and explain why things couldn't be rushed. If this administrator was in charge, my serum would already be in mass production."

"Who is the administrator?"

"Grayson Everet. The chief financial adviser at Boston U."

Van pulled a sleek black phone from the back pocket of his cargo pants and texted something.

"Do you know him?" Aliesa asked.

"No. But he's on the list of people I'd like to have a word with."

Maybe to corroborate her story. Van could go and speak with Grayson. Aliesa had nothing to hide and he'd find out soon enough.

She changed the subject. "How much longer are we going to hide out here?"

"Those two are just getting started over there. It'll be a couple of hours before they pack it in."

"That long?" Aliesa shivered. She felt violated. Those two goons were pawing through her personal belongings.

Van faced her. "Why don't you go and rest for a while. I'll wake you when they finish."

"I can't sleep in someone else's bed," she said.

"Why not?" Van asked. "You think it's okay to break into a place but not to lay down on the bed?"

"That's not what I meant."

"Afraid I might attack you while you're asleep?"

Aliesa recoiled.

"Don't flatter yourself," Van said. "You're not even remotely my type." He opened the art book on the coffee table and continued reading.

Attraction never crossed her mind. Men like Van had never taken an interest in her. In fact, his off-the-cuff remark baffled her—she'd been thinking murder, not making out.

Her heart raced. She grabbed her purse and headed to the primary bedroom. She swung the door closed, leaned against it and squeezed her eyes shut.

How did things get so out of control? Aliesa prided herself on always being in charge. But right now she wasn't sure of anything. She questioned her decision to stay with Van. She should have chosen to go into police protection, but with all the negative press about cops on the take, would she have been any better off?

Her mind raced in circles.

Enough. Despite being exhausted, she knew she wouldn't be able to sleep. She opened her eyes and appreciated the luxurious five-piece bathroom—-shower, tub, sink, toilet and bidet. The Largo Bank had done a great job renovating this place to make their clients feel like royalty. Darn shame really. In all the time she'd lived in the building she'd never seen anyone ever use the condo.

A shower. She'd let the hot water pummel her, wash away her troubles, if only for a short while. She might as well add the illegal use of a towel and soap to the breaking and entering charge.

She hurried through the primary bedroom and into the bathroom, locking the door behind her. Gilded gold taps shone. Smoked mirrors reflected her image ad infinitum. An oversized tub sat on a pedestal in the center of the room. Aliesa always showered, never having the time to luxuriate in the tub. But a soak in the tub somehow seemed apropos and might relax her.

She set her purse on the marble countertop and pulled the clip holding her hair. Long strands spilled across her shoulders.

Two plush robes embroidered with the words *His* and *Hers* hung on the back of the door. She stepped out of her clothes, meticulously folding each piece because she would have to put them on again later.

Naked and chilled, she grabbed the terry robe marked *Hers* and slipped it on while she set the water temperature.

Van knew he'd been downright mean.

He had no sympathy for drug dealers.

Why was he so mad?

This woman had every right to be freaked out. Up until this afternoon, she'd been going about her own business. In the last few hours her whole life had come apart at the seams. She needed a little space.

Why did he say she wasn't his type?

He hadn't been exactly truthful.

Intellectual smarts always turned Van on. And the dossier picture he'd downloaded from Drew hadn't done Dr. Atworth justice. The mousy hair in the picture now glistened like freshly brewed Columbian coffee. She wasn't pencil thin with a gray pallor—her skin glowed like amber and her figure held a gracious curve.

Anger bubbled beneath the surface of his calm. He took several deep, cleansing breaths.

Suddenly, loud peals of laughter drew his attention to the front door of the condo. Company, out in the hall.

Van surveyed the room to ensure nothing was out of place. He hurried into the bedroom, stood with the door slightly ajar, and listened.

Chapter 9

A man and woman burst into the penthouse. Lips locked, they spun in a circle, with him struggling to remove his suit coat, and her wiggling out of her black leather bomber jacket.

Abruptly, she stopped, craned her neck and blinked her eyes. Then she raced over to the wall of windows on the far side of the living room and opened the slider to the balcony. Her long red hair tossed in the breeze as she surveyed Boston's cityscape. Tall leather boots covered her long shapely legs. "Wow," she said, snapping her gum. "This is a really nice place you got here."

The small Asian man smiled and dashed through the living room into the open concept kitchen. He reached inside the stainless fridge, pulled out a bottle of Dom, and a huge bowl of fresh strawberries. "I use this place whenever I come to Boston," he said. He popped the champagne, splashed some bubbly into a couple of flutes and hurried out onto the balcony to join her.

Van eased the bedroom door shut and rushed over to the bathroom. It took all of two seconds to open the locked door.

"We've got company," he whispered.

Aliesa, clad in a white robe had been testing the water

and nearly toppled into the tub. "What do you mean we have company?"

Van pulled the plug and prayed the water would drain quickly and silently. Then he grabbed her folded clothes off the counter, handed them over, and hustled her into the bedroom.

Voices headed their way. With nowhere else to go, Van hauled Aliesa still clutching her clothes, shoes and purse tightly to her chest like a life preserver, into the closet. He slid the mirrored door closed, leaving it open barely a crack. Both held their breath as a woman burst into the bedroom tearing away her clothes to reveal a black leather bra and thong.

"Now, pay attention," she commanded. The woman withdrew a short whip from her belt and slapped it against her palm. "Have you been a good boy?"

The man nodded like a wide-eyed eight-year-old.

"Take off your shirt," she said.

The man shucked his button-down shirt and awaited his next command. The dominatrix pushed him back onto the bed and straddled him. She bent and ran her tongue along his chest, but he became impatient. When he grabbed her butt, she bit one of his nipples. His loud yelp pierced the silence.

"I didn't give you permission to touch."

Van couldn't believe his luck. Of all the worst-case scenarios, this one took the prize—he had a half naked woman sitting beside him in the dark and they were forced to watch a sordid peep show. Then he gave himself a shake. It could have been worse. He could have been watching two people having hot sweaty sex, the way he liked it. Not this passive-submissive crap. The more he thought about the woman sitting beside him, the more uncomfortable he became.

Right now, comfort didn't even remotely come into play. A multi-pronged shoetree poked him in the small of his back.

Once his eyes adjusted, he examined his surroundings—to his left stood a bank of drawers and shelves—to his right stretched an empty space for long hanging articles. They had to move over there if they were going to endure their stint here in the closet. And they had to do it without making any noise. They'd still be cramped, but neither of them would have to watch the escapades transpiring in the boudoir.

Van gave this woman credit—she remained calm despite the dire circumstances, even when he'd dragged her out of the bathroom into the closet. She trembled. At first, he thought she was frightened. Rightly so. They didn't need this complication right now. Then, after they switched positions, he figured her shaking might have been from something altogether different.

Van had always had particularly good night vision—an asset on many classified missions. Who knew what she'd been hiding beneath her lab coat? She was well put together and, judging by the gold ring dangling from her necklace, another man's woman.

Ten minutes ago, Aliesa would have bet money her day couldn't get any more hellish. But she would have lost, big time.

Perhaps she needed to view her situation from an entirely new angle. Put a positive spin on things. She'd been fortunate Van barreled into the bathroom when he did, because ten seconds later she would have been stark naked.

Aliesa sat with her back to the wall and watched the goings on through the open crack. She knew some people got off on these types of sexual exploits, but she'd never witnessed them first-hand before. Grateful for the darkness, he'd never see her heated blushes.

His hot breath tickled her ear.

"You need to get dressed."

"Where?"

"Right here." He scrubbed his hand across his brow "Get busy when things get louder out there."

So Aliesa watched and waited.

The dominatrix had stripped the man naked. Her male slave knelt on all fours on the bed. Then, she started his spanking. The thwack reverberated throughout the room and a large red mark blossomed on the man's bare ass.

Amid the yowling, Van nudged Aliesa. She loosened the robe and let it drop to her waist. She grabbed her shirt and shoved it over her head and struggled to find the armholes.

The squealing serenade continued. Van's eyes were shadowed. Seconds elapsed.

Again, his hot breath caressed her neck. "It's backwards."

He could see her clearly enough to know she'd put her shirt on wrong? And if that wasn't bad enough, her body decided to play by Sir Isaac Newton's rules—every action elicited an equal and opposite reaction—her nipples tightened and hardened painfully into little ball bearings while she straightened her top and pulled on her pants.

A gut-twisting yelp emanated from the bed.

Both Van and Aliesa turned to see through the opening over to the bed.

The dynamic in the bedroom had shifted.

The dominatrix no longer held the position of power. Her submissive partner had her pinned on the bed, both of his hands manacled her neck—a move the dominatrix hadn't anticipated because her arms windmilled and clawed at him.

She gasped and couldn't seem to stop watching the horrific scene in the room. This was no act. As the man's hands tightened around her neck he seemed to get more and more aroused. He pumped his hips furiously and pounded into the woman who seemed to become sluggish, even lethargic.

A shiver coursed across her spine and she leaned away from Van. She'd put her life in the hands of a monster—someone with no regard for human life. The man sitting beside her was no better than the frenzied rutting animal on the bed. She couldn't bear it so she squeezed her eyes shut.

Van's anger boiled over.

He pulled his phone out of his pocket, slid open the closet door and slipped quietly into the room. He held his finger on the button and snapped a series of rapid photos. Then he dragged the man off the dominatrix and onto the floor.

On the verge of ecstasy, the man grunted and squealed at being interrupted. Van punched him right between the eyes and he face planted on the floor, out cold.

The dominatrix gulped air. She moaned and coughed and pulled herself to the edge of the bed.

"Are you okay?" Van asked. He pulled a blanket from the bed and wrapped it around her.

She nodded. Her mascara had smudged and black streaked her cheeks. "Thanks," she said, her voice no more than a whisper.

Van bent in front of her. "What do you want to do?"

She blinked tears from her eyes. "I want to go home," she said.

Van opened his phone and made arrangements for a cab to wait for her at the curb. When he finished he turned. "What's your cell phone number?" he asked.

He saw the uncertainty in her eyes.

"I'm going to send you the photos I took," Van explained. "They're your insurance. They'll make sure your friend here doesn't bother you again. The photos are yours to do with whatever you see fit."

Within a half hour the woman was composed enough to leave.

Van grabbed a hold of the man's arm, dragged him into the bathroom and hefted him into the tub, and switched on the cold water.

The man sputtered and screeched and Van turned on his heel and walked out of the bathroom. He stopped at the door of the closet, leaned over and reached out to help Aliesa to her feet. "It's time to go."

Chapter 10

Aliesa couldn't get out of the other penthouse fast enough.

A variety of smells wafted through Aliesa's designer chic apartment. Overturned drawers, couch cushions, and unshelved books lay in shambles on the living room floor. She opened the sliding balcony door in an attempt to fill the rooms with fresh air, but the crisp spring breeze had been subzero and warmer than the blood coursing through her veins.

With detachment, she surveyed the damage. Thankfully, she'd never considered this apartment her home. Hell, she'd barely sat upon the leather sectional in the living room. Her emotional attachment had been for the family home where she was raised, the one she recently sold because she didn't have the time to properly maintain.

Her work had consumed her. Work never allowed her the time necessary to do justice to what had always been her parents' pride and joy. Her job became the pat answer she gave the realtor or anyone who asked her reason for selling. It had nothing to do with the haunting memories assailing her day in and day out—the constant reminder of what she had and lost.

She sold the house fully furnished. The only things she'd taken were the clothes on her back and some jewelry—keepsakes from her parents. She wore her mother's eighteen-karat gold chain and on it hung her father's wedding band.

What about their watches?

She raced into the primary bedroom and snagged the overturned jewelry box from the floor. Empty. She attacked the pile of clothes and shoes heaped on the bed, tossing aside shirts and pants before she struck gold—the contents of her jewelry box. There, beneath the clutter of costume necklaces and earrings, lay her mother's and father's watches. The crystal of her father's pocket watch had been shattered, but the second hand continued to sweep. She took a deep breath and clutched them tightly to her chest.

"Find something?" Van asked, from the bedroom door.

Aliesa brushed a tear from her eye. "They were my parents'. They're all I have left." She patted the necklace and the ring around her neck too.

Too bad he didn't have the same attachment to the gold medallion around his neck. There were days it felt like the hangman's noose.

He stepped over the contents of her dresser drawers and stood beside her. She held the watches out for him to see. First chance she got, she would drop them into her safety deposit box in the bank for safekeeping.

"Why don't you jump into the shower?" Van said. "I'll straighten the living room." Quietly, he walked back through the bedroom, closing the door behind him.

Hot water massaged Aliesa's tense muscles. She'd never been in the best physical shape because she never really took care of herself—a situation compounded by her poor diet, lack of sleep and exercise. She spent hours hunched over her studies, which accounted for her disheveled appearance, and she rarely wore makeup because it would be lost beneath her thick prescription eyeglasses. But everything changed with her first stem-cell injection. The steamer trunks beneath her eyes shrank to overnight bags. The constant muscle pain in her back and neck had become the odd twinge. She could barely believe the physical changes within her own body. Her dull, mousy hair shined lustrously. She'd thrown away her reading glasses and she had energy galore.

Energy she'd put to good use.

By the time she left the confines of the primary bedroom, she'd hung and folded her clothes, tidied both the bedroom and the bathroom, and taken a shower. Clad in fleece, she padded into the living room to help Van with his cleanup efforts, but he'd already put everything in order.

He sat on her sofa, texting a message on his phone and eating a slice of pizza. Her stomach growled in protest, another of the many changes occurring in her body. Aliesa had gone from never being hungry, to hungry most of the time.

The sight of the pizza triggered another memory and quite suddenly she found herself back in her BU lab, two short weeks ago.

Evelyne barreled into Aliesa's office balancing her books, two hot drinks, and take out. "Since you've taken to practically living at the university, I thought you could use some sustenance," she said. She placed the takeout on the desk.

The aroma of French vanilla and mocha filled the small room, drawing Aliesa from her chair. She pulled the coffee from the tray, pried open the lid, inhaled the heavenly scent before taking a sip. Evelyne ripped open the bag and passed her a muffin.

"What a surprise," Aliesa said. "Bird seed muffins. Again. Couldn't you bring cinnamon rolls just once?"

"As long as I'm toting the food it's going to be healthy. And they're not bird seed muffins, they're seven grain. They're good for you."

"Why does everything good for me have to taste like cardboard?"

"Be thankful I brought you coffee and not green tea."

Aliesa narrowed her eyes. "How do you get it past your nose? It smells like someone steeped a pair of dirty socks."

"It's an acquired taste," Evelyne said. "It's not bad once you get used to it. And it's very good for you. Full of antioxidants."

"I'm sure. But I'd never get it past my nose, unless I put it in a hypodermic."

Van pocketed his phone and turned toward her.

Aliesa startled. "What?"

"Help yourself to some pizza," he said.

She lifted the lid of the box and grabbed a slice. Despite the hunger pains, she couldn't stop thinking about her friend. She folded the piece of pizza lengthwise in her hand. "Evelyne ordered my last pizza."

Van's eyes were unreadable and Aliesa desperately needed to talk about her best friend. "One night, a couple of weeks ago, after a particularly bad day in the lab, she called to tell me she'd ordered pizza."

Van straightened. "What constitutes a bad day in the lab?"

"All of my cultured stem cells euthanized."

"That sucks."

"The right cytokine doesn't do much of anything unless you have the right enzyme to activate the protein in the DNA chromosome." She'd lost him. His eyes glazed over with her science talk. "Anyhow, Evelyne called to give me another pep talk. She told me I'd figure it out. She said she'd help me re-culture all of the cells because she didn't want me to give up."

A lump formed in Aliesa's throat. With Evelyne gone, she had been rendered virtually friendless at age thirty.

"How did her pep talk translate into pizza?"

"She knew I'd go home and since my cupboards were almost always bare, she ordered me a pizza."

"She knew you pretty well. I tried to make something

to eat in your kitchen. I found an over-ripe container of kung pao chicken and a moldy brick of cheese in the fridge. I chucked both."

"See." Domestically challenged, Aliesa made no excuses. "So I thanked her. She laughed and told me not to be too hasty. She said she ordered a tofu pizza. I was so hungry by then it didn't really matter, I would have eaten anything."

He shuddered. "Tofu pizza?"

Aliesa smiled. "It smelled like regular pizza. I only hoped it didn't taste as gross as it sounded."

"And..."

"She'd been messing with me. She ordered cheese and pepperoni, just like this." Finally, she took a bite and devoured the slice. Van held open the box and offered another, which she took.

She sat beside him on the couch.

Again, he pulled out his phone and pushed several buttons. She strained to see the screen but the man took the word "secretive" to a new level.

"What are we going to do first?" she asked.

Van flashed a get-real stare. "Who said you were going to help me do anything?"

Not knowing what to do with his comment, she sat back on the couch. It never occurred to her that Van didn't want her help. Shades of grade school all over again. She'd never once been *chosen* to be on the team.

"Evelyne meant more to me than you know. I can't sit around and do nothing. If you don't want my help, I'll do it myself."

Her statement got his full attention. "And what do you think you're going to do? I've saved your ass twice in the past twenty-four hours."

"There's got to be something I can do." She rubbed her hands together. "I'm pretty good at problem-solving."

A loud crack resounded in the outside corridor.

Van jumped, instantly alert.

Aliesa cowered.

He grabbed her hand, tugged her along the hall, and tucked her behind the front door. He leaned toward the peephole and checked the hall. He exhaled on a sigh and his head fell forward.

"What is it?"

"Molly Maid's here to tidy next door."

Aliesa took a turn and peered through the peephole. A woman wheeled a cleaning cart into the suite across the hall. When Aliesa turned to say something, he stood staring into space, deep in thought.

Finally, he snapped out of it. "There's someone we need to see."

Chapter 11

After Aliesa's earlier conversation with Van, she didn't think he'd take her anywhere. She'd been shocked when he told her to get ready.

First, he took a three-minute shower. She knew the exact length of time because she'd barely been able to conceal her two remaining stem-cell injections. She could stash them in the refrigerator, but it would be too obvious and they'd be easily spotted. And if this did turn out to be a case of corporate espionage, there would be no reason to keep her around once the serum had been procured. She opted for door number two and placed the injections inside her wine fridge behind a very expensive bottle of Beaujolais.

Moments later Van came bounding through hall. She grabbed her purse and her coat. "I'm ready when you are."

He eyed her up and down. "Lose the purse."

Okay. She dug out her wallet and dropped the bag on the kitchen counter.

"Dead people don't use credit cards."

"But..." She'd better clam up or he'd leave without her. He opened the purse and she tossed the wallet inside. He placed the bag back on the counter, turned and walked to the door.

Aliesa stopped. "Oh, we need a key," she said.

"I've got one," Van said. He opened the closet and handed her an overcoat, a scarf, and gave her a pair of dark glasses to put on. When he was comfortable with her makeshift disguise they left her building and walked to the business district of Boston's downtown core. She followed Van into a high-rise, rode the elevator to the seventh floor and entered the office of ABC Inquiries. A woman sat behind the computer desk in the neatly kept office.

"He's expecting you," she said.

"Thanks, Simone." Van nodded introductions. "Aliesa Atworth this is Simone Seville."

Simone shook Aliesa's hand; long red, white, and blue airbrushed fingernails skimmed her skin. Simone had lustrous midnight black hair and wore a tight skirt and low cut blouse designed to turn heads—nothing at all like Aliesa's baggy pants and shirt. Just once Aliesa would like to draw the appreciation of all the men around her. Instead, she schlepped through the room. The inside office could have passed for the bridge of the Starship Enterprise with the captain sitting in a customized wheelchair surrounded by six state-of-the-art computers.

"What have you got for me?" Van asked.

The man swung around in his chair. "I believe that's my question. Did you bring the stick?"

Van dug a flash drive out of his pocket and handed it to him.

"Good to see you too, Van," he said. He wheeled forward and stuck his hand out to introduce himself to Aliesa. "He's a nice guy, but his manners leave a lot to be desired. I'm Drew Nystyshyn. You must be Aliesa Atworth."

Aliesa shook Drew's hand.

"Based on your dazed expression, the big guy over there didn't mention I was a paraplegic."

She shook her head.

"I had to trade in my Special Forces Tiddlywinks when I got shot in Mogadishu. Bullet severed my spinal cord. All my calisthenics are mental now."

Special Forces? Drew's casual reference to the unit made it sound like Van might have been one too. For the first time, hope bloomed. Once upon a time, Van had been a good guy.

"Are you finished? Talk much?" Van asked, his brow furrowed, his face red.

Drew shrugged. "What can I say? I don't get out a lot." He swung the chair around and rolled back toward the main frame. "Lucas and Devine uses a firm called Spit and Polish."

"Did you uncover any names and addresses of their night-shift employees?"

"I did." Drew handed Van a printout.

A moment later, Simone poked her head inside the office. "I'm all set, Aliesa, if you are?"

Aliesa straightened. She regarded Van with wide eyes.

Van tugged Aliesa aside. "You need to change your appearance if you're going to tag along with me—insurance to keep you safe."

Aliesa blinked and listened to Van despite the heat rising in her cheeks. She worked hard to keep her expression unreadable.

"Simone has generously offered to take you shopping and help you make some necessary changes."

Aliesa had her doubts about Van, and Simone. At this particular point in time, Van held all of the cards, so she'd go with the flow. She turned and faced Simone. "Let's go," she said, sailing past Van out into the hall.

Simone's eyes threw daggers at Van. "We have a lot to do so don't expect us back soon. I'll call if we have any trouble," she said, slamming the door.

Outside the office, Aliesa already held the elevator.

"Sorry," Simone said, joining her.

"About what?"

"Van should have asked if you wanted to change your appearance before he had me make the arrangements."

"It's okay." Evelyne mentioned a make-over a while back and these extenuating circumstance made it a priority. The roller coaster Aliesa rode had been speeding along for so long she barely noticed this latest bump on the track. "I understand why he's doing it. He's trying to protect me."

"He could have been more diplomatic."

Aliesa pictured Evelyne smiling. It's not like her best friend ever practiced diplomacy with her either. "I'll survive," Aliesa said, feeling so ashamed she could still draw oxygen in and out of her lungs.

The two women walked out of the building and hailed a cab.

"Where to?" the cabbie asked.

"The fashion district. Armando's."

The cabbie made a face. So did Aliesa.

Simone turned toward her. "I know it's not far, but Van made me promise not to parade you around, out in the open." Simone opened her purse and took out a ten-dollar bill. "You've got an appointment with Armando. He's going to give you a fabulous new haircut, while Kat does your nails."

Aliesa reeled. "How did you get all of this organized so quickly?" Had Van been truthful with her? What if she wasn't in any real danger? What if he'd simply been trying to scare her so she'd tell him about her research?

"What's wrong? Are you feeling all right?" Simone asked.

"When did Van tell you we were coming?" Aliesa asked, in a small voice.

"Only about an hour ago. You're really lucky. Armando just happened to have an opening."

She relaxed and exhaled the breath she'd been holding, but her hand still shook as she adjusted the scarf on her head. She had to stop questioning Van at every turn.

"It's all right to be afraid," Simone said, patting Aliesa's arm. "I don't know exactly what's going on but I know people are after you. Add a new hairstyle to the mix and your stress is probably off the scale. I can't put your mind at ease about the other but Armando is a master. You're in very good hands. There isn't anyone more qualified to do the job. I trust him implicitly."

Aliesa couldn't have cared less about a new hairdo. Her appearance had never been a priority with her. She had to figure out who killed her best friend and why.

The cab pulled to the door of Armando's on Newberry Street. Simone passed the cabbie ten dollars for a four-dollar fare. "Keep it," she said, winking at Aliesa. "Van's footing the bill."

They walked inside the salon.

"Simone, darling." A man completely outfitted in black dragged his tortoise-shell glasses to the tip of his nose. "Is this her?"

Simone nodded. "Yes, this is Aliesa."

"Come here, sweetheart." Armando waved her over. "Let me see you."

She walked over to where Armando stood. He lifted her hair, twisted it into a knot, and studied her from several angles.

Armando wore both face and eye makeup which took about ten years off his age. He grabbed a handful of hair and inspected the ends. "When was the last time you had a haircut, honey?"

"A long time ago," Aliesa said. In fact, she couldn't remember. In the last few months, she'd never had enough time to make an appointment so she grabbed the scissors, trimmed her bangs and tidied her ends.

"Well, never mind. You'll be ready for the runway when I finish.

Drew inserted the flash drive into his computer to transfer the information. "You did everything I told you to do. The email file is intact. You copied a couple thousand emails on this drive," he said. "I'll run it through another program to compile a list of repeating contacts."

"Perfect," Van said. "I knew it had to be a pretty big file because it took several minutes to download." At one point during the process he wondered if he'd be able to get out of Hernandez's lab without the custodian noticing.

"Okay," Drew said. He pushed print and snagged the copy. "Here's it is."

Van sat and read it. For the amount of emails the list didn't seem to be as long as he expected. There were four. The top hit was Panacealla Pharmaceuticals, then an organization called Lucas and Devine, Capill Industries, and lastly Dr. Aliesa Atworth. "You wouldn't happen to know if these four hits have in anything in common, would you?"

"Give me a few minutes and I'll see if I can find any correlations," Drew said. "Go and grab us a coffee from the lobby."

Van did as Drew asked and by the time he returned Drew handed him another list.

"Panacealla Pharmaceuticals funded Dr. Marcus Hernandez's research," Drew said. "And Panacealla owns Capill Industries, in Quincy. The company fills capsules and presses pills. Most of Panacealla's formulations are sent there."

"I see." Aliesa had been telling Van the truth about Panacealla. "And Lucas and Devine?"

"It seems Panacealla Pharmaceuticals hired Saul Devine to terminate Hernandez's contract."

"Recently?"

"Last month."

"I think I've heard the name Saul Devine before," Van said.

"Probably. Lucas and Devine is a very up-and-coming law firm in Beacon Hill. He sits on the committee running Aliesa's condo corporation."

"For Bayfront Towers?"

"One and the same."

Van stood and put on his jacket.

"Going somewhere?" Drew asked

"I think I'm going to pay Saul Devine a visit."

"What makes you think you'll get in to see him without an appointment?"

Van pulled out a leather billfold and flipped it open. It was photo identification for a DEA field agent.

"Weren't you supposed to turn that in when you quit?"

"Ooops."

Van strode out of Drew's office and walked ten minutes to Beacon Hill and the prestigious firm of Lucas and Devine.

He intended to shake the bushes to see if anything slithered out.

He flashed his identification and was asked to sit in the waiting room.

"Elliot Vance," the secretary said. "Mr. Devine will see you now." The unsmiling, fifty-something woman rose from her desk and opened the office door.

Van had been watching her for the last twenty minutes. The cut of her suit indicated she'd lost several pounds. No wedding ring, no family photos on the desk, red-rimmed eyes, gray pallor. "Thank you," he said, pushing past her.

He strode inside across the jewel-toned Tabriz rug to one of the leather wingback chairs in front of the antique desk. Bookshelves flanked the far wall, lined with volumes of gold embossed leather legal journals.

Saul Devine, Esquire, stood and stretched out his

hand. "Nice to meet you, Mr. Vance. May I call you Elliot?"

"Not if you expect me to answer." He shook Saul's hand. "I prefer Van."

Saul sat in his tufted leather chair. He removed his half-moon spectacles and cleaned them with a cloth. "What can I do for you, Van?"

Van undid his jacket button. "This is more of a courtesy call," Van said.

"How so?"

"I understand Panacealla Pharmaceuticals is one of your largest clients."

Saul steepled his fingers. "It's not common knowledge, but we have been working on their behalf recently."

"I thought you might want to give your client a heads up," Van said. "One of their South American contractors was murdered recently."

"I see," Saul said. "Does this contractor have a name?"

"It's Dr. Marcus Hernandez out of Trujillo, Peru."

Van watched Saul very closely for any telltale reaction.

"How did you come by this information?"

"He was under investigation for manufacturing cocaine."

No reaction. Nothing seemed to rile Saul's poker face. He sat back in his seat.

"It seems the Alarcon Cartel put Hernandez out of business permanently."

"I see." Saul shook his head. "Thank you for the information. I don't believe this information will impact the company I represent. Mr. Hernandez had already been released from his contract. But I will be sure to pass this information along to the owner."

Van nodded, buttoned his jacket. At the door he turned.

"Is there something else?" Saul asked.

"An observation," Van said. "Your secretary is ill."

Saul's eyes widened. "Yes. How did you know?"

"I pay attention," he said. Then he turned and walked through the hall toward the exit. Along the way he came upon a door with a housekeeping sign on it. He nearly walked right on by it, but suddenly he thought about the cleaning cart he saw this morning headed to the penthouse across the hall from Aliesa's. He cracked the door. Nestled inside was a wheeled cart with the words *Spit and Polish* stenciled across it.

Outside on the street he shrugged into his jacket and called Drew. "I need the address of a custodial service called Spit and Polish, here in Boston."

"I'll send the address to your phone," Drew said.

Before Van could disconnect his phone dinged.

The address.

Not far. Located in the North End—more commonly referred to as Little Italy—a brisk twenty-minute walk. He double-checked the address Drew had given him on Hanover Street, not far from the Paul Revere House. No number hung on the door, but through the process of elimination he knew the residence had to be sandwiched between Mama Mia's Pizzeria and a Giovanni's Groceteria.

He knocked.

No answer.

When he was about to leave, an old man came out of

Giovanni's and called over to him. "What do you want?"

Van spun to face the older man. "Where's Joe Spina?" The man narrowed his eyes so Van sweetened the pot.

"I borrowed fifty bucks off him last week at work and I came to return it." He fished a fifty out of his pocket and waved it at the older gent. A lie, but the bold ruse routinely worked.

The old man's brow relaxed and he waved Van toward the rear of the store. "Joe's in the back alley, unloading a delivery."

Van wormed his way through the store's narrow aisles of foodstuffs and into a storage room. The alley door of the store stood open and a man unloaded a dolly by stacking the boxes against the far wall. Then he disappeared outside.

Inside the panel truck, Joe shoved boxes closer to the bumper. Van studied Joe. Slivers of gray streaked his dark hair. His work clothes, despite being well worn had been pressed to hold a sharp crease. He appeared to be in his mid-thirties.

"Who are you?" he asked when he noticed Van staring.

"The name's Van."

"What can I do for you?" Joe asked, sliding more boxes forward.

"I have a business proposition for you," Van said.

"What kind of a business proposition?"

"A lucrative one."

"Do I have to do anything illegal?"

Van shook his head. "I'd like to pay you to take the night off. Why don't I buy you a late lunch so we can discuss it?"

The expression on Joe's face went from mildly

interested to skeptical. "Can't," he finally said. "I still have a couple of hours left here before my shift tonight at Lucas and Devine."

Van rolled his sleeves, grabbed the dolly and began stacking boxes. "If I give you a hand to get this truck unloaded in half the time, will you hear me out, then?"

Joe eyed Van guardedly. He slid another box forward. "There's no harm in listening."

Chapter 12

Angry was Van's new state of mind. The angrier and busier, the better.

He never expected to meet anyone like Aliesa. He expected her to be brilliant; he didn't expect her to be so damn needy. A woman involved in the cocaine trade should have a thick skin. She should be spoiled, egotistical, and a snob with a God complex.

Not.

Losing Evelyne affected her. When she rushed into her bedroom to locate her late parents' keepsakes, Van had gotten a close up of her pain. Lucky for him, the ring on the chain around her neck had to be her father's. He'd found nothing to corroborate any involvement in the cocaine industry when he cleaned her living room either.

It only left him with more questions. If she'd been involved with Hernandez, why had she been so upset by her assistant's death? And the obvious question—where the hell was the missing cocaine?

She was hiding something.

At one point, Van thought she might be carrying a brick of uncut cocaine inside her purse. But his theory dissolved the moment he dumped her purse out on the coffee table in the adjacent penthouse. The contents of her lunch bag had been the only thing he hadn't thoroughly examined. And its small size discounted his uncut cocaine theory. One squeeze told him there were two small containers inside—containers which easily could have been a sample or test kits for prospective buyers.

Until he had proof to the contrary, he had no choice but to stay mad. Staying mad would maintain his focus.

Late afternoon, Van returned to the ABC Inquiries office. He strolled through the door and set a shopping bag on top of Drew's desk.

"A present? For me?" Drew asked in a syrupy voice.

"Not likely," Van said. He pulled a pair of coveralls out of the bag. "Think these will fit Aliesa?"

Drew eyed the utilitarian work clothes. "Hard to know. Couldn't see a thing because of the trench coat she wore this morning."

Van had been grateful for the cover up. He remembered Aliesa's form all too well from their night in the closet. The baggier the outfit the better. "I think the coveralls will fit. Might have to roll the sleeves, but we'll make it work."

"I guess you're going to be working the night shift at Lucas and Devine." Drew wheeled his chair over to his main frame.

"Uh huh," Van said.

Drew shook his head. "How the hell did you get someone to trust you in less than an hour?"

Van shrugged. "Simple. I earned it."

"And?"

"I helped him unload a truck. And I made him a

promise."

"Your firstborn?"

"Not quite. I simply told him no one would ever know he didn't show up for work. He itemized a complete list of chores to be completed on site."

Drew wouldn't have been any more surprised unless his friend sprouted horns.

"I need to gain access into Saul's computer," Van said, sitting on the corner of the desk. "Any suggestions?"

"A Trojan horse might work," Drew said.

"What's that?"

"It's a program which installs a back door in his system so I can return later and gain access."

"Won't Devine know his computer security has been breached?"

"Not if you follow my instructions to the letter. This program mimics a Microsoft security update. He'll download it to protect his computer. Most people don't question anything sent to them by Microsoft."

"Brilliant."

"Thanks," Drew said.

The door in the outer office sprang open. Simone hurried inside and dumped several shopping bags on top of her desk and removed her jacket. Aliesa came through the door next. Same overcoat, dark glasses, and scarf.

Van and Drew turned toward each other then at Simone. "She doesn't appear any different now than from when she left this morning," Van said.

"Patience," Simone said. "Something you seem to have very little of." She raised a brow and rubbed the corners of her eyes.

Aliesa removed her dark sunglasses.

Her indigo eyes pierced deep, seducing him. Had they always been so rich and vibrant?

Slowly, she pulled the scarf off her head.

The transformation made his mouth drop. Her shoulder-length hair had been neatly shaped into a sassy bob. Blonde shimmered on the smooth strands and warmed her entire face. Blood rushed through Van's veins like a runaway train and he struggled to keep his expression unreadable.

Then she undid the buttons of her raincoat and slipped it off.

Everyone else in the office disappeared and he fantasized her reveal was all for him. Her loose fitting track pants had been replaced with form fitting clothes. In fact, her skin–tight outfit might very well have been painted on.

He closed his mouth and something deep inside him snapped. "I told you to change her appearance and make her unrecognizable."

"I know." Simone watched Van assess Aliesa. "She doesn't appear anything like she did when we left this morning, does she, Drew?"

All three sets of eyes turned toward Drew. He shook his head frantically.

"She's totally different, all right," Van said. "Only now, I have another problem. She might not be recognized, but she will certainly be remembered."

Van handed Aliesa her coat, scarf, and glasses and helped her put them back on. It turned out to be a cold and brisk walk back to Aliesa's apartment—one which had absolutely nothing to do with the temperature outside.

Aliesa had barely spoken two words to Van since they left ABC Inquires. She'd simply given Simone a hug, grabbed her parcels, and fell into step beside Van.

The quiet gave Van an opportunity to consider how cruel he'd been. He'd been a complete jerk. Perhaps he'd been working alone for too long. Being alone didn't make it all right. He'd fucked up.

They entered the Bayfront Towers and rode the elevator to the penthouse suite. Before he opened the door to Aliesa's apartment, he turned toward her. "I'm sorry," he said.

She faced him with wide eyes and tried with all her might not to cry, though he would have deserved it if she had. "None of this is your fault," he said. "I should have been more specific when I told Simone to alter your appearance."

He held the door to her penthouse and waited until she walked inside. She hung her coat and scarf, walked the hall and placed her parcels on top of the sofa in the living room.

He followed her.

She paced the length of the room. "What's next?" she asked.

Dumbfounded, Van stepped back. Nothing about this woman added up. Just when he thought he had her all figured out, she threw him for another loop.

"What's wrong?" she asked, when he didn't immediately respond.

"I'm confused," Van said. "What happened to you giving me the silent treatment? Why aren't you still mad at me?"

She raised her hand and quieted him. "You asked me

to change my appearance and I did. My appearance has never really mattered much to me. You may not like what you see, but I'm confident no one is going to recognize me so mission accomplished."

"You're right," Van said. Better to leave well enough alone. He tossed her the bag he'd been carrying.

"What's this?" Aliesa asked, peering inside.

"Your coveralls. We're working the grave-yard shift tonight."

She shook the wrinkles out of the jumpsuit and turned it around. "Spit and Polish," she said. "Where are we going?"

"A company called Lucas and Devine," Van said.

"And you think they have the cocaine?"

"Not exactly."

"Then why are we going there?"

"To try to get a handle on all of the players."

"I see. More guilt by association?" She rolled her eyes.

"The information we need isn't lying around in a filing cabinet. Likely, it's password protected on his computer."

"You're going to hack into his computer files?"

"In a manner of speaking. And we'll install a listening device on his phone."

"What do you need me for?" Aliesa asked.

"To help me clean." He didn't wait to hear her response. "I'm going to grab a quick shower."

Van grabbed his coveralls and headed into the main

bathroom. A moment later, Aliesa heard him singing in the shower.

She wondered when she'd stop being so pathetic. This topsy-turvy life she'd hazarded upon scared the dickens out of her. If that wasn't bad enough, every time she caught sight of her reflection, she barely recognized herself. She was a scientist, not a freaking secret agent. Subterfuge? Her? She'd do what ever it took to avenge Evelyne's death. Even clean an office.

But right now she needed an infusion of confidence.

The closest she could come would be a stem-cell injection.

With Van still belting out a tuneless chorus, she rushed over to the wine fridge and removed one of the two remaining stem-cell injections. She grabbed her parcels and padded across the hall, closing the door to her bedroom behind her.

Chapter 13

A cold shower.

He needed to focus and cool his revved engine.

While he waited for Aliesa to change, he went into the kitchen to grab a slice of stale pizza. Only then did he spot her purse, exactly where he'd tossed it when he told her she couldn't bring it to ABC Inquiries. The same purse she'd clung to like some sort of magic amulet.

Odd. She'd obviously removed the item she'd been protecting. Once again he turned the purse out onto the table. Everything appeared exactly as he remembered except for one thing. The insulated lunch bag was empty.

He opened the freezer and found the small freezer pack but nothing else. He searched through the various compartments of the fridge—the crisper, butter keeper, even inside the jar of pickles and jam.

Nothing. Maybe he'd made too much out of this. Maybe the lunch bag had simply contained her lunch. He opened the cupboard beneath the sink and checked the garbage. Nope. Empty.

He chewed the piece of leftover pizza and a sudden inkling took him into the living room and the wine fridge.

Bingo.

Hidden behind a bottle of wine he found an unmarked vial as long and twice as wide as his thumb. But only one. He could have sworn he'd pawed two items inside the bag when he handed everything back from her purse.

He lifted the vial to the light and shook it. Clear. Like saline. His mind darted. What the hell was it? And what had she done with the other one?

Then Aliesa came bounding out of her room, other things took priority. They took a cab and arrived ten minutes early for their shift at Lucas and Devine. Van let himself in with Joe's spare set of keys—keys he promised to leave behind in the cleaning cart—keys Van had copied so he could let himself in later to collect the surveillance equipment they planned to install tonight.

At half past nine, Van rose from Saul Devine's desk and stretched. While Aliesa pushed a mop and cleaned the women and men's bathroom, he installed the Trojan horse on Saul's computer.

Five minutes left.

Drew never mentioned it would take the better part of an hour to download the software. Good thing they had all night to put things in place. As long as he and Aliesa were out of the office prior to start of business the next day, the mission would be a success.

The search of Saul's office turned up no bugs or cameras. And Van took the added precaution of installing a digital transmission intercept on his phone. Since the device was voice activated, the battery on the unit should last upward of eleven days and he could safely locate the receiver somewhere out of the way in the housekeeping closet.

Finally, a notice flashed on Saul's computer screen telling Van the program had been successfully transferred. Just as Drew said it would. A little bubble floated at the bottom of the screen informing the user a Microsoft update sat ready to be installed. All Devine had to do was press enter.

Van collected the disc and went to the door of the office. He could hear the vacuum roaring in the outer offices. When he opened the door he needed to quickly duck out of sight. Saul Devine, the man himself, barreled through the hall toward him. Van turned to the left and right and figured it was game over when Aliesa nearly plowed into him with the power head.

Van watched them. Saul had immediately changed tack. He'd slung his suit jacket over his shoulder and turned to face Aliesa. The man stood transfixed, likely watching the sway of Aliesa's hips as she continued to push the vacuum to and fro.

"Are you new?" Saul shouted above the drone of the vacuum.

Aliesa switched off the beast. "I beg your pardon?"

"I wondered if you were new?" Devine said, his voice much lower.

"I'm a temp," Aliesa said, winding the cord on the handle. "The regular guy is out with the flu." She hefted the Hoover onto her cart and grabbed the rag to wipe surfaces.

"Your face is familiar," he said, narrowing his eyes. "Have you ever waitressed at the Hunt Club?"

Aliesa kept her head down and didn't make eye contact.

"Never mind," he said. He shook his head. Then he

turned and headed toward his office, swinging the door closed behind him.

Van crawled out from underneath the secretary's desk, and sprinted toward the janitor's closet. Inside, he found Aliesa sitting on the floor, shaking like a Parkinson's patient.

He sat and put his arms around her. "It's okay. You did really good."

Her breath was ragged. "I couldn't figure out why the name Lucas and Devine sounded so familiar. That man is part of the committee which governs the building I live in. I've met him a couple of times at condo meetings," she said, her bottom lip quivering.

"Breathe," Van said.

She took a deep breath and blew it out. "You saved my ass back there. If you hadn't tried to run him over with the vacuum he would have ran right into me. And since I paid him a visit this afternoon he certainly would have remembered me."

"I did?" she squeaked.

"You did," he said. Gawd, she filled his arms perfectly. He rubbed his hand across her silky hair and fought the urge to lift her chin for a kiss.

"What if he's on the phone right now telling the police Dr. Aliesa Atworth is still alive?"

"He thought he knew you from the Hunt Club, not as the doctor who owns a penthouse in Bayfront Towers. Guess you were right about that too."

Van reached into the inside pocket of his coveralls and withdrew the digital receiver which could easily be mistaken for a cordless telephone and switched it on. A light flashed indicating the unit had been voice activated. "He's on the line all right. But we won't know with whom until we get back to your place."

"You bugged his phone?"

Van shrugged. "I didn't have anything else to do while I waited for the Trojan horse to download."

"The hell you didn't. You could have helped me clean."

The light on the handset extinguished and Van popped the storage drive in the handheld and replaced it with a new one.

With the office squeaky clean they left Lucas and Devine, and under the cover of darkness they walked the several blocks back to Aliesa's apartment, grabbing some takeout at the corner deli on their way.

They sat at the dining room table eating corned beef on rye and Van inserted the storage drive into another handheld receiver so they could listen to it. Saul's voice crackled through the speaker.

You wanted to speak with me?

I thought you might be interested in some new information about the woman you asked me to investigate a few weeks ago.

Irrelevant considering she's dead, don't you think?

Aliesa nearly choked on her sandwich. "That sounds like Detective Lowry?"

"Shhh," Van said.

You believe everything you read in the papers?

Are you saying the woman is alive?

"Shit," Van said. He stood and paced.

I'm listening.

Can I expect the same compensation as the last time?

Absolutely. Where is she?

With someone very well connected. Whoever he is, he was able to get the victim's true identity suppressed for a few weeks

Why call me?

Because I thought you might like to know she's involved in some pretty deep shit.

Can you be more specific?

Somebody wants her dead. I think it was a professional hit.

When the red light on the handset went black, Van reached across the table and switched it off. A professional hit? Van would never call Jorge and Axel professional hit men. And no professional would kill the wrong person—unless they didn't have a choice.

"C'mon," he said, dragging Aliesa out of her seat. "It's time to go."

"What?" Aliesa said. "Go where?"

"Anywhere but here."

"I thought you said I would be safe here."

"Not now. People know you're not dead."

He grabbed their coats and got on the elevator. Van pressed P1.

"Why are we going to the parking garage?" Aliesa asked.

"We need to get as far away from here as possible."

"Are you going to steal a car?" she squeaked.

"We can't walk fast enough since you're back on the grid."

The elevator slid to a stop and the doors opened. He exited. She didn't. He jumped back across the threshold stopping the elevator doors from closing.

"I won't be an accessory to stealing anything," she

exclaimed crossing her arms over her chest.

"Seriously?" he said. "We're not stealing a car, okay? How the hell do you think I got here in the first place? On the T?"

"How should I know? And if you've had a car at our disposal all this time, why have we been walking and cabbing it everywhere?"

"Because walking is good exercise." He rolled his eyes. "And parking in the downtown core is a nuisance."

Van grabbed her hand and he led her out of the elevator. They walked ten feet or so and he stopped beside a sleek, black, motorcycle.

"This isn't a car." Her voice trailed off to barely a whisper.

"I never said I drove a car here," Van said. When he turned and faced Aliesa he noticed the color had drained from her cheeks. "It's like a bicycle only bigger."

"I've never ridden a bicycle before. When all the kids on the street were out riding their bikes I was inside making potions with my chemistry set."

"You're going to love it." He dug two half-helmets out of the saddlebag and handed her one.

She turned the helmet over in her hand and pushed it back toward him. "I don't think I will. I think I'd rather take my chances upstairs."

Fuelled by adrenaline, Van spoke through clenched teeth. "Listen to me. If the detective contacted Saul Devine to tell him you weren't dead, it's a safe bet he isn't the only person who knows."

"You have no way of knowing that. You seem to have a very low opinion of people." Aliesa rubbed her hands together. "You think the police force is incompetent, I'm a drug dealer, and the detective is on the take."

"If it sounds like a duck it usually is."

"Do you still think I'm dealing drugs?"

He thought back to this afternoon and the missing vial from the bar fridge.

She sighed. "I think I'm going to take my chances with the police."

Entirely preoccupied by their debate, Van hadn't noticed the dark sedan pulling into an empty spot at the end of the aisle until two burly figures bored toward them. He had to do something fast.

He strode toward Aliesa, who had already swiped her card to summon the elevator. He spun her around.

Her eyes shimmered with unshed tears. "I'm not a drug..."

Van did the only thing he could think of to stop her from completing the rest of her sentence. He swallowed the words on her lips by kissing her.

Chapter 14

—————————————————————————

Van could kiss.

A million sensations assaulted Aliesa—she burned hot and cold, the wire of desire tightened—painfully so.

He plundered, then serenaded, taking his time to linger. Only time must have been an abstract variable and as much as Aliesa tried to analyze and catalog her reactions, she found herself unable to do anything but follow his lead.

Through a fringe of eyelashes, she became vaguely aware of two men as they breezed past them to board the elevator.

"Get a room, why don't you?" one of the men said, pressing the button to close the elevator door.

She dropped the helmet dangling from her hand.

Van ended the kiss and set her at arm's length. "Now do you believe me? They were the two men who ransacked your apartment," he said.

Her brain took a moment to kick into gear. The one who made the snide remark did have a Spanish accent. She gulped. "Do you think they're the ones who killed Evelyne?"

"I'm not so sure any more. Lowry said the job was

professional. If so, Evelyne may not have been killed because of a mistaken identity. Maybe she surprised the killer and because she'd seen his face he had no choice but to kill her. I don't know exactly; all I know is it isn't safe here."

Aliesa struggled to process his statement and watched Van lift the helmet and hand it to her.

She relented.

Van walked her back over to the motorcycle and he helped her tighten the chinstrap. Then he straddled the bike and nodded for her to slide on the back. "Put your arms around me," he said, adjusting his helmet.

"Where are we going?" she asked.

"Grayson Everet's place."

"We're going to pay my boss a visit? Right now? It's after midnight. You must be pretty anxious to confirm my alibi." Her last remark had been intended to get a reaction out of him, which he neither confirmed or denied. She shook her head, climbed on behind him and then she put her hands on his sides.

He grabbed her hands and pulled them tight around his waist. "I don't want to lose you going around a corner."

She may have been an analytical genius but that didn't mean she couldn't ever be stumped. She didn't have a clue what to do next. She tried to put their kiss into perspective. He hadn't been overcome with desire—he'd simply created a diversion—so Aliesa wouldn't be recognized. Hard to identify someone when they were lip locked. Unfortunately for her, the diversion had been so successful she'd let herself believe it. She'd even moaned. Not just a little, a lot.

As she saw it, she had two options. She could ignore what happened, or pretend she'd gone along with it. Not likely, with her limited experience. Lust had flattened her like a steamroller. No man had ever kissed her like he had. Oh, she'd been pecked hello and goodbye, she'd been smooched on the cheek or lips, but never I-want-to-get-you-naked kissed. Of course, Van didn't have to know her dilemma.

She thought back to her meeting with Grayson on the day her life spun out of control. She loathed the odious little man who cranked the heat every three months and set her blood boiling.

"The money's gone," Grayson Everet said. "Your refusal to accept the termination of your project will only make matters worse."

"Worse?" This couldn't be happening, not now, when she'd recently discovered a promising new cytokine which could very well be her work's missing link. "It's a shame because I'm on the brink of success. I've doubled and in some cases tripled the life expectancy of my test sample."

The surly smile on his face gave her a modicum of hope. She hated playing money mind games. Finding funds was his job, not hers. She opened her folder and gave him the details of her success.

A genuine smile spread on Grayson's face from cheek to cheek. He listened intently. Every so often, he would nod, say something innocuous like "excellent", then he would jot a note on the pad in front of him.

She made slow headway.

He tapped his pencil on the pad. "You're saying the cells aren't dying—they're stronger and more resistant to infection?"

"Correct."

"You've stumbled across the proverbial fountain of youth."

She raised her hand. "Hold on a minute. Those are merely the lucky side effects of the study, not my original intent. If the Ethics Oversight Committee catches wind of your comment I would be shut down."

His smile cracked. "How long do you need to publish these findings?"

"A month, maybe more." Aliesa had to make him aware of the gravity of the situation. "These tests cannot be rushed. Moving too fast could cause mutation. And cell mutation is never a good thing. Cell mutation is cancer."

Grayson popped out of his chair and paced behind the desk. A blue vein pulsed at his temple.

"When will the results of the last test sample be submitted?"

"A few months."

"What?" Grayson squealed like a spoiled child. His face whitened and Aliesa realized he'd been on a fact-finding mission all this time. At thirty-two she could decipher DNA nucleotide polymers but couldn't read another human being's signals. And if the person also happened to be a man, a plethora of internal chaos often followed. Her heart rate spiked and her palms began to sweat. She hated how naïve she'd been. "Are you saying my funding is still intact?" Aliesa smoothed her hair back into the severe bun on top of her head.

"It hasn't been easy but yes."

"What kind of promises have you been making?"

"I've told the investors just enough to maintain their devotion. These people want assurances."

"What do you mean people? I thought we had corporate funding." She'd never once made inquires about who'd been footing the bill for her research.

"I'm afraid that ship capsized long ago," Grayson said. "I had to improvise. I needed a fast chunk of change."

"I need to know who is bankrolling this project."

"It's a private investor." He leaned back in his seat. His tone made the words private investor sound dirty.

"I thought you wanted to keep my research quiet?"

"I did until I found my back pressed against a wall. You needed money. And I had to be a tad more creative in my endeavors. Now it seems like I made the right choice since this project is going to require big bucks over the long term."

"A few months aren't exactly what I'd call long term."

Grayson's face had run the entire color gambit—pink, white, and now scarlet. "Whatever."

Aliesa stalked out of his office—anger boiling beneath her outward calm.

When Aliesa got off the motorcycle twenty-five minutes later, she followed him to the solid oak entry of a sedate brownstone across the river in Charlestown. Van pounded on the door.

"No one's home," she said.

"Keep an eye out." He hunched over the locking mechanism. She spun around and feigned nonchalance as she imagined Van inserting the pick into the old, keyed entry. She hoped no one had taken notice of them. Nothing stirred at this late hour. Behind her, she heard a click, a creak, and he hauled her inside the vestibule.

The heavy, wood vibrated shut. Shards of light from the street lamp shone through the etched glass on either side of the mullions and illuminated a tunnel-like corridor.

She tucked in behind him. Pressed against the wall, they slowly made their way down the hall. How many laws she'd broken in the last two days? Up ahead, a sliver of blue light eeked beneath a closed door.

A television blared in the next room.

He turned around and faced her. "Stay here. Don't touch anything," he mouthed. "If I'm not back in one minute, get the hell out."

Aliesa nodded. Why would he tell her not to touch anything? Then she saw he still wore his leather riding gloves. He slinked soundlessly inside the room. From where Aliesa stood, she could see part of a bookshelf and a television talk show host clad in a suspendered hot pink shirt and psychedelic tie. She moved closer to take stock, but still couldn't see Van. She reached out to open the door farther when it swung wide. Van walked over to the bookshelf and switched off the television.

A man sat at the desk with his face planted on the blotter.

"Is this Grayson?" Van asked, grabbing a thatch of thinning salt and pepper hair he tipped back the man's head.

As soon as she saw the thin goatee, she nodded. "That's him." She noticed something else—a gun shoved into the waistband of Van's pants. "Is he dead?"

"He's piss drunk."

A near empty bottle of Scotch stood beyond his fingertips.

"Drunk is worse?"

He nodded. "Much. It means I'm going to have to sober him up to get some answers." He paced the length of the office, stopped to admire a cluster of VIP photos on the wall.

"Why would he tie one on at the beginning of the week when tomorrow is a workday? Do you think he has a drinking problem?"

"I don't know. He never smelled like alcohol or ever seemed hung over in all the time I've known him. And he's not my friend. He was a scavenger. He loved watching academics squirm when he told them their funding had been terminated." His rabid dedication to ruining lives had been the only gossip she'd ever heard.

Van seemed to digest her observations and sat Grayson straight in his chair. "Wake up," Van said slapping one cheek and then the other. Grayson's head flopped from side to side.

Still nothing.

"He's completely out of it," Aliesa said.

"I'll be right back," Van said. He let Grayson go and the man flopped forward. He grabbed the trash bin from beside the desk and disappeared. Moments later he strode back through the door carrying a half-filled bucket of water, which he proceeded to dump on Grayson's head. Then he placed the bin back in its original spot on the floor.

Grayson's eyes were suddenly wide open. He'd jerked back in his seat. He sputtered and gulped like a half-drowned rat. When red-rimmed eyes settled on Van they registered alarm. "Who are you?" Drool leaked out of the corner of his mouth. He wobbled in his chair. "How'd you get in here?"

"I came to ask you some questions. You should really lock your front door."

Grayson didn't recognize Aliesa—a testament to the power of alcohol. She doubted he would remember anything in the morning. Grayson never questioned Van's open door story, and Aliesa knew if he'd been sober, he would be frantic over any breach in security. Drunk, he merely shrugged. His eyes began to close.

"Celebrating something?" Van asked.

He chortled, like he knew some private joke. "I've been saving this single malt for a special occasion." He patted the bottle top, missing it the second time and the bottle tipped.

"And the right moment happened to be tonight?"

"What?" Grayson shook his head with exaggerated movements. He scoured the desktop searching for something. "No. It's all over," he said, shaking his head back and forth. "Nothing left to throw a party for, so I thought tonight was as good as any."

Grayson's bloodshot eyes settled on something far off in the distance and he began rambling. "It shouldn't have happened this way. I'm supposed to be rich." The word trailed off. "I found the fucking fountain of youth, only to have it ripped from my fingertips."

Van followed his lead egging him on. "Really?"

Grayson's eyes settled on Van. "Damn straight. None of it would have happened without me."

Aliesa scowled at him and balled her fists. She wanted to club the bastard. With a quick nod, Van told her to keep quiet.

"I called in a lot of markers." He straightened. "Then the stupid bitch went and got herself killed." Spittle spewed on the s and b words.

"Who?"

"Dr. Aliesa Atworth." Grayson faced Aliesa. "Have we met before?" Simone had worked magic on her—the ugly duckling.

"You lost everything?" Van asked keeping Grayson on track.

"I thought I might still have a crack to salvage something, so I thought I'd talk to her assistant, but the bitch won't take any of my calls. What was her name?"

"Evelyne Mathews." Aliesa forced the name through her clenched teeth.

"Right," Grayson said, staring at her. He narrowed his eyes—obviously still unsure if he recognized her or not.

"Is the lab tech capable of continuing Dr. Atworth's work?" Van asked.

Grayson shrugged and eyed Van. "It's possible," he said, sounding less than convinced.

"You spun the story to your investors in order to buy yourself a little more time."

Grayson's wary eyes darted to Van's. "Who sent you?"

Van skirted Grayson's desk. "Let's go," Van said. "He

doesn't know anything and he's too busy wallowing in self-pity to be helpful."

Van grabbed Aliesa's hand and before they got to the edge of the office he turned. "Russian roulette is a risky game to play."

Russian Roulette?

Is that where the gun Van had tucked into the waistband of his pants came from? She never would have thought Grayson had the balls to put a gun to his head let along pull the trigger.

Outside, Van and Aliesa walked over to his bike parked in the alleyway, next to the dumpster. He pulled the helmets out of the saddlebag.

"It seems Grayson believed the newspaper reports and thinks I'm dead."

"It seems so."

"Now, do you think I'm telling you the truth?" Aliesa took the helmet from Van. "I didn't know anything about the shipment of cocaine Dr. Marcus Hernandez sent to me."

Van didn't know what to think.

Grayson had no idea Evelyne had been murdered instead of Aliesa. If Jorge and Axel mistakenly killed Evelyne, Grayson wouldn't have a clue, but then he wouldn't have a clue if this turned out to be about Aliesa's serum. He would be too far down the food chain to be informed. Since Van had no answers he did his best to ignore Aliesa's question.

The kiss they'd shared in front of the elevator in the underground parking still rattled him. Almost as much as it seemed to rattle her. The way she clung to him, and her sexy little groan had been quite the turn on.

"You can't ignore me forever," Aliesa said.

"At this point I'd be as successful at it as you would."

"What do you mean by that?"

"I think you know what I mean."

Owlish eyes blinked several times. "It means I'm not expendable until after you find the cocaine."

Did she really say that? They connected—she knew it and so did he.

"I'm tired of this game. Thanks for stopping Grayson from taking his own life and I appreciate everything you've done so far to get to the bottom of this, but I'm not a cut out for this nefarious stuff. I'm going to turn myself in and take my chances with the police."

They exchanged glances. This woman didn't act like anyone he'd ever met. She had no identification and no money, people were after her and still she'd abandon her best chance for survival, all because he didn't believe her. Could their kiss have frightened her more than it excited her?

"You know what," Van said. "It's late. Let's find somewhere to stay to grab some sleep. We'll talk about everything first thing in the morning. Study it with fresh eyes."

Van plucked the gun from his waistband and put it in his saddlebags along with the .38 caliber bullets he took from Grayson's desk.

"Do you really think Grayson would have killed himself?"

"Hard to say. If he borrowed the money for your funding from a less than reputable source it's only a matter of time before they come after him."

Suddenly a shot pierced the silence of the night.

Both Van's and Aliesa's heads turned.

"That sounded like it came from Grayson's place." Aliesa's voice cracked.

"Stay here," he said, handing her his helmet.

She refused to take it. Instead she placed hers on the seat of the bike. "I'm going with you."

"I don't have time to argue," he said, hooking his on the handlebar. He dug the .38 out of his saddlebags and a handful of bullets. "Keep behind me and stay close. We're going through the back door this time."

When they climbed the back stairs to the door, he noticed it wasn't locked. Van entered the kitchen with the gun outstretched in his hand. They moved through the living room and down the hall into the office.

"Clear," he said, shoving the gun into his waistband.

Grayson sat where they left him, head on the desk. A crimson puddle encircled Grayson's head. Blood trickled over the edge of the desk, the pool on the floor expanding with each drip.

"Is he passed out again?" Aliesa said, stepping out from behind him. Her eyes found the gun loosely held in his hand beside his head. "Oh my god, he did it. He killed himself." She closed her eyes and she wobbled on shaky legs. Van turned and pulled her into his chest.

"I'm sorry," Van said. "I know he was a friend of yours."

He heard her breath catch. "Grayson was never a friend of mine," she said. "But it doesn't make me feel very good knowing he killed himself because of me."

She pulled out from his embrace and took a deep steadying breath.

"I'm not convinced he committed suicide."

"What?" Her shaking hand covered her mouth.

Van circled the desk. He made sure he didn't step in the blood pool as he pulled open the side drawers. "Now I know he didn't kill himself."

"How can you be certain? He's holding a smoking gun."

"A gun he doesn't own. Most likely a gun with the serial number scratched off. See this?" he asked.

Aliesa moved closer. "The box of ammunition?"

"It wasn't in the drawer before."

"Maybe he had another gun somewhere else in the house," she said.

"You saw him," Van said. "He could barely sit straight, there's no way he could walk. Besides, the gun I took from him was a PPK, this is a Sig Sauer."

"It's a free country. Lot's of people own two different guns."

"Both are .38s."

Aliesa's brow wrinkled. "Huh."

"I doubt GSR will be found on his hands either."

"GSR?"

"Gunshot residue. If Grayson pulled the trigger, gunshot residue would collect on his hand and around the entry wound. Not to mention his head is turned on its right side. If he used his right hand to shoot himself, his head would be laying on its left side."

"How can you be so sure?"

"Think about it. You of all people should know Newton's First Law—any moving object will continue moving in the same direction unless acted upon by an unknown force."

Aliesa swallowed hard and she cowered. Then she eyeballed all of the dark corners of the room. "You think the unknown force was someone who broke in and killed him after we left? What if they're still here?"

"They're long gone," Van said. "See the tuft of hair on his shoulder?"

Aliesa stood perfectly still with her hands wrapped around her waist.

"This is how I think it happened. Grayson had probably passed out again. The killer pulled his head back by tugging on a fistful of hair, just like I did when we arrived the first time. He pressed the gun to Grayson's temple, pulled the trigger and when he released Grayson's head, it fell to the right side and the follicles of hair he'd uprooted sprinkled onto Grayson's shoulders."

Sirens sounded in the distance.

"Someone must have reported shots fired," Van said. "Time to leave." He grabbed her hand and they charged out of the brownstone and drove far away from the cluster of swirling red lights and wailing sirens.

Chapter 15

The double beds at The Get-Away Inn suited Aliesa just fine. The tired hotel had démodé art on the walls and a four-piece bathroom, but what it lacked in style it made up for in cleanliness.

Aliesa hadn't spoken a word to Van since they climbed on the back of the bike.

Poor Grayson.

The gruesome image of him would be forever stamped in her memory. At least she hadn't upchucked. Maybe she'd gotten used to seeing dead people.

Van crossed the room, closed the curtains, and set the thermostat. Then he rummaged through the saddlebag he carried inside. He dug out a clean T-shirt and tossed it to her. "This should be comfortable enough for sleeping. You can use the bathroom first."

Van's cell phone must have vibrated because he pulled it out of his pants pocket and answered it. She carried the shirt into the bathroom and closed the door.

The last time she went into an unfamiliar bathroom, she'd been hauled half-naked into a closet. Not wanting to linger too long on the memory, she swiped the shampoo and conditioner off the counter and set the water in the shower. She stripped and stepped under the spray.

With her hair partially lathered, Van called to her from inside the room. "I'm going out for a while," he said. "Don't put the chain the door."

He didn't even stick around for an answer. She heard the room door slam shut. Shampoo streamed into one eye and to stop the incessant burn she leaned her head back into the stream of water. She rinsed, shut off the water, and toweled dry.

After finger combing her hair, she donned Van's T-shirt and opened the bathroom door. With a little luck she'd be fast asleep by the time he returned. She circled the bed and came to an abrupt halt. The sheets had been turned down and a small tube of toothpaste, a toothbrush and a comb were resting on her pillow.

"Burning the midnight oil?" Van asked as he walked into ABC Inquiries.

"Couldn't sleep," Drew said. "There'll be plenty of time to rest when I'm dead."

"I got your message. How are you doing with Hernandez's computer disc?"

"I'm still reformatting it. It'll be ready very soon."

"How about Devine's Trojan horse? Did it work?"

Drew circled around to the main frame. He typed some commands on the keyboard. "Of course it worked. Devine downloaded my program and fired off an email a couple of hours ago."

"Just one?"

Drew typed another set of commands. "So far. Why do you ask?"

"Cause Devine returned while we were setting things up. Aliesa ran interference."

"I'm guessing you averted the crisis otherwise we wouldn't be having this conversation."

"He came back to the office after hours to make a phone call."

"Did you bring the storage drive for the phone tap with you?"

Van pulled the digital receiver from his pocket and they listened to Devine and Lowry's conversation.

"Shit," Drew said. "That's not good."

"Tell me about it. I barely got Aliesa out of the apartment before the two Alarcan cartel goons returned."

"I don't know what to tell you. Devine sent an email to Jules Wolcott, the CEO and owner of Panacealla." Drew pressed a couple of buttons and the email appeared on Drew's central screen.

> *Dr. Marcus Hernandez has been manufacturing cocaine and has subsequently been murdered. We need to prepare an official statement for the press denying any and all culpability. Get back to me asap with instructions.*

"I'm wondering if they knew about his other manufacturing activities. Maybe that's why they didn't renew his contract," Van said.

"It's possible," Drew said. "There had to be a reason they terminated his legitimate manufacturing contract."

"I'm sure it won't take long for them to find another doc willing to manufacture their anti-leukemic."

Drew closed the computer window.

"Is there any way I can view all of Devine's emails, incoming and outgoing, for say... the last three months?" Van asked.

"To the same address?"

"Yeah."

"Can I compile the list and have it for you in the morning?"

"Perfect," Van said. "I want you to dig up all the information you can on a man named Grayson Everet, the CFO of Research at BU."

"Okay. Do you think he had a personal relationship with Aliesa?"

"No. Why do you ask?" Van's head snapped around toward Drew.

"Because you get this territorial glint in your eye whenever you discover the good doc has had any kind of relationship with another man."

"I do not."

"Whatever." Drew shrugged.

"Focus on Everet's business relationships," Van said. "I'm thinking the man made one too many promises he couldn't keep."

"Is he a suspect?"

"Not anymore. He's dead. Someone killed him tonight and tried to make it look like a suicide."

Drew jotted a few notes. "Anything else?"

"One more thing." Van pulled Aliesa's insulated lunch

bag out of his pocket. He shook the contents out onto Drew's desk—an icepack and a small liquid filled vial. "Would you have this analyzed for me?"

Drew raised the vial and held it to the light. "Any educated guesses?"

"Yesterday I would have bet money on narcotics. Now, I'm not so sure," Van said. "Think you can get me a decoy vial, too? One filled with sterile saline would work."

"I'll see what I can do."

Chapter 16

Running water woke Aliesa from a sound sleep.

Klunk.

Startled by the sharp noise, she attempted to sit, not an easy task with the bed sheet wound around her body like a sari. She wrestled one arm free, then the other. Once her synapses started firing she realized Van must have dropped the bar of soap in the shower.

The bathroom door opened. Steam and light spilled into the otherwise dark room.

"You're awake," he said. Clad in a towel knotted around his waist he walked around her bed.

Moisture glistened on the well-defined muscles of his broad chest. Still in shadow, Aliesa let herself study the man who'd protected her these last few days. The towel rode low on those narrow hips and her less than innocent thoughts made her feel like a voyeur.

"While you're in the shower, I'll get dressed and go grab us something to eat."

Aliesa disentangled herself from the sheets. "Where are we going?"

"I thought we'd go to the police station and have a word with Detective Lowry. Then you can make an informed decision about who you want to trust with your life."

Aliesa cringed. She wished she could take back everything she said to him last night. She'd been hasty. Van had gone out of his way to corroborate her claims of innocence and keep her alive.

Based on Detective Lowry's telephone call to Saul Devine, he thought she was a drug dealer, too. At this point it made more sense to stick with the devil she knew than go with the one she didn't.

At the station, Van told the desk sergeant he wanted to speak with Detective Lowry. The sergeant grabbed the telephone and dialed. "There's someone here to see you." The sergeant motioned for them to sit. "He'll be right down."

With only one vacant seat, Van let Aliesa take the chair while he leaned against the wall.

Close to ten minutes later, Detective Lowry poked his head through the door, gave the waiting room the once over and turned to leave.

Aliesa stood.

Lowry stilled. "Did you want to see me, miss?"

Aliesa walked over to the door. "It's me, Aliesa Atworth," she whispered.

"Dr. Atworth? I didn't recognize you. You've changed your hair," he said, pitching his voice low.

Aliesa nodded.

Van strode over beside them. "Elliot Vance," he said, shaking the detectives hand.

"Let's go somewhere more private," Lowry said. He led them upstairs and opened the first interrogation room. Inside were the typical accoutrements—metal table and two chairs and a camera in the upper right hand corner of the room. Van studied the camera.

"Don't worry," Lowry said. "It's not on. I would have had to activate it before we came in here. Now what can I do for you?"

Aliesa sat. Van reached into his black leather jacket and removed the digital receiver. He pushed play and set it on the table. Once the detective heard the conversation he'd had with Saul Devine played back to him, his expression changed from accommodating to mutinous.

Arms crossed over his chest he spoke through clenched teeth. "Since you illegally obtained the wire tap all of the information would be thrown out."

"In a court of law it would. But I'm certain your Captain, his Commissioner, and the Admiral would be very interested to hear what you had to say."

The detective snickered. "What can Devine do? Issue a writ?"

"We've got ourselves a comedian," he said. In a flash he grabbed the detective by the arms, spun him around, and threw him against the wall. Van tightened his fingers around his neck, constricting the detective's windpipe and vocal chords. "You interfered with your boss's gag order. I'm sure he won't find this recording as funny as you."

Lowry squirmed against Van. First his face turned red, and finally blue, before Van released him. The detective doubled over. He wiped spittle from the corner of his mouth. "What do you want?"

"What I want is to conduct my investigation without having to worry about another attack on Dr. Atworth."

"Okay. Anything else?"

"When did Devine initially contact you for information about Dr. Atworth?"

"About two months ago," Lowry said, his voice grating.

"For what reason?"

"He wanted information. She moved into a building he managed."

Aliesa had spoken the truth. "Who else knows Dr. Atworth is alive?"

"No one," he whispered. "Not from me. I swear."

Van pulled out a chair. "You might want to sit, you're unsteady on your feet."

The detective refused. He angled his chin and stood straighter.

Van leaned close. "What did you mean when you told Devine Aliesa had gotten herself into some trouble?"

"The crime scene had all the earmarks of a professional hit. Debris from ransacking the lab landed in the blood pool not the other way around. The killer probably destroyed the lab as an afterthought—to make us think he'd been searching for something."

Aliesa sat in the seat shaking her head. "Are you saying there was only one perpetrator? Are you certain? There were two men who ransacked my apartment. I assumed they came straight from the lab. The only reason I'm sitting here right now is because Van saved me."

"I'm not wrong according to forensics. CSI could only find evidence of one perpetrator at the crime scene." Lowry rubbed his chin. "Unless you're withholding information."

Aliesa faced Van.

"Uncut cocaine," Van said. His mind had already kicked into overdrive. Forensics were a slam dunk. If it had be a professional hit, Evelyne would never have been mistaken for Aliesa, labcoat ID or not. Evelyne had been targeted too.

"Are you fucking kidding me?" Lowry said.

"Last night, the police responded to a shot fired in Charleston," Van said.

Lowry turned his head and regarded Van. "Yeah, what of it?"

"Homicide or suicide?" Van asked.

"ME ruled it a suicide," Lowry said.

"You need to have a second pass. See if the victim has GSR on his hands. And check for forced entry on the back door. See if forensics can find any consistencies from the lab crime scene."

"You think it was the same professional's handiwork?"

"Maybe," Van said. He reached for Aliesa who took his hand in hers. "It's time you did some good old fashioned detective work. You do that and I'll make sure you get the credit. Oh, and if you interfere with my investigation again by telling anyone else about Aliesa this tape will land on the Commissioner's desk. Capisce?"

The detective stood still and silent as they walked out of the interrogation room and headed across the hall where Van pressed the elevator call button.

Three people at the other end of the hall were having a heated discussion. Both he and Aliesa couldn't help but overhear the conversation.

"Our daughter has been missing for almost forty-eight

hours, there's got to be something you can do," the elderly man pleaded with the Captain.

The gray haired woman beside them dabbed a tissue to her nose and cheeks.

Aliesa's knees buckled and Van put his arm around her waist to steady her. The elevator doors slid open and Van helped her inside.

The doors closed and she sobbed.

"What's wrong?" Van asked.

"They were Evelyne's parents. They invited me to join them for their Easter celebration this past year. It's not right. I need to go back and tell them what happened to their daughter."

Van folded her in his arms. He rubbed her back and whispered assurances in her ear. "We will—I promise. As soon as you're no longer a target. You're not alone. We're going to figure this out together." Van lifted her chin with his finger and placed the gentlest of kisses on her lips.

The elevator came to a halt and they walked to the parking lot at Tremont and Ruggles where he parked the bike.

"Thank you," Aliesa said.

A vision of his mother and sister flashed in Van's head. "I know what it's like to lose someone you love."

Chapter 17

On route to ABC Inquiries, Aliesa couldn't help but wonder about Van's heartfelt comment. He'd obviously suffered some devastating loses in his life. His compassion made her think he might be starting to believe in her innocence after all. A lot like her, he tended to have tunnel vision when working on a case, neglecting even common courtesies—he strode right past Simone without so much as a hello.

"Hi, Van," Simone said. "I missed you, too."

"I'm sorry," Aliesa mouthed following Van into Drew's office.

Aliesa sat with Drew and Van to sift through computer files. Van focused on Saul Devine's incoming and outgoing email, specifically his correspondence with Jules Wolcott. All were professional and advisory in nature. Nothing questionable. Aliesa and Drew dissected the disc from Dr. Hernandez's computer and isolated a file recording all of his deliveries. While Aliesa compiled a list of alphanumeric numbers, Drew began tracking them through the FedEx website. By entering each code he could tell where and when the package entered the system and arrived at its destination.

Simone came into the office and whispered

something in Van's ear.

He faced Aliesa. His eyes were hot and demanding. They ravaged and plundered and caused an equal reaction within her—palpitations and an increase in her core temperature.

Thankfully, he tore his attention away from her and turned back to Simone. With a curt nod, he sent Simone back into her office.

Two hours crawled by.

"Here it is," Drew said. "It's the first of three shipments Hernandez sent to you. All of the others were sent to a company called Capill Industries, in Quincy."

Excitement bubbled inside of Aliesa and before she knew it she threw her arms around Van and kissed him. "You see," she said. "He sent me three separate deliveries of Camu camu fruit. I told you I had nothing to do with his cocaine operation."

"Hey," Drew said, smiling. "I'm the one who clears you and you give him the kiss."

Aliesa giggled and hugged Drew.

"What's the date of the last shipment to Aliesa?" Van asked, his expression a grim line.

"Nine days ago."

"That's not the last shipment he sent," Van said. "The final one would have been six days ago. Aliesa emailed asking for another shipment on the very day he was murdered."

"There's no record of it in these files." Drew pondered Van's remark. "Maybe Hernandez didn't have a chance to enter the last delivery code into his system."

"Or maybe he didn't want to have any record of it. Either way, I need to know the particulars of the last shipment." Van folded his arms across his chest.

Aliesa realized she'd been too quick to celebrate. Maybe Marcus did send a shipment of cocaine to her to keep its whereabouts a secret from the people he worked with. If she guessed right, she'd have a heck of a time convincing anyone of her innocence. Possession was nine-tenths of the law.

"It may take a few hours. I'll contact FedEx directly," Drew said, he clicked his headset and opened a new line on the phone.

Van typed the name Capill Industries into the search engine on the screen in front of him. Aliesa stood behind him reading the copy on their home page. Capill Industries was a pharmaceutical contractor. They manufactured patented drugs for a lot of the industry leaders, GlaxoSmithKline, Lilly, Panacealla, and Pfizer. "So, if I understand this correctly," Van said.

"Capill doesn't do any R and D of their own."

"Not that I can see," Aliesa said. "They follow formulas. They measure and cut the raw materials to make certain medications on spec. They press pills, fill gel caps, package and label products for distribution."

Van leaned back in his seat. "I think we need to go and check this place out, maybe have a little chat with the president of the company."

Aliesa touched the picture on the screen. The president, Jackson Mercante, seemed vaguely familiar in his power suit and slickened blonde hair. He had a dark mole on his right cheek beneath steel-blue irises.

Van went to close the web page but she stopped him. "Keep reading," she said.

Van scanned the rest of the page. She knew the very

second he saw it. With clenched teeth he read the last sentence, "Capill Industries is a subsidiary of Panacealla Pharmaceuticals."

Aliesa sat in the passenger seat of the mid-sized silver rental and waited for Van to open the door for her. Was it her imagination or was he more attentive to her than before? The old adage—keep your friends close and your enemies closer rang in her head. The door swung open and she tugged at her skirt and shifted her legs to get out, but probably not before Van got an eye full. And wham. Desire struck. So powerful it nearly made her knees buckle. Her heart sprinted in her chest. The scientist wanted to record these reactions and graph the curve. The woman wanted to take this attraction to the next level.

When they left ABC Inquiries, Simone handed her a parcel.

"What's this?" Aliesa asked.

"Clothes," Simone said. "Van asked me to contact the boutique where we shopped the other day. They sent over a couple of outfits I set aside." Aliesa had Simone to thank for the length of the skirt.

Van closed the car door and they walked across the parking lot of Capill Industries to the entrance of the building.

"Did you know we were going to be impersonating government officials when you had these clothes sent over?" Aliesa asked.

"If I did, I would have had my jacket pressed. More clothes were Simone's idea. Remind me to thank her later." He raised his eyebrows mischievously.

She swatted him. "Guess you noticed, huh?"

"A little."

On their way back to their hotel, they rented a car.

Back at the hotel, Van changed into a wrinkled suit and shirt from his saddlebags and Aliesa changed into her new clothes and they left for Quincy.

"Now, let's go over our cover story one more time," he said.

"Your name is Robert Blake and you work for the Department of Agriculture. My name is Jane Doherty, your trainee. You're showing me the ropes. We're checking transfer agreements between Peru and the USA."

"Good," Van said. "Let me do most of the talking."

He opened the oversized glass door and Aliesa stepped onto a mosaic of Carrera marble tiles. Her heels clicked on the polished stone as both approached the receptionist's desk.

"May I help you?" the buxom brunette asked.

"We're here to see Mr. Mercante," Van said, handing her a business card sporting the seal of the Department of Agriculture and the name Robert Blake.

"Is he expecting you?"

"That would entirely negate the purpose of a surprise audit, now wouldn't it?" He adjusted the dark rimmed glasses on his nose. "We're here to make sure his company is following government protocols."

The brunette lifted the phone and pressed an extension. "You have two people here from the

Department of Agriculture to perform an audit." Then she disconnected and pasted a wobbly smile on her face.

"He'll be right with you."

Aliesa clasped her hands together to stop them from shaking. She began to wonder what the hell she was doing? Van appeared calm and cool.

On the far side of the foyer a man wearing a silk suit approached. "Jackson Mercante," he said, not offering his hand. Piercing eyes doused her like a pail of ice water.

Van stuck out his hand. "Robert Blake, Department of Agriculture," he said. When he realized Mercante had no intention of shaking his hand he introduced Aliesa. "This is my associate, Jane Doherty."

Again, cold blue eyes prodded her.

"Why are you here?" Mercante asked.

There would be no finessing this man.

"We've come to audit your records. Over the last few years, you've been receiving shipments of vassicine hydrochloride under transfer agreement from Dr. Marcus Hernandez."

"Vassicine is one among many drugs we process here. Why are you interested in that particular drug?" Mercante asked.

Van figured Mercante's poker face served him well. "Because of Dr. Hernandez. We want to make sure all of the vassicine transferred is present and accounted for."

"Is he in some sort of trouble?" Mercante asked.

"Did you know Dr. Hernandez?"

"We roomed together at university. He majored in biochemistry, I majored in pharmacology."

Aliesa knew it. No wonder Mercante seemed familiar.

To make matters worse, he kept staring at her like a lion stalking its prey.

"I'm sorry to have to tell you this, but Dr. Hernandez is dead."

A flash of surprise lit Mercante's face—his pupils dilated and his nostrils flared. Thankful she was no longer the center of his attention, she took a deep fortifying breath.

"Sorry to blurt it out like that," Van said. "I thought you knew."

Mercante cleared his throat and struggled to regain his composure. He turned toward the secretary sitting at the reception desk behind them. "Call William Stiles and tell him to dig out the records on vassicine, brand-name Vasotec, for the last three months."

While the secretary followed her instructions, Mercante turned to face them. "Anything else?"

"Do you know when you received his last shipment?" Van asked.

"I haven't the foggiest. But Stiles will know. Follow me. I'll take you to his office."

Aliesa and Van fell into step behind him. Van's hand rested on the small of Aliesa's back. His gentle touch seemed to calm her frayed nerves.

An hour later, they sat in Stiles's office, comparing the computer printout of delivery dates Drew had compiled to Capill's quality control and production numbers.

"So all of these dates are present and accounted for?" Van asked.

"Yes," Stiles said.

"Can you explain why there are such inconsistencies in the production numbers? One would think each shipment would contain approximately the same amount of vassicine hydrochloride?"

"As with any manufacturing operation there is waste. Sometimes the quality of the vassicine is questionable. We dispose of it if it's no good. Once in a while the mixture is too rich and fillers must be added."

"And these tests are performed in the lab?" Aliesa asked.

"No longer necessary. We've developed simple test kit a child could use. When a shipment arrives, our receiver adds a small sample to get a reading. If the solution turns pink it's viable, if the solution turns blue the sample is tainted and is slated for disposal."

Suddenly, Van sat forward in his seat. His eyes alert and focused. "Who handles the disposals for you?"

"Good question," Stiles said. He went to his computer and opened a file. "It's a company called Medevac."

"Do you have their contact information?"

"Not off hand. But if you give me a few minutes, I'll get it for you."

"Wonderful," Van said. "Once we have the information, we can let you get back to your work. Would you mind calling Mr. Mercante so he can sign off on it?"

"I'll have him paged," Stiles said. "Be right back." He walked out of the office, leaving Van and Aliesa alone.

"I think Mercante knew about the cocaine," Van said when Stiles moved out of earshot.

Aliesa startled. "What?"

Van explained. "A normal cocaine identification test kit contains a vial with clear liquid. If cocaine is added, the solution turns blue. Would it be possible to add another test in the same kit? Say for vassicine?"

Aliesa thought for a moment. "Absolutely."

"With a background in pharmacology, Mercante probably designed it."

She jumped out of her seat, and paced. On her third lap, Van finally clued in.

"What's wrong?" he asked. "You need to sit."

"I'm freaking out," she said, on a short breath. "It creeped me out the way Mercante ogled me."

"Can't say I blame him. I've been having trouble keeping my eyes off you, too."

If Aliesa hadn't been so unnerved she might have allowed Van's compliment to warm her.

"Don't you think your over-reacting?" Van asked.

"Impersonating someone isn't something I do everyday," Aliesa said pitching her voice low. She rubbed her hands and tried to get the blood circulating. "I don't think so. Mercante said he and Hernandez were roommates in university."

"Why is it so important?"

"Because Hernandez was my lab partner in grad school. Remember?"

Damn.

That particular tidbit didn't make Van feel very warm and fuzzy. Of course he waved the whole thing off as nonsense because he didn't want Aliesa to have another melt down. He made light of it by shrugging and patting her hand, when what he really wanted to do was wrap his arms around her and get the hell out of there.

He tried to rationalize it.

Mercante couldn't have recognized her, it was several years ago and Simone had done a decent job of altering Aliesa's appearance. Besides, if Mercante hurt her it would only draw attention to Capill Industries and put his entire operation under a microscope.

"What are you thinking?" Aliesa asked.

Van shook his head. He pulled out his cell phone and dialed.

"Drew? I want you to find out who owns a company called Medevac? M e d e v a c. Thanks," he said closing the cover on his phone.

A moment later, Stiles re-entered the office. "The waste disposal company is located here in Quincy. Oh, and I'm sorry, but Mr. Mercante has left for the day. If you want to leave the paperwork behind, I will make sure he signs it when he returns."

"Thanks, but I'll email the entire report to him," Van said, rising out of his chair.

"Fair enough." Stiles remained on his feet. "I guess we're done"

Van reached out and they shook hand. "Thanks for all of your help," he said. "We'll show ourselves out."

As they walked the hall to the front foyer, Van's phone beeped. He read the call display. "Yeah," he said, nodding a couple of times before he disconnected.

"What did Drew say?" Aliesa asked, as they climbed into the rental car.

"Medevac is a numbered company. Drew's going to dig deeper to find out who registered it."

"So where do we go from here?"

Van withdrew the sheet of paper Stiles had given him from his pocket. "We go to Medevac."

Chapter 18

Medevac was located in an industrial park just beyond Quincy's city limits. Aliesa and Van drove the maze of streets between clusters of long, gray steel buildings. At the very end of the third street, they came upon a roll-down-delivery-door branded with a Medevac sign, beside which stood an entrance.

"It's not very big," Aliesa said. Van slowed the rental car and circled the block one more time, she assumed to make sure they had not been followed. He parked behind the building, out of sight. She unbuckled her seat belt and reached for the door.

"Where do you think you're going?" he asked.

"With you," Aliesa said.

"It's too dangerous," he said.

"It's too late to change the rules now," Aliesa said. "We've been working together right from the start."

She held her breath while he decided.

"Fine," he said. "But you have to promise to hang back and follow my instructions." He pulled out some nitrile gloves from his pocket and handed her a pair to put on.

They got out of the car and Aliesa followed. He knelt at the door of the warehouse and slipped a lock pick out of his pocket.

"Did you go to school to learn how to break and enter?" she asked.

"Do you mind?" he said. "I'm trying to concentrate."

She raised her eyebrows, closed her mouth and observed.

With one slender pick at the top of the key notch and another at the bottom, he finessed the internal tumblers. He smiled knowingly at Aliesa, twisted the knob, and the door sprang open.

"Let me go in first and do a quick inspection," he whispered.

"Don't you have a gun?" Aliesa asked. "For protection?"

"I don't like guns," Van said, right before he disappeared inside.

When she thought back to all of the close calls they'd shared, the only time he carried a gun was when he confiscated Grayson's. Something about Van made her feel safe.

Minutes ticked by before Van loomed in the doorway.

He had the oddest expression on his face—one of angry resignation. "It's all clear," he said. "You can give me a hand searching the place."

The warehouse wasn't overly large. Parked inside the roll-down-door was a white panel-van with the name Medevac painted on the side. Overhead fluorescent tube-lights hung from chains. Underfoot, shiny gray concrete stretched the length of the warehouse. A multi-tiered metal rack of cleaning products stood against the far wall and a mop and bucket leaned in the corner. The entire place reeked of bleach.

He slid open the side door of the van and climbed

inside.

Aliesa hopped into the passenger seat and checked the contents of the glove box and console. "What are we searching for?" she asked.

"We won't know until we find it."

She found the vehicle's registration and insurance, a manifest of pick-up and deliveries and a record of the visits to the hazardous waste facility.

"What do you have there?" he asked, opening and closing plastic cooler-like containers stacked in the back.

"Some receipts for dumping hazardous waste." She closed the glove box and decided to abandon her search of the vehicle and she paced across the floor to the office where she flipped on the light inside the door.

She startled when she spotted a man in his mid-twenties, sprawled across the desk with a tourniquet on his arm and a needle sticking out of a vein—his dead eyes staring over at her. She counted to ten to allow her heart rate to settle.

"What part of hanging back didn't you understand?" Van asked. He stood right behind her.

She spun around and faced him. "Why the hell didn't you say something to me," she said. She balled her hand into a fist. She wanted to strike him for deliberately being mean but the pain etched on his face made her stop short.

"My kid sister died of an overdose," he said, his brow creasing. "She was a sweet kid. Her name was Chela. She's the reason I turned in my Green Beret and got a job as a DEA agent."

In this very moment, Aliesa began to see Van clearly.

He may call himself a vigilante with a cause, but Green Beret to DEA agent made him one of the good guys. "I'm so sorry."

"Don't apologize." He all but barked. "I could have done something to stop it from happening but I was too selfish to spend any time with her."

"You can't blame yourself," she said.

"The hell I can't," he barked. "I was in between missions, on leave at Langley. Chela begged me to come home to spend spring break with her. I told her I couldn't—I had to ship out any day. While I baked in the sun on the beach, she nursed an aphthous ulcer, a canker sore in her mouth. By the time my mom called, it was already too late. The doctors tried to save her but she'd developed agranulocytosis."

"An auto-immune disorder?" Aliesa asked.

"No, she'd been snorting cocaine cut with levamisole, a veterinary deworming agent." Van scrubbed his hand across his face to conceal the tears gathering in his eyes. He stepped around her and walked into the office. "Now let's try to figure out what happened here."

Aliesa swallowed the lump forming in her throat. He'd trusted her enough to share something of great magnitude with her and she'd been humbled. Her shock at finding a dead body in the office had passed. And, truth be told, she'd spent many grad school lab hours working on cadavers. She took a deep breath and pasted on an objective face.

"Tell me what you see," Van said.

She swallowed hard and adjusted her nitrile gloves on her hands as she walked over to the corpse to make her observations. "The body is not in rigor yet. There's no blood. It's not messy. Everything appears to be neat and orderly."

"Agreed. Anything else?"

"The victim died from an overdose."

"Which is odd because typically addicts who die from overdoses usually have enough time to withdraw the needle," Van said. He opened the top drawer of the lone filing cabinet.

Aliesa circled the desk and took stock of the victim—jet poker-straight hair, brown pock-marked skin, in his mid-twenties, clad in a Medevac company shirt and blue cotton work pants. "There's a spoon, lighter, empty bag." She snagged the clear plastic envelope and held it to the light. The folds still held a residue of light pink powder. "This might have contained the cocaine."

Van studied the victim. "Judging by the track marks on his arm I'd say he's an addict."

All of Aliesa's experiments had called for her to make observations. She could analyze and put into perspective the smallest details. The time had come to put those skills to the test. "There's a telephone, antiquated PC and printer, but no paperwork out on the desk. Let's see what's on the computer." She switched on the hard drive and it whirred to life. A flashing cursor winked on the screen as the computer clicked through its opening sequences.

He walked over and shared the file he'd been examining. "Slow doesn't begin to describe the state of this business. According to these manifests, Medevac only serviced one client."

"Capill Industries."

"You got it."

"The company files are booting now. Let me try to access the payroll records." A moment later she scrolled through the past few months. "Whoa. Based on these figures it's a wonder our friend could support any kind of a habit."

"Unless he was being subsidized."

"By whom?"

"We'll find out soon enough from Drew. The logical suspect is Jackson Mercante. Mercante would have doled out the cocaine to feed his habit. It would have been one of the perks of this low-paying job."

"If you're right, Mercante's had to know Henandez's contract hadn't been renewed and the cocaine was about to dry up permanently. I'm sure our friend here had to be pretty desperate for a fix."

"This afternoon, Mercante left the office early right after we told him Hernandez had been murdered." Van came around the desk. He placed his hand on his arm. "The body hasn't had time to go completely cold yet."

She placed her palm on the man's arm and concurred. "If Mercante came here to tell him they were out of business this guy might have panicked—got a little carried away and killed himself. He had no job and no more cocaine."

"Or maybe Mercante came here to do a little housekeeping."

"Really? It's one possible scenario. Did you notice the calendar on the desk blotter? Tomorrow is circled and starred."

Van leaned closer. "Maybe Mercante told him they'd be back in business tomorrow. Then he gave him a little something to tide him over. A lethal dose of uncut cocaine."

"What's with you? Why does your mind always jump to the worst-case scenario?"

"I didn't jump to any conclusions. My theories are based on observations and prior experience."

"I'm a pretty good analyst. We've taken note of the very same details and I've come to an entirely different conclusion."

"Okay," Van said. He put his hands on his hips. "Let me ask you a question."

"Shoot."

"When you came into the office, what's the first thing you did?"

"I flicked on the light."

"Why?"

"Because the darkness in here reminded me of a cave."

"I rest my case," Van said. "A dead man can't switch off the lights."

Chapter 19

Van's phone chirped as he and Aliesa got into the rental car. He checked the screen. He pressed speaker so she could listen in. "What have you got for me?"

"Medevac is independently owned by Jackson Mercante," Drew said.

"I thought as much. Fits with my worst-case scenario." Van dispensed an I-told-you-so shrug. "Did you get any other information?"

"An address. Do you want it?"

"You bet."

"It's in Quincy. One Oceanvista Lane."

"Got it." Van said. "Any word on the other stuff we discussed?"

"Nothing yet. I'll be in touch." Drew disconnected.

Van turned to Aliesa who had already begun to plug the address into their GPS. "Oh, good."

While she programmed the town, street number and name, he punched numbers into his phone. "Detective Lowry? This is Vance. There's a DB in an industrial park in Quincy—a place called Medevac." He didn't wait for a response from the detective he simply ended the call.

He turned toward Aliesa because he sensed she hadn't

taken her eyes off him.

"What?" he said.

She blinked and shook her head. "Why did you call the detective?" she asked.

"I didn't do it for the detective," he said. "I did it for that poor shmuck in there. Even an addict deserves a proper burial."

Aliesa sat back and they drove in relative silence. Every once in a while the GPS would blurt out driving instructions. They turned off the main drag at a sign boasting beachfront property. The houses became larger and rested farther from the road. Million-dollar homes with views to match, overlooked the water. The crown jewel nestled at the road's end atop a rocky bluff. The house—a sleek, ultra modern design, sat on the ledge of the rock face like an eagle's nest. One Oceanvista had an elaborate wrought-iron gate and gate house, and the property was completely surrounded by an eight-foot-high stone walls with broken glass embedded on the top.

"How the hell are we going to get in there?" she asked.

"We're not even going to try," Van said. "Not until the sun sets."

She heaved a sigh.

"You sound relieved?"

"A little," she nodded. "Climbing a fence in this skirt would have been a real trick."

He bellowed a laugh. "We better turn in our rental and get you back to the hotel ASAP so you can slip into something to make it doable."

Locked in the bathroom of the hotel room, Aliesa could finally allow herself to wind down from the stress of the day. She'd never impersonated anyone in her life and stumbling across another dead person—three people, four including Hernandez, would give anyone the heebie-jeebies. She stripped off her power suit and tried to relax with a soak in the tub.

The old Aliesa had been a fine, upstanding, law-abiding citizen—a renowned professor who only took chances in a laboratory setting, a setting over which she had total control. Finding Evelyne dead reduced her into a quivering, crying mess—a woman who wouldn't be able to serve her friend well. She had to be strong and capable enough to push through the madness to get to the bottom of this thing.

Out of her element and out of character, didn't begin to describe her social behavior lately. It made her wonder if it might have been due in part to her recent stem-cell injection.

The physical changes in her were obvious—her lower heart rate and well-defined muscles were as buff as her skin, hair, and nails. Her emotional highs and lows confused her. Never a risk-taker outside the lab, her life always remained as dull as dishwater. She never cared about her appearance, her clothes, or what other people thought of her. She followed rules and never did anything outside of the law.

If her physical attributes had improved with the stem

cell injection, her personality could very well have gotten a face-lift also.

Too soon to draw a conclusion, she decided to take the wait-and-see approach. Surely her final injection would give her definitive proof one way or the other. Until then, she wouldn't rush to judgment.

If something as cataclysmic as Evelyne's murder hadn't happened, she wondered if she would have ever had the strength to do the things she'd done and still planned to do.

Aliesa?" Van called through the closed bathroom door. "Are you okay?"

She shook off her ruminations. "I must have dozed off for a few minutes," she said, "I'll be right out." She dunked her head under the water and pulled the plug. She dried her hair and dressed in a cat-woman outfit—compliments of Simone—black-leggings and black form-fitting shirt, and she walked into the room where Van shoved chopsticks and a carton of Kung Pau chicken into her hand.

"If you're tired I can fly solo tonight," he said, sitting at the table.

"You make it sound like I have a choice in all of this," Aliesa said.

"You do." Van stilled.

"No, I don't. I need to find out why Evelyne is dead. I won't stop until then."

"The answer won't bring her back."

Aliesa thought for a moment. She could argue the point. With her knowledge and technical base she had everything she needed to be able to clone her friend. But, like her stem-cell research, the ethical debate made it a very slippery can of worms to hold. "You'd be surprised what I can do," she said. While she attacked succulent strips of spicy chicken and rice, Van showed her the Google Maps app on his phone. "Have you figured out how we're going to get past the gate?"

"We're not," he said. He tossed his empty food carton into the garbage and pointed to spot on the map. "We're going to climb over the wall."

Her appetite fizzled out like a comet entering the earth's atmosphere. She set the carton on the edge of the table.

"Are you ready?" he asked.

"As ready as I'll ever be."

In the parking lot of the Get-Away Inn, she threw her leg over the motorcycle's seat and put her arms around Van. Human beings were masters of adaptation. A couple of days ago riding on the back of Van's bike made her really nervous. Now she snuggled into the small of his back like a contented house cat.

They drove out of Boston and turned inland. She knew when they were close—the air became thick and salty. They zipped past the Oceanvista gate. He continued along the road for a few thousand feet and pulled onto the soft shoulder. "Hold on," he said.

They dipped into a gulley and thicket. Despite the low gear and speed, she felt like popcorn on the back of the bike. Branches and leaves swept across her body from shoulder to ankle. She had no concept of direction in the matrix of underbrush and even doubted they were headed in the right direction until she spotted the clearing ahead.

"I'll be damned. It's the stone wall?"

He took off his helmet and covered the bike's light. The thick brush allowed him to drive right over to the stone fence without being seen from the road. He removed his knife from the leather case on his belt and handed it to her. "Cut some branches to cover the bike, just in case someone happens by."

While she trimmed some greenery, Van stood on the seat of the bike and examined the compound with his binoculars.

At dusk, the sun had all but disappeared inland to the west. The temperature and visibility plummeted. Soon complete darkness would prevail.

Aliesa returned with an armful of brush. Van turned off the gas and wedged the bike on its side against the wall and she proceeded to cover it with branches as best she could.

With the saddlebags slung over his shoulders he hoisted himself to the top of the wall. He set the thick leather across the shards of glass and straddled the wall.

"Climb onto the bike seat and give me your hand," he said.

She balanced on the seat and reached for him. In one smooth motion he lifted and held her until she swung a leg over.

"I'm going to jump down on the other side." He swung his leg over and pushed off the top, hitting the ground with a thud.

The wall may have only been eight feet, but it seemed much higher from her vantage point.

"Your turn," he said. "I'll catch you."

She swung her leg over, closed her eyes, and jumped. Strong arms cushioned her impact. When she opened them again, he'd already turned and was on the move.

"Follow me. Stay low."

She did exactly what he did. They used rocks and trees as cover as they made their way across the yard and over to the house. This side of the home didn't have an ocean view so there were fewer windows to worry about. They checked all the windows on the ground floor. Every one of them locked.

"Wait here," he said, putting his hands into gloves.

Tucked behind an ornamental hedge at the side of the house, she watched him shimmy the drainpipe attached to the façade, disappearing through an open window on the second floor.

And she waited.

She hunkered close to the ground and heard a low grumbling. It happened again. Another low and menacing grumble reverberated right behind her.

Slowly, she turned.

In the twilight a large Doberman stood licking its lips. Beady, black-pearl eyes pierced her. The grumbling turned into a full-fledged growling and drool glistened on its sharp, dagger-like teeth.

Chapter 20

Like the exotic puffer fish, Aliesa inhaled and tried to make herself as large and looming as possible. Still, the growling persisted. Drool sluiced from the Doberman's bared and jagged teeth as he circled her.

Careful not to make any sudden movements, she unzipped, slipped off her jacket, and wound it around her right arm several times. She thought about shouting at the animal but decided against it. The ruckus might alert Mercante. She'd rather face a hungry guard dog than confront the creepy man again. Something about him unhinged her.

The dog's unwavering focus caused her to take an offensive stance. In the next second, as if a matador's red cape had been waved, it attacked. It lunged at her face, jaws wide.

She raised her padded arm.

The dog's teeth sliced through the layers of cloth. Jaw locked, the animal held on tight and tried to shake her. She could smell its sour breath as it clamped its jaws even tighter. The dog's empty black eyes sent chills coursing down her spine. She had to do something quick.

The sliding door off the patio slid open and Van

charged full tilt toward them. Like a field-goal kicker he swung his leg at the dogs mid-section. His foot impacted the animal with a thud. The force of impact caused the dog's jaws to release. Droopy tailed, yelping and squealing, it scurried out of sight.

Van turned and unwound the coat from her arm.

"It's all right," she said. "I'm okay."

"I'm not. Not until I make sure you're unharmed." He held her arm like it was a delicate bone china. He had a pained expression on his face. "I never should have left you outside all alone."

She put her hand on his cheek. "I'm fine. Really. My arm is only bruised."

"I saw the dog from the upstairs window. Most guard dogs are trained to bark."

"I'm guessing Mercante isn't home."

"I really don't know. I haven't had a chance to clear the ground floor yet. I fully expected an alarm to sound the moment I opened the door." He put his hand on top of hers and held it. "C'mon. We've got work to do."

Van and Aliesa walked through the sliding door and into the living room. The sparse interior of the house contained sleek, ultra-modern furniture. Low-profile, white leather couches were flanked with glass and stainless tables and sat upon a thick white polar bear skin rug. The entire east face of the house was floor-to-ceiling glass and showcased a breathtaking view of the rugged Atlantic shoreline. At the far side a black Mercedes had been parked in front of one of four garages.

"There's a car in the drive," he said in hushed tones. He eyed the keypad on the wall. "Something's not right.

The security system's been disarmed."

"Maybe he forgot to reset it when he arrived home."

"It's possible. But I doubt it. Anyone with this type of security system doesn't forget. I don't think we're Mercante's first visitor tonight."

"Stay close."

"Don't worry." She tucked in behind him. Back to the hall wall he poked his head in the room between the living room and kitchen. He pulled her inside.

The office contained a massive black onyx desk. Nothing marred the gleaming surface—the computer monitor had been mounted on the facing wall.

Van crouched behind the desk.

She peered over Van's shoulder at a dismembered computer hard drive. He snagged the black box off the floor.

"What's that?" she asked.

He opened the case and shook it. "It's the housing for the computer's hard drive. It's empty."

"I don't understand. Why wouldn't Mercante just delete the information from his hard drive? Why destroy the whole computer?"

"Because deleted files can usually be recovered. Destruction of the hard drive is the only way to permanently delete information."

"I guess there was incriminating evidence on the hard drive."

"Based on the mess, I think so," Van said.

"Is it possible Mercante had another partner? I mean someone other than Hernandez?"

"It's possible."

"I'm not as well-versed in this stuff as you," Aliesa said.

"What are you thinking?"

Van stood and continued to survey the pristine office. "There are three possible scenarios, the way I see it. One—Mercante disassembled his hard drive to use it as insurance to stay alive. Two—he removed his hard drive and pitched it into the ocean, destroying all of the incriminating evidence. Or three—someone other than Mercante removed his hard drive and killed him before he became a liability."

"Do you ever think happy thoughts?"

Four loud beeps pierced the silence.

He grabbed her. "It's time we got out of here."

Aliesa clung to him like a silk stocking as they hurried toward the kitchen.

The smell of copper hit her like an impenetrable wall long before saw it. Blood. Lots of it. The puddle spread wide, coating the dips and ripples of the slate floor.

Another corpse.

Mercante lay sprawled on the kitchen floor between the stainless AGA and the climate-controlled wine pantry, his throat cut. Discombobulated limbs indicated bones had been broken.

On the wall the alarm system blinked a silent warning.

"The fail-safe's been triggered. Help is likely on route."

Aliesa turned her head away from Mercante.

Help would come too late for him, but too soon for them, if they didn't get the hell out of here.

"Follow me," he said. He sprang over Mercante's body like a gazelle. He turned and reached for her. "Jump."

She raised her head and prayed.

Even dead, Mercante frightened her. When she

jumped she fell short. The blood pool proved to be as slippery as a banana peel. Her heel slid and she fell forward. Down. Flat. Face to face with the corpse.

The thin layer of blood on the slate floor might as well have been a hundred fathoms deep. An invisible hand dragged her beneath the surface. Air seeped out of her lungs. Mercante's dead, black eyes mocked her and her muscles were lethargic and unresponsive.

She could imagine the headlines now. *Hypothermic Doctor Drowns In a Micrometer of Blood.* She had to get a grip.

Before she could get it together, Van lifted her off the ground, set her on her feet, and dragged her along behind him. They ran from the house back to the stone fence, unfettered by the dog likely off somewhere licking its wounds. He gave her a boost and quickly followed.

Her teeth were chattering and her fingers were numb as she tried to fasten the helmet chinstrap. Van cleared the bike of brush, set the saddlebags across the seat, and swaddled her in his leather jacket. He got on and she settled behind him.

"Hold on tight," he said.

She laced numb arms around his waist and snuggled close.

Oh, God, he felt really good. Even through the leather, she could feel warmth radiating from him. The man was a veritable furnace. She closed her eyes and nestled even closer.

He ratcheted the bike and they set off through the thicket. The headlight illuminated the inky darkness—he navigated the rocks and stumps as they tunneled their way through the trees. When the bike popped onto the rural road, he set a sure and steady pace. Not too fast, not too slow.

She could hear sirens in the distance. At the Oceanvista cut off, three police cruisers screamed past them with lights twirling. They maintained their pace to the Get-Away Inn where he parked the bike in the lot and switched it off.

He lifted her limp hands from around his waist. They were sticky and as cold as ice cream. He helped her off the bike. Her teeth chattered and she stumbled along beside him like a mindless zombie. Her eyes were open but blank as she followed him inside the motel room. He stood her against the bathroom vanity, pulled off her shoes, then his, and set the water in the shower.

Still nothing.

She didn't blink or utter a word. He lifted her, fully clothed, into the shower.

The water washed over her body, turning red as Mercante's blood dissolved and rushed toward the drain. He poured shampoo into his palm and washed her hair and clothes. When he searched her eyes, the defeat in them robbed him of breath. He'd seen the same hollowness on the faces of men in combat. Men who'd seen too many days in battle.

"C'mon, baby. Come back to me," he crooned, rinsing her hair. He rubbed his hands up and down her arms.

Despite the warm water, she continued to shake as if

her clothes were frozen lead weights. Nothing seemed to be working. He had to do something drastic to snap her out of it. He tugged her shirt over her head and peeled her pants from her long legs and tossed them to the far end of the tub.

All of his army training came rushing back to him. He didn't dare risk scalding her by raising the temperature of the water. The most efficient way to raise her body temperature was to share their body heat. He stepped out of his pants, shucked his shirt and leaned her against him. He tried to completely envelope her with his body. He rubbed her with his arms, legs, and chest. Her cold, blue skin made his breath catch. Her hardened, dusky nipples scored the surface of his chest, and would forever mark him.

He'd taken too many chances with a civilian. She was no more a drug dealer than he was a scientist. He should have taken better care of her.

When the lightning bolt struck he knew with absolute certainty he'd gone and broken the cardinal rule. He'd fallen in love with his suspect. He stood transfixed and owned it. "I believe you."

Chapter 21

Those three words lifted the fog in Aliesa's mind. She'd had enough. The demands of the last few days had taken a toll on her and she'd lost the will to keep beating her head against the wall.

Until Van said he believed her. Those powerful words put the fight back inside her.

Her heavy, stiff limbs tingled and warmed. He held her through the shivers. She became aware of every square inch of her naked body. And his.

Above his square and determined chin she noticed his concern. She loved the way his chest muscles danced as he kneaded her tendons and rubbed her skin. That's when she knew she needed more.

Warm water trickled over her like rain. Through a curtain of wet hair she saw his eyes darken when he dragged the soap across her chest. His light touch ignited a fuse that burned like magnesium within her—white-hot and blinding. In the flash fire, her heart rate doubled and her nipples hardened into raised peaks.

Her core sizzled. She burned in her most intimate places. These carnal sensations transported her to a different place—a place she'd never been before—a place she wanted to explore. Before thinking it to death, she plunged in. She wound her arms around his neck and drew him closer, covering his mouth with hers.

Their kiss exploded—like a spark bursting into flames the moment it found oxygen. The pull of her desire stronger than anything she'd ever known.

His lips were demanding and she gave willingly.

Nothing she'd experienced before compared to kissing him. She ran her hands through his hair, touched his face, his chest, she couldn't seem to get close enough. A guttural gasp escaped her lips and when she finally opened her eyes she saw the same desire smoldering within him.

He leaned forward. Not once did he break eye contact. His focus was almost feral. He nuzzled her neck and she felt more alive than she ever though possible. She didn't feel awkward or inexperienced she knew what she wanted and went after it.

She ran her lips across his neck and across his chest. Her hands plied his sculptured skin beneath the fancy gold medallion hanging around his neck. She kissed her way down his rippled stomach. His breath caught when she stroked him.

He lifted her back to eye level. "Slow down," he said, reclaiming her lips.

Their tongues danced.

Aliesa always thought intimacy meant making your partner lose complete and utter control, but that was only part of it. Empowerment had to be shared. Making love involved so much more. It shouldn't be rushed. Unlike a race, there should never be a winner and a loser.

He turned the tables on her and began his own decadent descent. This man knew how to pleasure a woman. His light touch and soft caresses nearly made her heart stop. He suckled her breasts and when her nipples hardened into tight pearls he made his way lower.

He didn't give her any options—not to hesitate or resist. He ran his tongue across her abdomen then moved even lower. Waves of liquid heat came to the boil. The force of her reaction caused her knees to buckle.

He steadied her. "Maybe we should take this into the bedroom." He shut off the water, wrapped her in a towel and carried her to the bed.

Aliesa burned hot. She felt like the most desirable woman on the face of the earth and fleetingly wondered if this feeling was a pleasant side effect of the stem-cell serum.

When he moved on top of her all thoughts flew out of her head. Poised at the apex of her thighs, she felt him pressing against her. "Is this what you want?" he whispered. His erection pressed against her swollen folds and she could feel the agony of restraint. He rocked himself gently back and forth. Then he gave her a series of soul-shattering kisses.

"Please," she begged. She felt singed by the onslaught of heat radiating from him. He leaned his forehead against hers.

"I love the way you respond. You act as if this has never happened before. Like no one has ever touched you here." He grazed her nipple with his thumb. "Or here." Then he put his hand between her legs.

"I've never wanted this so desperately," she

whispered.

Van continued his machinations for several seconds. "Let's see how long we can stretch it out."

"You already have," she said. She grabbed his buttocks and angled her pelvis so he was poised for immediate entry. Instead of complying he held himself perfectly still and let her rock against him.

She did everything in her power to get him to slide inside but to no avail. She gyrated and clung to him like a pole dancer.

Van almost lost it.

His emotions had run the gambit tonight. He thought she might have had a psychotic break at Mercante's house when she came face to face with someone she feared, even if he was dead.

He tried to coax a response out of her but nothing seemed to have an impact. In a last ditch effort, he played his last card by giving her the only thing which mattered the most.

His trust.

From that very second she came back to him—not only did she come back, she turned into the most seductive woman he'd ever met.

He'd always considered sex a biological function. He'd chosen his partners carefully, so he didn't have to worry about entanglements. It was all about finding a release. Selfishly, he never wanted his emotions to cloud his judgment or interfere with his dutiful cause. As Aliesa caressed and nipped at his chest he knew he would never be happy with unfettered sex ever again.

Lord, she knew how to kiss. Her satiny tongue slipped across his and when she sucked on his lip what little circulating blood supply he had left, traveled south.

He throbbed to get inside her almost as much as he wanted her to set the pace. He didn't have much restraint left. He only had to change the angle of his pelvis and he'd slip inside. Her back and forth rocking motion felt amazing and he didn't want to interrupt because she seemed to be enjoying herself. She looked damn hot, squirming to and fro beneath him. She mewed, chewed on her bottom lip, and her breasts were nipped hard and dusky pink.

Then without any warning, she sat and shoved him over on his back. She straddled him, impaling herself, inch by succulent inch, and took him to the hilt.

He groaned, his voice a strangled mixture of pleasure and pain. Breath whistled out of his lungs. "I'm not wearing a condom," he said between clenched teeth.

Her brow creased and she squeezed her eyes shut. "You needn't worry," she said. "I'm sterile. Pregnancy won't be a issue."

Pregnancy hadn't only been his concerns, he knew he was disease free but was she? He guessed so—her inner tissues were as tight as a vise and each one of her contractions were lightning strikes against him. He held onto her, not daring to move or it would be all over for him.

The moment she relaxed, he took a deep breath and rolled her onto her back and got his second wind. One languid kiss reignited their passion and the steady pace he'd set caused the pressure to return with a fury.

She clung to him as he took them both into the eye of the storm and beyond. This time when her inner muscles began to contract he couldn't stop his own floodgate from opening.

Exhausted and spent, with him still planted firmly inside, they fell asleep wrapped in the other's embrace.

He dosed and woke abruptly to a loud trill. His phone. He'd taken it off silent.

"What was that?" she asked, her eyes still half closed.

"My phone," he said. He retrieved it from his pants pocket, checked the call display and sat on the side of the bed.

"It's Drew," Van said. "What's up?"

"Got some information for your eyes only," Drew said. "It's about Aliesa."

Van rolled his wrist to check his watch. "I'll be there in twenty minutes."

Chapter 22

Aliesa bolted upright. "Where are you going?"

Van leaned over. He kissed her so gently she settled back on to the pillow. "You're going to stay right here in bed and keep warm. I won't be long. An hour, tops."

He prayed she'd acquiesce—be too tired to argue. When she closed her eyes, he knew he'd been lucky.

Van dressed quietly. The relaxed, even cadence of Aliesa's breathing told him she'd drifted back to sleep. He tiptoed through the darkened room. Aliesa trusted him implicitly—a sentiment he only recently shared. His objectivity had flown south and taken his reservations about her right along with it.

One tug and the door clicked shut. He hopped on his bike and drove across the slumbering city to the offices of ABC Inquiries.

Only one thing kept nagging at him. He'd broken the rule. He'd fallen in love with his suspect. He'd ditched basic training one-o-one—things not to do while conducting an investigation.

He should have known the very second he read the bio on Dr. Aliesa Atworth. Something about her ensnared him even before he'd laid eyes on her. Her inner strength and conviction drew him like a lodestone. Not to mention her smarts. His downfall. She'd bloody well outmaneuvered him.

He got off the elevator and strode inside Drew's office. "What have you got for me?"

Remote in hand, Drew drove his wheel chair over to the file on his desk.

"Two things." He tossed a small plastic evidence bag to Van. "Here's the vial you wanted analyzed." He placed one on the table and then held another. "This is the dummy vial filled with sterile saline. It's not an exact match, but close enough."

Van eyed both vials. "It's perfect." He grabbed the dummy vial and put it in his right pocket.

Drew crossed his arms. "The real vial tested negative for narcotics."

"Did the lab identify the contents?" Van asked.

Van plucked it from the table and placed it in his left pocket.

Drew snagged the lab report. "Biological material."

"What kind of biological material?" Van asked.

"I asked the technician the very same question."

"And?"

"She said it contained stem cells."

Van shrugged. "She's been up-front from the very beginning."

"Hold on there, big fella," Drew said. He slipped another sheet of paper out of the file and slid it toward Van.

"What's this?"

"It's the FedEx bill of lading from Hernandez's last shipment."

Van focused on the fine print and scanned the document.

Sender: *Dr. Marcus Hernandez, Universidad of Trujillo.* **Contents:** *Vassicine Hydrochloride.*

Destination: *Biochemistry Lab 2B, Boston University, Boston, Massachusetts.*

Attention: *Dr. A. Atworth.*

"Fuck me," Van said. He bit hard on his lip and tasted blood. "Hernandez wasn't lying."

Drew turned toward him. "I did some research on vassicine hydrochloride. Why was he sending her an anti-leukemic?"

I don't think he was. I think there was only enough vassicine hydrochloride to pass inspection. The bulk of the shipment is cocaine hydrochloride."

"I hate to be the one to point out the obvious but innocent people don't ordinarily have uncut cocaine delivered to their doorstep."

With his right hand balled into a fist, Van shook. "You read the emails. Each time she asked for Camu camu, there was a FedEx shipment within a day or two. This last shipment was sent before an email."

"Hey, don't kill the messenger. I'm just sayin."

Van wanted to hit something. Hit someone. His cocked arm wavered and he slammed it into the desk. He closed his eyes. Inside, he shook. He wadded the piece of paper in his other hand and paced. He knew Aliesa had been honest with him. All he had to do was prove it.

"How do you want to handle this?" Drew asked.

"I'm going to go back to the hotel and pretend everything is peachy."

"And you think you can pull it off? Aliesa's pretty smart. She's going to want to know why I summoned you."

"I'll think of something."

"Oh, gawd." Drew shook his head. "You're sleeping with her, aren't you?"

Van came to an abrupt halt. Drew's eyes drilled him. He nodded. The old Van would have thought she suckered him. The new Van bought her whole act. Hell, he swallowed the entire fishing pole. He walked over to the desk and withered into the chair. "I think I'm in love with her."

"Oh, shit."

"Tell me about it. I know. I fucked up."

"Why not confront her? You'll know in an awful hurry if she's been playing you."

"I don't have to. I know she isn't."

"I hope you're right. I guess you'll have to figure it out. There'll be repercussions if you've miscalculated."

Van gritted his teeth and all but hissed. "Don't you think I know that?"

"Sorry," Drew said. "It's just I've never seen you like this. You've always been so careful."

Van rose and turned to leave.

"Let me know if there's anything else I can do."

"Thanks. But there's really only one thing left to do and I'm the only one who can do it."

Van left Drew's office in a daze. He hopped on his bike and headed back to the hotel.

How could he prove Aliesa was innocent? He knew her to have staunch morals. Hell, she recoiled at the sight of dead people. It didn't make sense she would have a hand in supplying something so toxic it would kill people. Unless she'd been played. Maybe Hernandez had something on her? He never considered the possibility of coercion or even blackmail.

He opened the room with his key and stepped inside. Beneath the covers he noticed the curve of Aliesa's hip. His instant arousal made him want to strip and make love to her until she surrendered any secrets she'd been keeping.

Reluctantly, he walked over to the bedside table and flipped on the light. When he lifted the sheets, his stomach bottomed. Bed pillows were neatly arranged beneath the coverlet. His precious Aliesa, the woman who he believed had been exploited, had performed one hell of a nifty disappearing act.

Substance volatility never ceased to amaze Aliesa. States could change. Physical properties could be manipulated. During her laboratory experiments, what she expected to occur and what she observed were often two very different things. Only recently, had she discovered the principle applied in real life, too.

A couple of hours ago, she basked in a blanket of security. Wrapped in Van's strong, loving embrace, far from the trappings of Evelyne's murder and this cocaine investigation. She'd drifted to sleep on a cloud of happiness and contentment. She awoke with a start and reality sent her reeling.

She got out of bed to think and paced the room.

Having sex with Van complicated everything.

Up until then, Van wanted her tagging along with him. It didn't take a genius to know men tended to lose interest once they got a woman into bed. Her neediness had likely been the catalyst. She'd handled every situation he placed her in.

There was no scientific explanation for her abrupt change, though she'd seen it happen time and again, in and out of the lab. She tended to go with her gut when a substance became unstable and changed states. Nine times out of ten she'd be right.

When she came face to face with Mercante on the kitchen floor she knew he'd already changed states. His soul eeked close to her and whispered alongside her. It slithered along her skin, clogged her pores like battery acid. She shivered as she remembered the burning cold. Unsure how to handle Mercante in his new state, Aliesa shut herself down—for protection and insulation. Something else she'd never been able to do before.

The ability to witness and react to this type of phenomenon made her wonder if her stem cell serum had rendered her more sensitive to things on another plane? Maybe it opened a neural pathway allowing her to tap into her sixth sense. She would never really know, even if it sounded unbelievable to her own ears. She would never tell anyone. Who would believe her? Some things were better left unsaid.

Van's admission of trust snapped her out of her defensive cocoon. She'd fallen in love with him—the plain scientist and the hot guy. Oh gawd, now she had some time to evaluate everything from a clearer vantage point she wondered if it hadn't been anything more than a mercy fuck.

When she began her experiment, she'd been trying to discover a cure for cancer, not the fountain of youth. She'd been very surprised when one of the side effects of the serum had been a more youthful, vital appearance. She'd never had the desire to be the perfect woman before, but that was then. She wanted Van.

Now, not only did she want to be a better woman, she decided she would do whatever it took to ensure she didn't slip back into geekdom. To prevent it from happening she needed another shot of stem cell serum and fast. Dressed in the only dry outfit available—the short skirt and jacket she'd worn this afternoon, she slipped out of the room and hailed a cab to her condo.

Outside her building, she slapped a twenty in the cabby's outstretched palm and told him he could expect another two if he waited for her at the curb, she'd need a drive back to the motel.

She rode the elevator to the penthouse level and listened outside and tried the handset. Locked tight. She slid the key into the slot and opened the door and poked her head inside. The two men must have gotten tired waiting for her and left. She hurried into the living room and removed the bottle of Beaujolais from the wine cooler and reached into the back to retrieve her last remaining vial of stem-cell serum. Her hand scooped air. She bent and peeked inside.

Nothing.

Perhaps the vial had fallen behind another bottle. Carefully she removed several bottles, placing them on the floor to examine the space behind.

"What are you doing?" Jorge asked with a thick

Spanish accent.

She spun around.

Jorge and Axel appeared at the end of the hall. Neither wore a jacket or shoes and she assumed they'd been asleep and using her penthouse as their home base.

"I really needed a drink." She laughed and tried to act as confident as possible. On the inside, her heart leaped into her throat.

Jorge moved. He drew his hand out of his trouser pocket and a shiny metal blade flashed. Aliesa snatched two bottles of wine, one in each hand, and slammed them together. Wine and glass shards scattered, circling her like spike strips. She wore thick-soled shoes. Approximately, a three-foot impenetrable perimeter surrounded her. In her hands, she wielded the jagged bottlenecks like daggers. "If you know what's good for you, you'll stay back," she said. She kept her hands moving so the two wouldn't see how bad she was shaking. Her lips were taut, but her voice rang out loud and clear.

Jorge started to laugh. Axel stepped backward to the very end of the hall and spoke a few Spanish words to his chuckling friend. Then, with the determination of a bull, he ran full bore down the carpeted hall, past Jorge, toward her. When he reached the highly, polished hardwood floor he planted one foot in front of the other and slid, plowing through the wine and glass shards like a snow blower. He slid right through her perimeter and knocked her feet out from beneath her.

Too stunned to do anything else, she dropped the broken bottlenecks and wobbled, struggling to maintain her balance.

Axel grabbed a handful of her hair and pulled her upright. "I live to surf," he said.

Jorge walked through the path Axel had cleared. "Where is it?" he asked.

"Where is what?" Aliesa asked.

Jorge slapped her. "The cocaine, bitch."

She pressed her hand to her face to stop the stinging. Her eye teared and she'd likely have a monster bruise. Play dumb. "I don't know what you're talking about."

Jorge grabbed her, spun her around and pressed a cold, hard blade against her throat. Axel chuckled.

"Okay, okay," she said. She racked her brain. "It's at the university, in my lab."

The men conversed with each other. Spanish words were shouted.

Aliesa guessed since these two were the ones who destroyed her lab she needed to do some fast-talking to stay alive. "Without me you won't ever find it."

More conversation.

Axel pushed her forward. She placed her feet in the cleared streaks on the floor. He plucked a silk scarf from the hanger in the front hall closet and tied her hands together. Jorge returned wearing shoes and his jacket and he held her at knifepoint while Axel did the same.

She'd made a mistake.

In hindsight, venturing back to her apartment hadn't been the smartest thing she'd ever done. Her brain must have been high on endorphins and unable to compute the danger quotient.

No doubt, Van would be royally pissed. She had to fix this. Leave some sort of clue where they were headed.

Axel shoved her toward the front door.

"Wait," Aliesa said. "I need my university identification cards in the kitchen."

When Jorge returned, he carried the lanyard with her cards. Axel nodded and he thrust her through the door toward the elevator.

Chapter 23

Forced into the front seat of a dark sedan, Aliesa's insides roiled. Axel leered at her like she was his favorite chocolate bar.

He spoke Spanish to Jorge who slid behind the wheel. She'd once considered learning the language, now she wished she had. Even still, she knew what Axel wanted. Sandwiched between the two men, she could smell his rancid breath and body odor. He slid his hand along her skirt to her knee.

She flinched, then faced him with a haughty calm and issued a threat. "Take your hand off me," she said, her voice belied the terror in her heart.

He pulled back ready to hit her, but before he could follow through, Jorge grabbed his hand. "Not until we have the package."

Axel grunted and sat back. Jorge started the car and exited the parking garage.

What had she done?

Not only had she disobeyed Van and left the safety of their room at the Get-Away Inn, she'd walked right into the arms of the men Van had been trying to keep her away from. He told her they were watching her apartment. He'd been right.

What had she been thinking?

It's what vanity did to a person. She'd been so convinced she couldn't hold on to Van without another stem-cell injection she willingly put her life in danger. The old Aliesa wouldn't have cared about keeping a man. Hell, the old Aliesa didn't even have time for a man.

Now she had an even worse situation on her hands. Her attempt to buy some time could very well put other lives, at the university, at risk. These two men had already demonstrated they killed people. They'd left a veritable trail of bodies all over Boston and the surrounding area. The early morning hour might be her only salvation. In her past experiences working around the clock, she knew there were fewer people roaming the halls.

The car sped through the empty streets of Boston's downtown core. They turned onto Cambridge, then Storrow.

She had to think. She needed a plan. But what? These two weren't going to let her live, even if she could produce the missing shipment of cocaine.

The dark sedan sped along Storrow, under the Harvard Bridge and exited at Carlton right before the BU bridge. Slash parked the car in a *No Parking Zone* in front of the Kern building.

With a little luck the car would be tagged for being improperly parked and towed to the impound, stranding them. Of course she'd already be dead. Visions of Evelyne's body flashed in her head.

Jorge got out of the car and Axel dragged her along with him. He closed the door and pressed her against the side of the car. "Don't try anything cute." She surveyed her surroundings. No people coming or going and she didn't see any security vehicles.

The trio walked the slate stairs. She inserted her ID into the slot and the door buzzed open. The halls were dark and deserted. A dozing security guard sat in a chair at the end of the hall. She recognized him. He regularly worked the night shift.

They headed for the stairs.

Yellow crime scene tape crisscrossed the entrance of Aliesa's lab. Jorge flipped open his switchblade and sliced the plastic with a flick of his wrist.

Thankfully, the lab had been cleaned.

The crime scene floor which had sparkled with broken glass now appeared matte and dull. The smell of blood redolent in the air had been replaced with the odor of bleach and disinfectant. Black tape still clung to the floor, outlining where Evelyne had fallen.

"Where is it?" Jorge asked.

"Good question. Someone's cleaned the place." More for her own benefit, she began opening and closing cupboards and drawers to see if any part of her research still existed. All of her samples, all of the raw data gone. She scanned the desk and noticed her laptop was missing. She flipped the switch on her BU computer, not even the light worked. Maybe the police had taken her laptop to the crime lab for analysis. Maybe they'd taken the hard drive of her BU computer too.

"What are you trying to pull?" Jorge said, turning on her. "There is no package here?"

Metal gleamed in his hand as he moved stealthily toward her.

"Wait," she said. "The package might have been waylaid in the mailroom."

"Where is that?" Jorge asked.

"This way," Aliesa said. She led the pair back out into the hall.

Halfway down the stairs, Jorge pulled her aside. He grabbed her hair and yanked it hard, to expose the curve of her neck. He pressed the cool metal to her throat.

"The package better be in the mail room or you're as good as dead," he said. When he released her she nearly fell and toppled to the bottom.

Van hated being made a fool of.

From the hotel room, he hopped back on his bike and nearly broke the sound barrier driving to her condo. He knew exactly where she'd gone because the key card to her condo had been missing from the night side table. A pain, since he'd have to once again disable the building's security system. He didn't bother parking underground, he simply left his bike at the front door of the building and barged into her apartment.

He stopped when he walked to the end of the hall. Broken wine bottles were scattered across the living room floor. He bent and examined the footprints tracked through the mess.

She'd had company. There were three people and there'd been a struggle.

Van scouted out the bedrooms. Unless he missed his guess, Axel and Jorge had been waiting for her to return.

They'd surprised her. He hurried back into the kitchen. The contents of her purse had been scattered on the table. As he took stock of the remaining items on the counter he soon realized her keys and BU ID were missing. They were headed to the university. He dug the real vial of stem cells out of his pocket and whipped open the refrigerator door. Virtually empty—except for a selection of condiments. Relish, ketchup, marmalade, olives. He grabbed the jar of olives and dropped the small vial into the brine and returned it to the shelf. Then he place the dummy vial in the bar fridge.

He sailed out of the condo, jumped on his bike and raced to the campus. He parked beside the black sedan, took the front steps of the Kern building two at a time and reached for the door.

Locked.

He started pounding on the glass. A security guard appeared.

"We're closed," he said, through the glass door. "The building opens at eight."

Van pressed his DEA ID against the window. "Open the door. Now!"

The security guard nodded and stood back.

Van made for the stairs and took them two at a time. Half of the flight behind him, he turned to head to the second tier of stairs when he heard a ruckus on second floor. He stopped and listened. "The package better be in the mail room or you're as good as dead," a thick Spanish voice echoed.

Mail room.

He'd seen the sign at the end of the hall on the first floor when he entered the building. He turned and headed downstairs. The security guard must have gone on a tour of the place because he was no longer at the door. Van ran toward the mail room. He stooped in the small alcove, picked the lock and slipped inside.

With not much time to spare.

He tucked in behind the door and waited. In less than two minutes the door burst open and Aliesa, flung off-balance, stumbled into the room.

Van leaned into the metal mail cart beside him and drilled it into the two men following her.

The force of impact caused Axel to fly over the desk and land on the floor in a heap. Jorge must only have been winged and jumped back out of the way. Van reached over and yanked Aliesa behind him.

Jorge shoved the cart out of his path. He tossed the knife from his left hand to his right. "I see lover boy's come to the rescue." He arced the knife and swiped air.

With a kick, Van sent the knife skittering into the corner. He lunged at Jorge, knocking into him. They fell onto the desk, their hands locked around each other's throat. Both rolled onto the ground and Van landed on top. He hit him once. Twice.

"Watch out," Aliesa screamed. Axel had staggered to his feet and grabbed Van's fist mid-punch. Axel flung Van off Jorge and sent him flying into the filing cabinets. Then, Axel straightened to throw a punch, but Van twisted out of the way and his fist impacted metal. He yelped and danced in pain.

Jorge had gotten off the floor and grabbed hold of the office chair, driving it like a battering ram into Van. But Van saw him coming. He jumped into the seat of the chair and lamb-basted Jorge between the eyes.

Axel kicked the office chair and it careened into the desk, catapulting Van overtop. Van's head hit the wall hard. His vision blurred and things started to move in slow motion.

By the time he shook off his dizziness and stood, Jorge had retrieved his knife and had it pressed against Aliesa's throat. "Make my day," he said.

Van straightened only to have Axel drive his fist into Van's gut. Axel grabbed a roll of packing tape and wound several layers around Van's upper and lower body. He did the same to Aliesa.

It seemed like a tornado had struck the mailroom. With both Van and Aliesa contained, Jorge delegated. "Let's check out the storage room, shall we." With their legs wrapped in tape both Van and Aliesa took baby steps.

Axel and Jorge followed them through the door. Inside the room, larger packages had been stored in alphabetical order on metal shelves. While Jorge held Van and Aliesa at knife-point, Axel pulled a clip board from the wall hook and examined the paperwork.

Then he walked over to the first spot on the shelf. "To Dr. Aliesa Atworth, from Dr. Marcus Hernandez," he said, removing a large brown-papered package from the shelf. He walked it into the office, set it on the desk, ripped open the shipping paper to reveal four bricks of pink powder. He opened the first brick and tasted a sample. He nodded to Jorge.

Jorge tossed his blade back and forth between hands and trembled in anticipation. Van had seen him perform the same ritual with Hernandez.

Van leaned in front of Aliesa.

"Before you do anything you'll regret you need to see the medallion hanging around my neck," Van said. When Jorge paid no attention he made the same statement only in Spanish. "Antes de hacer cualquier cosa que usted II pesar, creo que deberiamos echar un vistazo a la medalla colgando de mi cuello."

Jorge stopped tossing his knife. He spread the lapels of Van's shirt and lifted the chain with his knife. His eyes widened when he recognized the crest.

Van didn't blink. "I need to speak with Santino Alarcon."

Chapter 24

Aliesa and Van stood in the middle of the mailroom with packing tape wound around their bodies and mouths. Aliesa listened to Jorge's conversation on his cell phone. She couldn't understand a word, but she hoped Van could.

She didn't know if Van still believed her. The missing shipment of cocaine had landed in her mailbox despite her denying any knowledge of it. All of which didn't make her seem very trustworthy at this particular moment. She said a silent prayer. Van had come after her, though right now she couldn't be sure he hadn't come for the cocaine not her.

Inside she felt scooped out and hollow.

When she turned toward Van she couldn't read his expression—yet another example of her social ineptitude. Had sleeping with her been a manipulation? She hoped with all her heart it had not been, though she knew she would have been an easy mark. She only wished she hadn't fallen for him in the process. Her naivety had left her wide open and her heart ached.

Jorge disconnected. "Let's go." When Van didn't start moving, he shoved him.

Axel led the way through the office toward the door.

The door burst open and a security guard stepped into the room "How the hell did you get in here?" he asked. Then his eyes flitted to Van and finally Aliesa gagged and bound in countless meters of tape. He reached for his firearm and as he did Axel head-butted him. The security guard wobbled on his feet and Axel spun and kicked him with a roundhouse. Impact drove the guard to the ground and Axel grabbed his .45 automatic Colt pistol and hit him over the head knocking him out cold. Axel dragged the guard further inside the room and out of the way and Jorge poked his head out into the hall.

"Keep you heads down and don't stop," Jorge said.

Axel carried the cocaine. He took the lead once again and Jorge rode shotgun behind them. They made it to door and outside to the black sedan, still illegally parked at the base of the outside stairs. A jogger with ear buds ran toward them. He never saw Van or Aliesa until he was almost upon them. His eyes widened when he noticed how they'd been taped like mummies and he slowed until Jorge stepped out from behind Aliesa and waved his knife under his nose. The jogger did a complete about face and ran in the opposite direction.

Axel popped the trunk of the car and when he stepped out of the way he pulled the security guard's gun out of his waistband and slammed it over Van's head, dropping him like an anchor inside the trunk.

Aliesa braced herself for her knock-out blow but none came. Axel dipped and lifted Aliesa, tossing her in the trunk on top of Van.

Right before the trunk swung shut and darkness descended, she caught a glimpse of Van's Kawasaki Ninja parked on the other side of the car. A few short days ago she'd been frightened to ride on a motorcycle. Seemed like a lifetime ago. Now she was being shoved in the trunk of a car and taken at gun and knife-point to a cartel kingpin. It made her wonder if she'd even be alive tomorrow.

Van moaned beneath her.

Hands still taped to her torso, she wiggled onto her side and nestled in beside him. She placed her head on his chest and listened. His pulse punched a staccato beat, strong and fast.

It made her realize the here and now was all anyone ever had.

Van drifted.

Somewhere in the darkness he could hear a woman assuring him he'd be okay.

His mother?

He couldn't quite seem to focus. His mind kept swirling. He tried to open his eyes but they seemed glued shut. He couldn't move his arms either.

Had he been shot? He began the process of elimination—moving body parts to determine whether he'd been hit. He wiggled his toes and flexed his legs. He shifted his pelvis, clenched a fist and strummed his fingers.

"Wake up, Van," a woman's voice said, this time closer.

Not his mother. It couldn't be. His mother was dead. Burying her had been the hardest thing he'd ever done.

Hot breath brushed his cheek. The back of his head

throbbed.

"I need you. Please wake up. Where do you think they're taking us?"

They. Ah, yes. Axel and Jorge. Aliesa. Cocaine.

Hernandez had sent the last shipment of cocaine to her. It made sense. Sending it to someone who owed him a favor and Aliesa owed him more than one.

If he'd sent it to Capill Industries he'd have to split it with his partner. If he sent it to Aliesa, the entire shipment would be his and his alone.

Now Axel and Jorge had what they came for he knew he had to do something to keep both of them alive. He played the only card he had left.

He pried open his eyes. The inside of the trunk was pitch. Aliesa leaned against him, the tape hanging half on, half off her mouth.

Van stretched and moved his mouth to loosen the tape across his. "How long have I been out of it?" he asked.

"We've been driving for about an hour. Axel hit you pretty hard. I was starting to worry. Thank God you're awake."

No sooner were the words out of Aliesa's mouth and the car lurched to a stop. Van listened and waited. The car idled. The passenger door opened and slammed shut.

A buzzer sounded on the other side of the trunk and a voice crackled through a speaker. "Hola."

"Open the first door," Axel said.

There was a beep and a motor droned. Metal rattled as an aluminum door jerked into motion.

Then the car reversed. This time when it stopped so did the engine. The trunk popped and light from the garage spilled inside.

The shock of brightness made Van squint. Axel reached in and scooped Aliesa out, placing her on her feet. Van didn't get the same consideration. Axel dragged him out and dumped him on the concrete floor.

He checked his surroundings. They had to be inside a funeral home. A hearse was parked right in the next spot and an adjustable coffin gurney was pressed against the back wall.

"A little premature, don't you think? We're not dead yet," Van said. His head pounded like a son of a bitch.

"That could change at a moment's notice," Jorge said, waving his blade.

"How about using your knife to slice off some of this tape?" Van had pins and needles in his arms from being restrained in one position for so long.

Axel and Jorge bent and grabbed a hold of Van's jacket to pull him to his feet. "Not going to happen," Jorge said. Axel nudged Aliesa toward the door leading inside the funeral home.

Visitation rooms brimmed with plush taupe carpet, jewel-toned wallpaper, and comfortable furniture groupings. They were hurried into a freight elevator and taken to the embalming room where they were shoved inside a storage closet.

He listened at the door and heard Axel clomping away.

Before the closet door slammed shut, he noticed a light switch on the wall inside the door. He slid against the wall and when he came to the switch he used his shoulder to flip it on.

"I need you to see if you can find the end of this tape

so you can unwind me." She sidled next to him and with her fingers she pulled at the tape. Van did all he could to help. He tried to keep the lower rings of the tape taut. Finally, one of the layers ripped. She worked at the torn edge and pulled. Van turned as the tape around his upper legs loosened. The tape broke on more than one occasion and she would have to work at finding the next piece she could pull at. It seemed like it took forever, but soon Van's hands were free which allowed him to tear at the layers too. Once Van cleared his body of the tape he did the same for Aliesa.

Then he went over to the door and listened.

Nothing.

He wiggled the knob.

Locked.

He searched the room for something he could use to pry the door open, but he couldn't find anything. He pushed on the door. Then he put his weight into it.

It didn't budge.

"I guess we're going to have to stay put for the time being."

On the farthest wall there were two maybe three shelves filled with medical supplies, catheters, hoses, and towels. Van pulled a stack of towels from the shelf and spread them out on the floor. "Might as well conserve our energy," he said. "Sit."

Both of them sat with their backs against the back wall.

"Why do you think they brought us here?" Aliesa asked.

Van had been wondering the same thing himself. "I can think of a couple of possibilities. Either they're going to kill us and toss us in with people about to be buried, or…"

"Inside the same casket?" Aliesa asked.

"It won't matter, you'll be dead, too."

"What's your other idea?" Aliesa asked.

"They're waiting to hear back from someone?"

"The man called Santino Alarcon?"

Van nodded.

Aliesa became very quiet. "It's not mine, you know." Aliesa said.

Van knew what she meant but he gave her more time to pull her thoughts together.

"You have every right to doubt me since Hernandez addressed the last shipment of cocaine to me. But I swear, I knew nothing about it."

He turned to her. "Do you think I would have made love to you if I thought you had anything to do with the cocaine?"

"I don't know."

He felt bad enough. He never once mentioned Hernandez sent the last shipment of cocaine to her. It was never really a matter of where but when. "Though I am curious how you knew the cocaine would be at BU?"

She shrugged and her eyes filled with tears. "I didn't. I thought if I told them the cocaine had been sent to the university it would give you enough time to find me."

Van put his arm around her and pulled her close.

Drew told Van the last shipment from Hernandez arrived at BU the day after Evelyne's murder. He never mentioned the kaleidoscope of emotions which bombarded him when he discovered her missing from the Get-Away Inn. Hot pokers of need skewered his heart. He'd jumped on his bike and streaked to the penthouse and then the university like a crazy man.

"Who is this Santino Alarcon?" Aliesa asked.

"It's a long story," he said. "It all started before either of us were born."

"I don't think Axel or Jorge will be back anytime soon."

Van put his head back against the wall and closed his eyes. "My dad was one of the first agents sent to South America on assignment during Nixon's war on drugs. A jungle raid had wiped out his entire team. He'd been shot and near death when a young woman, a local, found him and hid him in a nearby village. He teetered on the verge of death for weeks. Everyday she would come and tend him."

"She didn't live in the village?"

"No. She knew she couldn't take him to her family's hacienda because he would have been killed. You see, her dad ordered the raid on the team."

"Oh, I see."

"Do you?" Van asked. "My father hid in the village for a couple of months and they spent everyday together."

"Didn't they wonder where she went every day?"

"One person did. A fraternal twin. After her eighteenth birthday all attention seemed to be focused on her brother to learn the business. She was left to her own devices." Van scrubbed his hand across his face. "You want to know what really gets me?"

Aliesa nodded.

"I didn't know any of this until about six months ago."

"What happened six months ago?"

"I'd been shot in the line of duty so I took a hiatus from the DEA and came home to spend some time with my family. When I got home, my mom was pretty sick. The doctor ran a bunch of tests and told me she had stage four breast cancer."

"I'm so sorry," Aliesa said.

"She died three weeks later," Van's eyes ere glassy. "She wanted to go to be with my father and sister again."

"Was your mom the woman in the story?"

Van nodded. "She escaped from South America with my father. Gave up everything to be with him. My dad retired from the DEA when they returned and my mom got her United States citizenship. In her last hours she called me to her side." He rubbed the medallion hanging on a chain around his neck. "She told me her secret. Alejandro Alarcon, the head of the South American cocaine cartel, the man the DEA's had in its sights for the past twenty years, is my grandfather."

Chapter 25

Aliesa heard the tension in Van's voice reach the breaking point. She sat in a daze trying to assimilate what he'd told her. She knew all about conflicts of interest. She'd crossed the line when she began using her stem cell serum on herself. It had been their fixations which brought them together. Given his history she understood why he made this cocaine shipment his priority. He'd lost everything to the drug trade. "Is that why you quit your job with the DEA?"

He huffed a near laugh. "I'd lost my objectivity. My mother's confession made my mission too subjective. I had no choice but to turn in my resignation. My fight had turned very personal. It consumed me."

"I'm sorry for your loss," Aliesa said. "Were you close to your mother?"

"I guess not as close as I thought."

"Don't be so hard on yourself," Aliesa said. "She didn't tell you because she knew you'd single-handedly try to dismantle the cartel."

He closed his eyes. "And she was right. After I buried her I went charging back to South America. I'd already put several small ops out of business but I couldn't seem to get close to any of the larger ones, not until I caught wind of Hernandez. Too bad the cartel had been downwind as well."

"The reason why Jorge and Axel camped out in my living room."

Van nodded. "Pretty much."

Aliesa remained silent for a few moments, then she remembered something. "Who was the one person you mentioned who knew your mom had been nursing your father back to health?"

"You don't miss a thing, do you?" Van said.

She shrugged.

"It was Santino, my mother's twin brother."

"Is that the reason you asked Jorge and Axel to speak with him?"

"I had to do something. I'm pretty sure they would have killed us if I hadn't."

"Why do you think Santino will spare us?" Aliesa asked.

"It's a crap shoot, but Santino is the only relative, on my mother's side, who knows I exist. I'm hoping he hasn't changed or forgotten about her. Otherwise I've only prolonged the inevitable."

"It's been a long time," Aliesa said. "Do you think he still cares?"

"Santino and my mom were born into privilege. Their father, Alejandro, was the richest and most notorious man in all of Peru and he held his children to an impossibly high standard. They lived in a third world country, one with extreme poverty and a stunted infrastructure—they had absolutely everything and Santino hated his father for it."

"How did Santino figure out your mom's secret?"

"He watched her leave the hacienda first thing in the morning and not return until after dark. One day he followed her."

"Oh, no," Aliesa said.

"He confronted her and threatened to expose her. He gave her three days to say goodbye and end it with my dad or he'd take the information to their father."

"Is that when your parents' escaped?"

"If only they had," Van said. "No, Alejandro had become curious about his daughter's whereabouts also. He'd had his men follow her. When he learned what she'd been doing, he disowned her and took revenge on the entire village."

"How could he do that?"

"Pride makes people do awful things. He had no idea his daughter was already pregnant with me."

"Did he ever find out?"

"I don't think so." Van shook his head. "And if Alejandro ever learns his only son lied to him it could very well be his death warrant."

"What do you mean?"

"Santino loved my mother. He didn't think falling in love meant she had to die. Somehow he got both of my parents out of the village before it completely burned to the ground. He snuck them onto a freighter bound for America. My mother worried her father would come after her, so Santino promised to tell him he positively identified the charred remains in the village as theirs."

Aliesa released the breath she'd been holding. "I don't know what to say."

"There's nothing to say."

A commotion in the outer room quieted both.

Van hit the switch throwing them into darkness. He tugged her behind him.

The door swung open. Van, ready to pounce, waited. He heard the unmistakable sound of the cocking mechanism of the automatic Colt Axel confiscated.

"We can do this the easy way or the hard way, it's your choice," Axel said. "Both of you put your hands on your head and come out very slowly."

Van closed his eyes and tipped his head back against the wall. Then he did what Axel asked and stepped into the open door. Aliesa did the same, falling in step behind him. They stepped out of the closet and into the embalming room.

Stainless steel tables gleamed.

While Axel held them at gunpoint, Jorge talked to another man sheathed in a white apron who stood with his back to Van making preparations at the counter. When he turned he pulled the contents of some unknown vial into the hypodermic he held.

In the corner of the room there were two particleboard coffins. Van's last-ditch effort for reprieve had obviously been denied. In the blink of an eye he reacted. He rammed his boot with all the ferocity he could muster into Axel's shin and knocked the gun out of his hand. Then he barreled head first into Jorge.

Both Axel and Jorge toppled to the floor followed by a tray of stainless steel instruments. When Van leaned over to grab Axel's gun the aproned man plunged the needle into Van's neck. The pinprick sent a chilling tide of some unknown substance racing through his veins and numbing darkness burrowed deep, penetrating his consciousness.

Aliesa stood with her hands in the air and saw the very moment Van's body go limp. Axel picked up the gun from just beyond Van's reach.

"No," she screamed, thinking Axel would put a bullet in him. She dove onto the floor and tried to cover Van with her body.

She squeezed her eyes shut waiting for a cold slug to burn into her body like a laser, but nothing happened. Instead she heard Axel and Jorge talking to the man who injected Van. All of them spoke Spanish at what sounded like the speed of sound. She opened her eyes and noticed a sticker on the box across from her. *Full Wood Combination Trays for Shipping Embalmed Remains*. Below it—a bulleted list—Leak resistant interior liner and tray, Foam padding, Body straps, Packing envelope, Body shroud, Polyabsorbent sheet and foam pillow. Underneath the bulleted points read the caption, *Containers For Precious Cargo*.

The three men lifted one of these two boxes and placed it on top of a stainless gurney.

Both she and Van were goners. Tears streamed down her cheeks. If only she'd told him how she'd fallen in love with him. Now he was dead and she'd never have the chance. She'd never be able to tell him how much his trust had meant.

Axel limped across the room and held her while Jorge and the other man lifted Van and placed him on the leak proof liner. She howled and squeezed her eyes shut. Her shoulders slumped forward and she prayed her demise would be as swift as Van's had been.

She had nothing left to live for. Everyone who had ever mattered to her had been ripped away. More tears filled her eyes. She hardly noticed the pinprick in the meaty muscle high on her arm and never even made it to the count of three.

Chapter 26

Van couldn't snap out of it. A million sensations swamped him. First, bitter cold nipped at his fingers and toes. Then the sizzling heat made sweat pool at the base of his spine. The temperature extremes made breathing difficult. Like a bellows, he dragged air in and out of his lungs.

A continuous drone screamed in his ears.

An engine? Maybe. The differences in pitch could be racing RPM's.

He hovered in and out of awareness.

A thump jarred him. He bit his tongue and tasted the coppery tang of blood. Something squealed. Then came the acrid smell of burning rubber.

Had he died? Was this hell?

The wailing ceased and he came to stillness.

Moments of clarity mingled in the haze.

A door hissed and opened. Heat struck him like a flamethrower. Distant shouting, and not in English.

With a bump and a scrape, the wood beneath him creaked as he was lifted. Then there was a thump and another slide. A door closed and then complete and utter silence prevailed. The temperature cooled.

And, once again, he knew he was on the move.

To his utter shock he slept. When he finally awoke, he found himself lying in a wooden tray. He blinked several times to clear the fogginess in his head, grabbed the raised edges of the tray, hauled himself into a sitting position and noticed his tray sat on top of a stainless steel gurney.

Beside him, on another table, lay Aliesa.

He had one hell of a headache. When he lifted his arms to touch his scalp, he felt crusted blood. Oh yes. Axel had whacked him on the head with the butt of his gun to get him into the truck. He pushed through the pain and climbed off the tray to stand on the floor. His legs wobbled like rubber bands.

"Aliesa," he whispered. He touched her cheek and called her name once again. "Aliesa, can you hear me?"

She groaned and rolled her head from side to side. One eye opened a fraction and then closed tightly again. Van examined the room. Unless he missed his guess, this was another embalming room. A somewhat antiquated one. The sloped floor angled toward a central drain for the disposal of bodily fluids. Van stumbled to one of the two closed doors. The first door opened to reveal a sink and toilet within. The second door was locked.

On the counter were two bottles of water and, he guessed, two wrapped tortillas. He grabbed one bottle, wet a paper towel in the sink and dabbed the cool cloth on to Aliesa's forehead.

Again, her eyes flickered open. This time she smiled. "Hey," she said.

"Hey, yourself. How do you feel?"

Aliesa blinked several times. "Like I've been drugged." Her hands wobbled and her eyes were glassy and unfocused. "Take it slow." He cracked open the bottle of water and tipped it to her lips. Water trickled across her cheek.

Van slid his arm beneath her shoulder blades and sat her up.

"Where are we?" she asked. She plucked the water bottle and gulped.

"I need to use the ..." Her voice trailed off.

Van pointed to the open door. "Think you can manage?"

She nodded, but when she went to stand she nearly toppled over. Van grabbed her and steadied her. "Are you sure?"

Aliesa took a few minutes to regain her balance. "I'm sure." Then she turned and shuffled into the bathroom closing the door behind her.

The other door burst open and a dark skinned man with a goatee came into the room. He carried two shopping bags, one in each hand. "You're awake."

Van nodded. "Where are we?"

The man's brow creased. "I was told you requested a meeting with señor Alarcon?"

"I did," Van said. "Are we in Peru?"

The man smoothed his facial hair with his hand. He chuckled. "Not quite. Welcome to Bahia Santa Cruz."

"Mexico?"

"Si," the man said. "Señor Alarcon is inspecting his lanes of distribution. He's staying at his villa."

"Business must be good."

"Señor Alarcon has many villas in many different places."

Van ran his hand over the particleboard container

he'd traveled inside. "I bet Santino has found many uses for these crates in the past."

"His cargo is not usually breathing. I hope the ride wasn't too uncomfortable?"

"I can't remember most of it," Van said scrubbing his face with his hands. "And where is Axel and Jorge?"

Aliesa came out of the washroom.

The man with the goatee bent his head. "Senorita."

Aliesa took a wide berth around him and stood beside Van.

"I was asking our host where Axel and Jorge had gotten to."

The man's forehead wrinkled. "They could not obtain a direct flight on the same plane. No available seats."

"Only room for shipping crates," Van said.

"Si. Mex Air is very sensitive when it comes to transporting the remains of loved ones. I've used them many times in the past."

"I bet you have."

"Our Boston counterpart sent your measurements to me and I've sent some appropriate clothing ahead for the both of you. I've sent it along to señor Alarcon's hacienda. He is hosting a party this evening. You will be taken there to rest after your travels."

"And if we refuse?" Aliesa asked.

"Señor Alarcon's instructions were very specific. A car will be here within the hour to collect you." The man turned and left, locking the door behind him.

"Don't bother to make it sound like we're guests when we're locked in here. We're prisoners." Aliesa eyeballed the fiberboard containers they were transported in and she shuddered. "Thank god I didn't regain consciousness on the way here. I'm claustrophobic."

"It would be difficult not to be under the circumstances," Van said.

Aliesa crossed her arms. "Is it me or is this pretty weird?"

"You mean the party?"

She nodded. "Why wouldn't Santino come here to talk to us?"

"I can think of a couple of reasons." Van scratched his chin. "I suspect he's being watched. If there are enough people present our arrival will essentially go unnoticed. And his attention will appear to be nothing more than him being a gracious host."

"It will also be the perfect diversion if he intends on killing us."

"Always a possibility, too."

Axel and Jorge arrived within the hour.

Aliesa stayed tucked behind Van as they followed Axel and Jorge out of the funeral home and into a Jeep parked in the courtyard. They lurched out of the Funeraria and onto dusty streets. The vehicle rocketed through town and Aliesa studied the local architecture—the colorful row of cement buildings painted a rainbow of pastels. A scrawny mutt panted beneath a bougainvillea, fanning himself with his plumed tail. Ahead, on the corner, a thatched umbrella protected café patrons from the grueling sun.

The color palette deepened. The buildings thinned

and the foliage thickened. Soon they were tunneling upward through the fringe of the jungle.

"Hold tight," Axel said, turning in his seat. "Parts of the roads in the Sierra Madres can be washed out by the rains."

They bounced and climbed the narrow roads. Every once in a while the green canopy would thin, and Aliesa could see across the landscape to the pearly Pacific.

One word kept resounding inside her head.

Azure.

She couldn't tell where the water lapped the sky on the horizon. Brilliant sunlight blazed. Van had become very quiet, seemingly deep in thought.

Little wonder. Aliesa knew he never would have asked to meet with Santino Alarcon if they hadn't run out of options. If he hadn't been so quick thinking both of them would likely still be in the BU mailroom, their bodies surrounded by police tape, as Evelyne's had, subject to the ME's prodding. Van compromised his morals to keep them alive. He had every right to be uneasy. In a few short hours, he would meet his uncle, the son of a South American drug lord who he'd never met or knew existed until six months ago.

The Jeep slowed as the road wound back and forth, scaling the mountainside. They came upon a crowded scenic lookout showcasing the lush valley. Minutes later, Jorge nosed the jeep onto a private driveway. Branches heavy with blossoming bottlebrush, palms and grasses swayed in the breeze candied by the sweet scent of nectar.

Jorge parked in a vacant spot and they all jumped out. Aliesa and Van followed Jorge and Axel, along the crushed seashell path, past two catering vans brimming with trays of food and drink, and into the Mediterranean-style villa dug into the side of the mountain.

She loved the open concept of the house and despite the soaring temperatures the interior remained cool and comfortable. Overhead fans spun lazily. The sprawling house clung to the mountain like a beauty mark. Numerous servants hustled about, moving furniture and getting the place ready for tonight's party.

"This way," Jorge said. "Your room is in the guest's wing, across this hall."

They followed him past three closed doors and he opened the last. Aliesa and Van walked into the richly appointed room. A king-sized bed with sculptured shell headboard floated on top of a raised platform. All of the windows were open and she heard cicadas buzzing amidst the foliage outside.

"Señor Alarcon welcomes you to his home. He wants you to rest and refresh yourselves. He has some business to attend to this afternoon and has made time for you later tonight. The party starts at seven. For your safety he asks you to stay on the grounds of the property." Jorge didn't wait for a response—he merely backed out of the room and closed the door behind him.

Van walked into the room and sprawled on top of the bed. Aliesa walked over to the carved armoire and opened the door. Inside there was a slinky shimmering dress and a pair of matching heels. She grabbed the dress and held it to her body to imagine it on. It would fit but it certainly wouldn't cover much. She'd never worn anything like it in her entire life.

A whistle from Van made her glance over her shoulder.

Van had gotten up from the bed and came to stand right behind her. He leaned and whispered in her ear. "Why don't you and I get naked and have a shower?"

Overwhelmed with emotion she exhaled and her shoulders drooped. Her eyes filled with tears.

"Hey," he said. He turned her around to face him. "What's wrong?"

"Why aren't you furious with me? If I hadn't gone back to my apartment we wouldn't be in this mess. You wouldn't have had to make a deal with the devil to keep us alive."

"Shit happens. We all make mistakes. I'm sure it'll be the first of many we'll inflict upon each other. I don't want an apology. And if you think it's made me feel different about us, you couldn't be more wrong." Then he kissed her.

Desire hit her bloodstream like a powerful narcotic—it ignited a heat akin to a bushfire. The dress she'd been holding dropped from her fingers and her hands trailed low to undo his pants.

He steered her out of the bedroom and into the master bathroom. She shoved his pants over his hips. While alabaster fixtures adorned with gold taps glittered in the background, he pulled her top over her head and flicked the clasp on her bra to open it. Then his hands and lips were on her, kissing her neck and shoulders. She felt him hard against her stomach and she hooked her fingers in the waistband of her pants and dropped them to the floor.

She stroked the length of him.

"I thought we were going to have a shower?" she said, half whisper half sigh.

"We are." He stepped out of the circle of clothes at his feet and reached inside the glass door to set the temperature of the water. He made some adjustments to the large gold showerhead so it dripped like afternoon rain. Then he reached for her and pulled her inside the enclosure, water cascading over their naked bodies.

They lathered each other, slow languid strokes which brought them to the brink of their control. He dipped his fingers and rubbed his thumb over her swollen folds, she stroked his liquid steel length in her hand. She placed him between her legs and pushed him inside.

Van groaned.

She wrapped one leg around his strong thighs and he lifted and pressed her back against the granite wall and thrusted.

He filled her completely. Pressure built.

All coherent thoughts fled from her mind. She strained against him—her body charging toward completion. Waves of pleasure rippled in her core and spread through her body like spikes on a seismograph.

"Now," Van said through clenched teeth.

And she joined him in their ecstasy.

They held each other close for several moments before he placed her back on her feet. He washed them again and rinsed before he reached and turned off the water. He unfolded one of the gold bath sheets and wrapped her inside it and snagged one of his own.

Maybe it was the events of the day, the residual effects of the sedative but suddenly she couldn't seem to keep her eyes open. He led her into the bedroom and both crawled between the silky sheets and slept.

Chapter 27

Aliesa awoke to music. It took her a moment to get her bearings.

Santa Cruz.

Santino Alarcon.

She rolled over to nudge Van and startled when she realized he was gone.

The bathroom door opened and Van strode into the room dressed in a pair of chinos, silk dress shirt, and sandals. "Thought I would give you a tad longer before I woke you. It's party time." He walked over to the armoire and pulled out the slinky dress and shoes.

Two could play this taunting game. She flung off the sheet and stood stark naked, pausing long enough to stretch and yawn. Then she sauntered over to him and plucked her outfit from his outstretched hands, darting away as he reached for her.

Inside the bathroom, she brushed her teeth and hair and fixed her face as best she could with the complimentary products. She held the dress and realized she'd have to go braless because of the plunging back. It took her a few minutes to wriggle into the designer dress because the fabric had little give. She checked her reflection in the mirror. Three weeks ago she couldn't have worn a dress like this. The fabric would have draped from collarbone to collarbone. Now it clung to her body like a second skin. It fit her to perfection; hell it appeared as if it had been custom made for her. Her breasts were high and firm and the fabric hugged her shapely curves in all the right places. The shoes were going to be a problem. She'd only ever worn sensible footwear. These shoes were not. She stepped into them and took a few practice paces. She'd manage as long as she took it slowly.

When she came out of the bathroom Van turned, his mouth dropped open. His eyes darkened and the air in the room seemed to crackle with an electrical charge. He closed the distance between them. No words. No finesse. No patience.

The force of his kiss made her teeter on her heels. The only reason she stayed on her feet was because he supported her with one arm. He ran his hand along every one of the curves her dress showcased.

A knock at the door made them come up for air. He set her aside and opened the door.

Axel stood in the entranceway. His eyes ravaged Aliesa. The way he ogled her made her skin crawl. Van must have felt it too because he wound his arm around her waist and pulled her close.

"Esa mujer es una pieza caliente de asno," Axel said.

Van narrowed his eyes and his angled toward him. "She's mine, got it?"

Axel raised his hands. Slowly he moved his right hand and pulled a cell phone out of his pants pocket. "This is yours," he said tossing it to Van. "Señor Alarcon has returned. He wants you to enjoy the party and food.

He will send for you later." The stalky man turned and walked away.

Van pressed buttons on his phone. "Battery's dead." He put it in his pocket. "Lets go and scout around."

He laced his fingers through hers and they walked out of the guest wing and into the throng of people. He snagged a couple of flutes of champagne from a waiter's tray and they mingled throughout the villa. Soon, the few people out on the lanai moved inside when the temperature began to drop. A cascading lap pool occupied the lower level. From this vantage point it appeared as if the water bled into the Pacific. Reflections of waning light from the setting sun made the water shimmer like marcasite. Soft music played.

Over the last few days, Aliesa had gotten pretty good at putting things out of her mind. The old Aliesa would have had multiple panic attacks after what had happened. Not this new woman. The woman she'd become could hold her own in most any situation.

"Are you as hungry as I am?" he asked.

"I'm starving."

He led her through the crowd to the dining room. They feasted on shrimp, lobster, and caviar beneath the frolicking dolphin ice sculpture.

When the band began their second set, Van set her plate on a side table and pulled her into his arms. They swayed in time with the music as he pressed himself close. His heart thumped against her. She rested her head against the rock hard muscles of his chest. The light touch of his hand on her back made her want more.

Her head swirled when he dipped his head and his lips found hers. He knew exactly how to kiss her.

"Ready for a little excitement?" Van asked.

"I wondered when we were going to venture off on our own to do a little field work."

He tightly clenched her hand in his and they walked in and out of rooms, away from the crowds and the throng. They climbed and descended stairs. In a secluded wing, they happened upon a cordoned hallway.

Van lifted the braided cord and tassel and both of them ducked underneath. Then they silently slipped down the hall and through the closed door at the far end.

It was an office—possibly Santino Alarcon's private domain. He strode over to the oversized desk. Cherry bookcases lined the wall behind—the dark rich wood tones in the room reminded Van of Saul Devine's Boston office—funny how a lawyer and a drug dealer could have very similar tastes. Van slid the chair away and jiggled locked drawers.

"Where do you think this leads?" Aliesa asked. She walked toward a door on the far side of the room. She twisted the knob and went inside.

Van searched the bookshelf. He ran his hand along the buttery leather spines of the books. Shakespeare, Joyce, Dickens, Hemingway, Doyle, Fitzgerald, Woolf. His finger stopped at a well-worn book—one of his mother's favorites, *The Enchanted Castle* by Edith Nesbit. He plucked the book from the shelf and flipped to the copyright page, a first edition. He studied the colorized plate of the magic ring and rubbed the medallion hanging around his neck.

"Van," Aliesa said. She stood in the opened door. The tone of her voice made him turn. Her color had blanched.

He slapped the book shut, slid it back onto the shelf and hurried over to her. She stepped to the side to let him through.

It was a bathroom. Mahogany paneled walls, smoked mirror, and Chippendale vanity. A dead man sat on the floor, propped in the corner, with blood trickling from a neat round hole in the center of his forehead.

Aliesa gasped behind him.

Van turned to reassure her. Another man stood with a Glock pressed to her temple. In his other hand he held a cell phone. "Mi oficina. Ahora," he said before he hung up. He told his men to come to the office.

The man had olive toned skin, the same high cheekbones and the same delicate nose as his mother. The family resemblance astounded him.

"This is my personal office," the man said. "You should not have come in here."

"Did the man in your bathroom take a wrong turn too?" Van asked.

The man waved Van over and he patted him down. Then he lowered the pistol and put it in his waistband. "Unfortunately it seems Pedro Gustavo's loyalty is to my father, not with me. A situation which has plagued me my entire life." He flicked his wrist inviting them to sit. Once Van and Aliesa complied, he shut the bathroom door and sat opposite them behind the large cherry desk. Leather hissed.

Axel and Jorge raced through the door.

"Pensé que te dije para mantener un ojo sobre ellos?"

Jorge opened his mouth to explain but Van cut him off. "They couldn't very well keep an eye on us, what with having to make all of the arrangements to dispose of Pedro's body."

"You speak Spanish?"

"Fluently. It's my first language. My mother taught me even before I learned English."

"What's your name?"

"I'm Elliot Vance and this is Dr. Aliesa Atworth." Van turned toward him.

"Do you know who I am?" The man asked.

"You're Santino Alarcon. My uncle."

Santino's expression remained impartial; he offered no light of recognition, no smile of victory, nothing. "What kind of a doctor is she?"

"She's a biochemist. She's the woman Axel and Jorge targeted after they slit Hernandez's throat."

"Another cook?" Santino asked.

"She has nothing to do with Hernandez's cocaine. She's a legitimate scientist who inadvertently got stuck in your crosshairs."

"Axel and Jorge acted on my orders. Alejandro insisted we go after the cocaine and I complied. My father wanted to set an example. It was sad really. Hernandez never threatened our operation. I found out about him months ago and Jorge and Axel kept an eye on him for me. I didn't bother Hernandez because he used discretion and kept to himself. But Alejandro does business differently."

"How did your father find out?" Van asked.

"I'm guessing it was Pedro. I've had my suspicions

there was a mole for a while, so I set a trap. I told everyone I wouldn't be home and I caught him riffling through my desk drawers this afternoon. He'd taken pictures of several documents with his phone and there were emails and texts containing information he had no way of knowing." Santino stood and walked over to the sideboard and poured clear liquid into two crystal glasses. He gave one to Van and drank his. Then he eyed the medallion hanging around Van's neck.

Van tossed back the shot. Tequila burned.

"How is my sister?" Santino asked. He wiped his mouth with the back of his hand. "Does she ever talk about me?"

"My mother died three months ago."

Santino recoiled. He squeezed the medallion hanging around his neck and lifted it to his lips and kissed it. He pressed his fingers to his eyes and took a few deep, fortifying breaths. "How?"

"Cancer."

The drug lord walked straight over to the bookshelf and tugged out Nesbit's *The Enchanted Castle*. "Why did you remove this book from the shelf?"

Van guessed Santino had installed cameras to catch Pedro in the act and knew he and Aliesa were in his office. "My mother used to read it to me when I was a child."

Santino opened the book and flipped pages. "Yes. My mother used to read this book to your mother and me when we were little. When I said goodbye, I told her the medallion you are now wearing was her magic ring. It would transport her to a wonderful new land." He slapped the book shut. "Alejandro would have killed her if she stayed. He never would have accepted you or your dad."

Van had rehearsed what he wanted to say to his uncle a million times, but the sadness and hopelessness in his face stole the words from him.

"I'm very happy she got away," Santino said. "Lived a good and noble life. Is your father still alive?"

Van shook his head. Underlying sadness scored Santino's words. He lived in luxury's lap but had no illusions about being righteous, nor good. "Are you certain Pedro was the only mole in your operation? What about Axel and Jorge?"

Jorge who'd been standing sentinel at the door, turned toward Van. He reached for his knife and flipped it open.

"Enough," Santino said. He faced Van. "I trust Axel and Jorge implicitly. They work for me, not my father."

Van thought back to the mailroom at Boston U. Jorge had called Santino on his cell. "Do you always use cell phones?"

"Si. Why do you ask?"

"Do you ever change the handsets?"

"New phones are distributed every month. Alejandro has a techno-geek on his payroll whose sole responsibility is communication. He sends out new hardware and we dispose of the old."

Van's shoulders slumped. "You're kidding right?"

The expression on Santino's face said otherwise.

"You've got an even bigger problem than Pedros," Van said. "Alejandro's cloned your phone."

Chapter 28

"Alejandro's cloned my phone?"

Van could see the disgust in Santino's eyes. "A 100 percent. He listens in on all of your calls. There isn't anything he doesn't know."

Santino pulled his cell out of his pocket and dropped it on the desk. He wiped his hand on his shirt as if it had been tainted with some sort of poisonous venom. Then he grabbed the swirled glass paperweight from the corner of his desk.

Before he could crush the phone Van stepped forward. "Think about what you're doing. Knowledge is power. From now on you can feed Alejandro only the information you want him to know."

Santino seemed to be considering Van's words. He returned the paperweight to the surface of the desk. A slow smile curled his lips. He reached out and called Jorge over to his desk. "Teléfono." Jorge handed his phone to Santino. "You and Axel take Pedro to my boat to dispose of the body."

Jorge nodded and left the office. "Excuse me for a moment, I need to alert my captain and crew."

Van nodded. While Santino made a telephone call, Van turned toward Aliesa whose face had turned a brilliant shade of red. He walked over to her. "What's wrong?"

She kept her eyes on Santino across the room. "What is wrong with him? He must not have any respect for human life what-so-ever."

"I know it's hard for you to understand. In his business it's kill or be killed."

"Is there a problem, señora?"

Jorge and Axel filed into the office and disappeared inside the bathroom. A few minutes later the men came out of the bathroom lugging Pedros. Aliesa watched in horror as Jorge and Axel rolled the body in the carpet.

"You said Alejandro insisted your men follow Hernandez's cocaine."

"Correct," Santino said.

Jorge and Axel lifted the carpet onto their shoulders.

"Were you the one who gave them the green light to destroy my lab and murder my best friend?"

Brow furrowed, Santino halted his men from carrying the corpse out of the office. "Did you do this thing?"

Jorge shook his head. "When we arrived the lab had already been destroyed and the woman was dead. We barely made it out before the policia arrived."

Santino nodded and sent his men on their way. "I'm sorry, senorita. But my men did not do this."

Van couldn't believe his ears. If it wasn't Jorge or Axel, who was it? "Do you know anyone by the name of Grayson Everet or Jackson Mercante?"

"No," Santino said. "Should I?"

Van didn't know what to make of any of this right now. Only one thing rang true right about now. He'd been chasing his tail all this time.

Aliesa hadn't stopped staring at Santino. She put her hand on Van's arm. "I've been watching Santino very carefully and I'm positive he's not telling us everything."

Van's uncle's skin blanched.

"Is Aliesa right? Are you hiding something?"

Santino gulped and nodded. He lifted his personal cell phone, the one Alejandro had cloned and went back through the history of calls. He scrolled through several items and abruptly stopped. "I think we might have a problem," he said through clenched teeth.

"What kind of a problem?" Van asked.

"Jorge mentioned the Alarcon medallion around your neck."

"Lots of people wear necklaces," Aliesa said. "Surely you can't think something so benign could have repercussions."

"There have only ever been two Alarcon medallions—mine and your mother's. When I told him the medallion was not on the body he had his men scour the ashes from the village in search it. Finally he assumed it was either lost in the jungle or my sister had used it as a bargaining chip to secure passage out of the country but died before she could get away."

"Do you think he knows anything about me being his grandson?"

"I don't think so."

"How curious do you think he'll be about the necklace?" Van asked.

"Curious enough to hop on a plane to come and see for himself." He switched to Jorge's phone and checked his watch. "But I have an idea how to find out, if she's still awake. I had a fling with Alejandro's housekeeper a while back." He dialed a number from memory and put the phone to his ear. "Catalina? Donde es Alejandro?"

Santino's eyes widened. He nodded and confirmed the time on his watch again. Then he pressed end and swallowed. "Alejandro's on his way here. He should be here within the hour. We haven't a moment to lose."

"We? Are you going to run too?" Van asked. "You'll have to give all this up?"

"No. My father will not live forever and I've invested too many years to walk away now. After he passes things will be different. Until then, I will bide my time. But I don't intend to cast you out and leave you to your own devices. My sister would never forgive me if I let something happen to you now. Once I make sure you're safe, I will make certain my father believes whatever I tell him."

"Please tell me you have a plan," Aliesa said.

Van put his arm around Aliesa. The frightened jack-rabbit he'd met several days ago had been replaced with the sexy fox standing beside him.

"I've always had a contingency plan," Santino said. "Several years ago, I spread a rumor about the lost medallion being found. I offered a reward for its safe return—a very handsome amount. Several people have tried to collect." He picked up his phone and Jorge's and pocketed them.

"Have you ever thought of standing your ground?" Van asked.

"Many times," Santino said. "Believe me, the best course of action is to kill you, just like I killed your parents. If I don't, you will never be free. You're Alejandro's one and only heir because I already told him I would never marry. I will never give him any grandchildren because he'd never let them live their own lives. If he knew you existed, he would keep you here, against your will. He'd manipulate you through the people you love. Now, please. We must hurry to catch my boat before she departs the harbor."

Santino, Van, and Aliesa left the villa through the servant's quarters and climbed into another jeep.

"You drive," Santino said, settling into the passenger seat. "Jorge and Axel should arrive at the dock any time now and I have to call the Captain to tell him not to cast off without us."

Van helped Aliesa into the back of the jeep. She steadied herself between the two seats by holding onto the roll bar above. Once she gave the okay, Van put the jeep in gear and peeled out of the driveway.

Instead of leaving the mountain the way they came, Santino told Van to turn in the opposite direction. "I thought we were headed back to the marina?" Van asked.

"We are," Santino said. "But I don't want to run into Alejandro's entourage on the mountain road. There is a less travelled road not far from here. It's been closed all season because parts of it were washed out in the rains."

The jeep climbed another one hundred feet before Van had to hair-pin to the left. "This can't be a road."

"This can't even be a jungle path," Aliesa said.

All of them held on.

The jeep crawled along the road jostling its passengers like popcorn in a skillet. When the jeep's headlights illuminated a road-closed sign. Van stepped on the brakes and they slid to an abrupt stop.

A sinkhole.

"Wait here," Van said, setting the brake. "I need to go and figure out our options."

Santino waved his acknowledgment. He'd only made contact with the captain a moment ago due to poor reception.

Aliesa followed Van around the barrier and over to the edge. "What do we do now?" she asked.

Van faced the crevasse at least fifteen feet wide and deep.

"I think it's safe to say if you get too close we're going to get stuck," Aliesa said, pointing to her feet.

Van noticed her high heels had sunk into the mud. She bent and pushed the straps over her heels and struggled to pry her feet out. "This is what will happen to the jeep if we try to make it across."

They started to walk back to the jeep when Van stopped and put his hand on the barricade.

Santino came toward them. "Do you think we make it?"

Van sent Aliesa back to the jeep and he and Santino placed the barricade flat on the lip of the sinkhole.

Then both of them came back to the jeep. "I want you to sit in the back seat and buckle up," Van said. Then both he and Santino put on their belts.

Van ground the gears into reverse. He didn't waste time trying to turn the jeep around; he kept the tires in the same grooves as he climbed back to the very top of the incline.

With the jeep in first gear, Van let his foot off the brake. Instead of taking it slow like he previously had, he hit the gas, and soon popped the clutch and shifted into second. The jeep lurched across the uneven ground—metal grinding the rocky path. The downward slope of the road made them quickly gain speed.

"Almost there," Van said. "Hold on."

The wood from the road sign gave them traction on the edge, launching the jeep into the air. They sailed across the gap, literally hanging in the breeze. The nose of the jeep angled down and Van said a silent prayer because it would be close. He only hoped the other edge didn't collapse on impact.

The concussion sent everyone thudding into their seats. The front of the jeep absorbed most of the thrust, bouncing them forward. The rear axle slammed into solid ground a moment later.

Van struggled to keep the jeep on the gravel path and pumped the brakes to slow them down.

"Nice work," Santino said.

"I can't believe we made it," Aliesa said in a small voice.

"You sound surprised?" Van said.

"I am," she said. "The odds were not in our favor."

They thumped and bumped along the rest of the slippery slope.

Moments later the battered, mud-covered jeep limped out from the mountain trail road and lumbered onto a deserted village street. The engine hissed and ticked all the way to the marina and to the end of the pier where a huge silver Palmer Johnson Sport Yacht, named Laila III, stretched from one end to the other.

Aliesa got out of the jeep and approached the massive cruiser. Well over a hundred feet of sleek fiberglass glimmered like cubic zirconia in the moonlight—a gem which outshone every other boat in the marina.

"Laila III?" Van faced Santino.

"I named all of my boats after your mother. They have always been my sanctuary. Your grandfather has refused to step aboard any of them."

When he got to the top of the access ramp he turned to help Van and Aliesa step aboard and became distracted by a series of headlights cutting a swath across the mountain toward the town.

"Get us out of here," Santino screamed.

The captain leaned over the rail of the upper deck. "Toss the lines," he said before he turned and returned to the bridge.

Van studied his uncle's eyes and knew he spoke the truth. He couldn't explain, but he trusted him—a nefarious drug dealer. Van had already put his life, and Aliesa's life, in his hands.

Headlights cut a swath through the darkness in the distance.

"Shit. Get us out of here," Santino screamed at the captain.

Santino hit a button and the telescopic walkway pulled away from the dock.

Aliesa pointed toward the valley. There was a convoy of three vehicles turning toward them. Their lights bobbed and intensified as they closed the distance.

Santino grabbed a knife from a hatch and tossed it handle first to Van. "Slice the bow and spring line."

Aliesa heard the whir of the engines. A huge wake roiled behind the boat, but the lines held them firmly in place.

Van hurried along the sleek rail of the cruiser to the cleat on the vessel's bow. He sawed the line. Nylon strands unwound and sprung from the jagged cut. A loud ping signaled the line snapping free and the remnant ricocheted to shore. Then he hurried to repeat the process on the stern line.

The engines continued to whine. Now the bow of the boat bucked like a bronco.

Aliesa noticed the cars shooting through the marina gates, sprinting toward the pier. Out of the corner of her eye, she saw a glint of metal in the moonlight.

"Van, watch out," she screamed.

Van dove sideways as an axe crashed on top of the stainless cleat, severing the line. As the boat lurched forward, Santino staggered. With his head down he shouted. "Turn around and hit me. Make it realistic. Like you're overpowering me!"

Van rolled onto the balls of his feet. He drew back and slammed his fist right between Santino's eyes causing him to hit the deck. Van collected the gun and tucked it into his waistband before he pulled Santino to his feet. He twisted Santino's arm behind his back and all three staggered through the smoked glass sliding door into the salon.

Van dropped the gun on the coffee table and helped Santino onto the caramel-colored leather sectional.

Aliesa went around the bar and scrambled to fill a towel with ice. "Think Alejandro bought it?" she asked, rushing back with the compress.

"I hope so," Santino said. "Is my nose broken?"

She didn't know, but based on the growing lump she erred on the side of caution and nodded yes.

"Sorry," Van said. "Adrenaline rush."

Aliesa sagged against the sofa. "I would have thought a boat this size would have had enough crew on board to make casting off easier."

"Ordinarily there would have, but I'd given most of the crew shore leave for the next few days. The only person I called was the captain because Jorge and Axel were more than able to handle the lines."

"I see," she said. "Then you might want to have a word with the captain. It seems he works for Alejandro, too."

The pained expression on Santino's face told her he agreed.

One of the phones in Santino's pocket trilled. He pulled out both. "It's Alejandro," he said, placing it on the table unanswered.

"And where are Jorge and Axel?" Van asked. "They must be on board somewhere. We parked beside their jeep at the pier."

Santino dialed and put the other cell phone to his ear. "I'll call Axel." When no one answered he put it with the other phone on the table.

Santino stood and grabbed his handgun. "I think it's time we had a word with the captain."

Aliesa trailed behind Van and Santino, her bare feet sinking into the plush carpet. She'd never been on a luxury yacht before and this one had it all. They walked from the salon through the dining room, past a table large enough to seat a party of eight people. An arrangement of freshly cut frangipani scented the air. They walked into a hall past a luxurious state room with a king-sized bed and upstairs onto the bridge where the captain stood at the helm.

"Fredrico," Santino said, shaking his head. "I need you to set a course for the off-shore shipping lanes. You've got one hour to get us there," Santino said, raising the Glock he pressed it into his temple, "or you're a dead man."

"But señor Alarcon, it's impossible. It will take closer to two," Fredrico said.

Santino pulled the trigger.

The opposite side of Fredrico's head come apart in pieces. Blood and gore covered the control panel of switches and gauges. And the body fell sideways. Santino stuffed his gun and took control of the helm. "Nevermind. I'll do it myself."

Santino set to work. He wiped blood splatter from the chart and read the coordinates and entered them. Then he revved the engines and set the auto-helm.

Aliesa regarded the dead man sprawled on the deck. A puddle of blood grew beneath his lifeless body. She felt like she'd entered some sort of parallel universe. She stopped to do another body count. Six people dead.

Van pulled her against him and faced Santino. "So you're going back?"

"I don't have a choice," Santino said. "I'm not brave enough to kill myself. But don't worry I have a plan in mind and it would be a big help if you could locate Jorge and Axel as I need to stay on the bridge. Check the engine room. They likely stored Pedro's body in there." Santino pulled out his gun and handed it to Van. "Take this."

"What for?" Van asked.

"In case you come across any more rats."

Chapter 29

V an and Aliesa went back to the salon to collect Jorge's phone because he thought it might come in handy to ferret out their possible location. Van thought it was a good idea until they entered the engine room amidship. The roar of the V12 diesel engine in the room made it impossible to talk without shouting. The white and stainless V12 diesel sat in the middle of the room and virtually shone.

Van ushered Aliesa forward, they stepped through the engine room hatch and he closed and sealed the door. "Try the phone now," he said.

Aliesa pressed redial.

At the end of the hall he could hear a faint ringing. They passed cabins port and starboard. The ringing sound came from the last cabin on the starboard side.

"Am I the only one who sees the irony in this?" Aliesa whispered. "A few days ago we were trying to get away from Jorge and Axel."

"Shhhh," Van said. He made her stand on the opposite side of the hatch. He pulled Santino's gun out from his waistband, flung open the door, and charged inside.

"It's okay. You can come in now," Van called to her. "Give me a hand untying these two."

Jorge and Axel grunted and groaned. They'd been hog-tied and gagged, one on the floor and the other on a bunk. Both men were as mad as a couple of bulls. As soon as he and Aliesa released them the drone of Laila's engine ceased.

"You might want to go and give Santino a hand, he's on the bridge," Van said. "Tell him we'll be waiting for him out on the swimming platform."

Both Jorge and Axel disappeared.

Aliesa turned toward him. "Swimming platform?"

"Relax," Van said. "Santino won't throw us overboard or anything. At least not without a life vest."

"Oh, great. You're a comedian now."

When they made their way to the swim platform at the stern of the boat they stood against the back rail. It appeared as if they were in the middle of the Pacific. The sun had risen and sparkles of light glistened on the rippling water.

Voices interrupted their reflection. Jorge and Axel carried the captain's body. Van steered Aliesa clear of them as they tossed the body overboard.

Behind the diving platform, hidden inside the stern of the boat was a large dinghy bay with a twenty-foot inflatable powered by a hundred and fifty horsepower Merc.

Jorge and Axel disappeared again.

Santino bounded down the rear stairs. "I hope you understand, I cannot let you go in the dingy," Santino said. "Alejandro would become suspicious if I returned to port with it missing. I need him to think the both of you are fish food."

"I figured as much," Van said.

Jorge and Axel reappeared carrying Pedros rolled in the rug. On the count of three they swung the second corpse into the water. The weight of the rug quickly dragged the body beneath the surface leaving only a telltale trail of bubbles.

Van reached for his necklace and the clasp. "I guess you'll be needing this."

"No." Santino raised his hand. "It's yours. It kept your mother safe and it will do the same for you. Besides, Alejandro wouldn't be stupid enough to talk about the necklace because then he'd have to explain why he cloned my phone."

Once Jorge and Axel were finished getting rid of the bodies, Santino sent them into the equipment bay. Jorge walked into the darkened interior and muscled a valise from one of the shelves and placed it on the lip of the diving platform. He zipped open the bag and pulled a cord and a raft exploded outwards. In less than two minutes, air whistled into a six-person raft. Jorge tethered it to the back of the boat while Axel collected various items necessary for their survival.

A bright orange canopy shaded the black-bottomed mattress floor. A white nylon line ran around the circumference and an entry ladder and sea anchors were attached to add stability in rough seas, which today, thankfully, was not a problem.

Jorge held it steady for boarding. Axel appeared carrying a case of bottled water and various tins of soup, some beluga caviar, and tuna fish—all of which he tossed into the raft.

"Not a lot to chose from in the galley since nothing has been restocked for my return trip. The good news is you'll be bobbing along a very busy shipping lane," Santino said. "You should be rescued quickly." He handed Van a can opener.

Axel grabbed a small case from another locker, unlatched it, took out a bright yellow handheld, and pressed the activation button.

"This is an EPIRB," Santino said. "An emergency position indicating radio beacon. As of right now you're on the US Coast Guard's radar." Axel handed it to Van.

Jorge helped Aliesa board the bobbing raft.

Van threw his other arm around Santino and gave him a quick hug. "Thank you," he said. "Maybe we'll meet again some day." Then he climbed into the raft beside Aliesa and disconnected the tether.

In a matter of moments, the engine of the Laila III roared to life and she raced out of sight, quickly becoming a dot on the horizon.

Chapter 30

Aliesa sat in the center of the raft as it bobbed and rocked in the water. They'd only been floating for less than an hour. The rubber reeked and would become a barbeque in a few hours with the sun high in the sky.

Van had been very quiet since they climbed aboard the raft. So much had happened to them in the last forty-eight hours she didn't know where to begin.

"Are you okay?" she finally asked.

He turned to stare at her. She'd never seen him more tired.

"I should be asking you the same question."

"What did you think of your uncle?" she asked.

"He's a real great guy for a killer and a drug dealer."

Aliesa faced him. "I think he's caught in an untenable situation and he does only the bare minimum to get by."

"Yeah, right. He's just misunderstood."

"I know you're upset. Who wouldn't be under the circumstances? But none of us are able to choose our family."

Van ran his hand across his whiskered chin. "I know. Though I'm pretty sure my family is more dysfunctional than most."

"I'd have to agree with you on that front."

"The good thing is I might actually be able to lay this crazy personal vendetta against cocaine behind me. It started to evaporate the moment I realized my fixation, not the evidence, made me jump to the wrong conclusions."

"One of the hardest things to do is to read the evidence." Aliesa had been struggling with all of the new abilities she seemed to be acquiring. Was it her two previous stem cell treatments? Or did her emotional growth with Van have something to do with it? "It's very difficult. I struggle with my preconceptions when it comes to my research, too," Aliesa said. She wrapped her arms around her legs and rested her chin on top of her knees. "In your defense, the evidence was somewhat ambiguous. You came to the most logical conclusions. Cocaine did seem to be the common denominator in all of the murders."

"Yes, the man from Medivac and Jackson Mercante were directly connected to Hernandez, but Grayson Everet was not."

"Right," Aliesa said. "No connection there."

"Santino said he ordered the hit on Hernandez. No one else. Axel and Jorge came State side to intercept the cocaine, nothing more."

"Whenever I lose my objectivity in the lab I try to start back at the beginning. I try to see things from different angles."

"Okay. Here's one for you." Van sank back and sprawled out on the air mattress floor. He rolled to his side and supported his head on bended arm. "Evelyne Mathews."

The name of Aliesa's best friend caused a lump to

form in her throat. "What about her?"

"What if she wasn't killed because of mistaken identity? What if she'd been the target all along?"

Aliesa took a deep breath and thought back to that terrible day. The entire lab had been trashed. Someone had been given explicit instructions on how to completely wipe out her entire test sample. "This has never been about the cocaine." She rubbed her temples with her fingers. "It's been about my work."

He sat. "We need to get back to Boston to start working this case with fresh eyes."

She pulled away from him. "What if I don't want to go back and face reality?"

"What do you mean? Don't you want to find out who did this?" Van put his hand on her arm. "You'll never be safe until we put the person behind bars?"

"Why do you care?"

"I don't want anything to happen to you," Van said.

"But why?" Aliesa stared at him.

"Because I've fallen in love with you."

This time when he reached for her she went willingly. Desire ignited.

Aliesa didn't know who moved first. Her anger dissolved into pure unadulterated need. He pulled her close. Her fingers worked the buttons of his silk shirt and she skimmed her palms across his chest. His breath caught when she unhooked his pants and lowered the zipper. The force of her attraction to him frightened her. She'd never been driven to this kind of distraction by the opposite sex. All she wanted at this moment was feeling him planted firmly inside her. It made her think her stem cell injections had also intensified her libido. It didn't matter. Love was love.

She went to slip her hand inside his pants when he grabbed her wrist and pulled her on top of him. In one fluid motion he grabbed the hem of her dress and pulled it over her head. Then he rolled her back onto the mattress and kissed her so sweetly tears sprang to her eyes.

Tears didn't make him take pause. He kissed them off her cheeks and trailed even lower.

She shoved his shirt down his arms removed it as he circled her navel with his tongue.

"Please," she pleaded. She couldn't finish her sentence because he slid her panties down. His lips followed the same path. He kissed his way to her thigh and lapped the sensitive skin behind her knee. He skimmed his fingers along her calves and slid the panties free of one foot then the other. When she faced him, his eyes darkened, and he began nipping his return. She closed her eyes, tossed her head back and let the sensations of his mouth, tongue, and lips wash over her. When he latched onto her most sensitive folds she imploded. With no sheets to twist, she ran her hands through his hair and held onto him as shock waves rose to a crescendo and receded.

When her heart rate returned to a normal staccato she tugged on his hair and rolled him over. "My turn," she said, kissing him on the lips as sweetly as he'd kissed her.

Then she began her own sweet torment. She ran her hands over the planes of his chest, kissing every inch of bronze skin. Her lips traced his rigid abs and lower. She removed his trousers and boxers and she wound her hands around the length of him. She stroked, cradled, and sucked. He groaned and pulled her beneath him. Poised for entry, he kissed and sank into her, one throbbing inch at a time. When he reached full penetration, he set a slow and steady pace. His control made her head swim. Her nerve endings were on fire—stretching and contracting until she raged out of control. He must have sensed the change in her because he quickened his tempo. The ocean waves added to the rocking motion and she seemed to be racing toward completion. When his releases came, he laced his fingers tightly in hers so they would resurface from the storm together.

They held each other close. "Just so you know, I've been in love with you for a little while now.

"I'm glad," he said.

With her head resting on his chest she listened to the steady thump of his heart. Both were rocked into a deep sleep by the gentle sway and slap of the salt water.

"Ahoy!"

A deep voice rattled over a loud speaker, waking Aliesa with a start. She checked her watch. Their quick nap had turned into a solid six-hour marathon. Naked and nestled beside Van, she shook him awake.

Instantly alert he sat, grabbed his pants and put them on. Then he tossed Aliesa her dress, collected his shirt, and crawled over to the door in the canopy of the raft.

"Ahoy," Van shouted.

Aliesa pulled the dress over her head, but couldn't find her panties anywhere. She finally located them in the corner of the raft and put them on. She ran her hands through her hair to straighten it but gave up. Van sat in the door of the raft and jammed his arms in the sleeves of his shirt.

"Grab a hold of the line and secure it so we can haul you in," the voice said.

Aliesa peeked through the door of the canopy. Acres of ash-gray iron towered above the raft. A wide racing stripe of red and thin strips of white and blue slanted across the side. Sonar revolved and a radar dish perched on a metal turret peaked high above the pilothouse.

Within minutes a rope ladder rolled over the side of the ship and into the water beside them.

"You first," Van said holding the raft steady as she reached for the rope ladder. "I'll be right behind you."

The limp rope made every step an exercise in strength. As she pulled herself closer to the top of the ladder she knew she never would have had the upper-body strength prior to her stem-cell injections.

As she crested the rail of the ship four pairs of hands grabbed her and lifted her safely onto the deck. Immediately she turned to watch the same happen with Van as his head popped over the rail.

"Senior Chief, Petty Officer, Derek Faulkner of the US Coast Guard cutter, *Udesto*." The non-commissioned officer saluted.

Van returned the salute with one of his own. "Elliot Vance, Special Forces, and Dr. Aliesa Atworth requesting permission to have a word with the captain."

"A departure from protocol, sir. Normally all rescued

persons are required to report to sick bay."

"I appreciate regulations, Senior Chief, but we've been adrift for a while and I have some important matters I need to discuss with the captain."

The senior chief removed his cap monogrammed with the word *Udesto* and scratched his bald head. His rank had been prominently displayed above the two front button-flap pockets of his shirt. He faced a group of able-bodied ensigns and seamen. "Winch their raft onto the deck and secure it for getting underway."

He turned toward Van and Aliesa. "Follow me," he said.

They stepped inside a metal door and through a narrow hatchway. The smell of fresh paint hung heavy in the air. They had to turn sideways as seamen and officers passed them in the ash-gray metal corridor. They turned and climbed a metal stairway to the pilothouse.

The bridge of the ship held a two hundred and eighty degree view of the surrounding waters. Computerized screens and instrument panels ran the full length of the station beneath the windows. Several officers and enlisted men monitored the equipment.

Van stepped over to introduce himself. "Elliot Vance, Special Forces."

A thick-necked man at the center of the action chugged his coffee and placed his empty mug on top of the map he'd been scrutinizing. "Captain Jake McKay," he said. "What happened, Vance?"

"Call me Van," he said. "We've been involved in a criminal investigation. Eight hours ago, we were abandoned in the Pacific."

"Was this investigation drug related?"

"No and I'd appreciate you keeping a cap on all transmissions about our identities. I'll be happy to fill in the details, but first I need to make an important call on your satellite phone."

Chapter 31

Captain MacKay gave the nod to one of his men to activate the satellite phone.

"Where is home port?" Van asked the captain.

"Los Angeles."

"Are you headed there?"

"We're scheduled to return tomorrow," the captain said. The green light of the satellite phone flashed and he handed Van the handset.

Van stood in the center of the pilothouse and punched in the number he'd committed to memory two years ago. It took a few moments for the signal bounce before he heard the crackle of connection. He checked his watch and did the time conversion. Six p.m. Dinnertime.

"Morningside." A gruff pronouncement blared through the handset. The admiral had never been one to waste words.

"It's Van."

"Status report?"

"All of this time I've been circling the wrong drain, sir. This case has never been about the Alarcon cartel or cocaine."

"What's it been about then?"

"Too soon to say. I need a few more days to piece it

all together."

"Keep me in the loop."

"Will do, sir."

"Have you covered everything?" the admiral asked.

"Not exactly."

"I'm listening."

"I need transport for two, sir. Presently we're on the coast guard cutter *Udesto*. We'll be arriving in LA at o-two-hundred hours and could use a lift to Hanscom as soon as it can be arranged."

"How the hell did you get on the *Udesto*?" Another pause. "Never mind. You can fill me in later."

"Who's the captain?"

"McKay."

"Let me have a word with him."

Van passed over the phone. He covered the mouthpiece and whispered. "Admiral Morningside."

"Good evening, Admiral," the captain said.

Van scanned the bridge. All eyes were plastered on him, but quickly everyone got back to work. A few moments later the captain passed back the phone.

"You need anything else?" the admiral asked.

"My motorcycle's been squirreled away in the Boston U impound. Is there any way you can have it waiting for us at Hanscom?"

"I'll see what I can do."

"Oh, and Admiral, I think it's time to let the press know Dr. Aliesa Atworth is still alive."

"Well, that should stir things up," the admiral said.

"That's the plan."

Van ended the call and handed the Sat. phone back to the captain.

"You have friends in high places," Captain McKay said.

"Not as high as my enemies."

The captain's brow creased.

A uniformed woman topped the stairs, stood in front of them, and saluted.

"Take our two guests and get them settled. Show them where they can wash and give them a change of clothes. Have the cook whip up some grub."

Van saluted and shook the captain's hand. Then Van and Aliesa followed the lieutenant down the stairs.

Aliesa had no idea Van had the support of a United States Admiral. There had to be a story in there somewhere. Someday she'd find out why and how, but not now. Right now she had more pressing concerns; the fresh target on her back and Mr. and Mrs. Mathews would learn their daughter, Evelyne, was dead.

Jane, the female lieutenant, escorted them off the bridge and through the ship. Van and her chatted about military life. Aliesa had been so preoccupied with her thoughts, Van had to give her a nudge when Jane asked her a direct question.

He repeated it. "Jane is getting us some ODU's. What size do you wear?"

Aliesa blinked. If she'd been listening she might have a clue what ODU stood for.

"Operational Dress Uniform," Jane explained, probably because of Aliesa's blank stare. "It's more relaxed than the dress uniform."

"We're about the same size," Aliesa said. "Whatever size you wear should be fine. Oh, and size eight shoes."

From there, Jane showed them where they could take a shower and the location of the mess hall. The mention of food got Aliesa's salivary glands pumping. She all but drooled at the idea of eating a meal, so she ran to have her shower and promised Van she'd meet him back in the mess hall in ten minutes.

He must have been hungry too, because he was already waiting for her when she arrived.

"Feel better?" he asked.

She slid into the chair across the table from him. "I feel like a person again."

"How the hell do you do it?" he asked clasping her hand in his.

"What do you mean? I didn't do anything."

"You had a shower, dragged a comb through your hair and donned military tropical blues, and still you're beautiful."

Warmth spread through her. He leaned across the table and captured her lips with his. "I can't get enough of you."

She'd always believed relationships hinged on honesty. It made her wonder whether or not she should tell Van her current sex appeal had been genetically engineered with her serum.

The kitchen door burst open and the chef wheeled out a cart with a large bowl of salad, fresh bread, and two steaming plates of pasta. "Hope you like Italian."

Van sat back and rubbed his hands together. As the chef placed the dishes on the table she decided to save her true confessions for another day. As hungry as she was she didn't enjoy her food the way she would have if she hadn't postponed the inevitable.

Her secret gnawed at her. It made her wonder if Van would have found the unaltered Aliesa as attractive?

She had one remaining stem-cell treatment. And what would happen when she ran out? Would she morph back into the dowdy professor? Right now, she had no idea how long she'd reap the benefits of her treatment. Not only had she noticed superficial changes in her appearance, there were the other changes—like the precognitive insights. She'd hoped the effects would be permanent. Maybe they would be, as long as she kept injecting more serum. She only had one vial left and once her supply ran out, she might lose the man she loved.

She cleaned her plate, but her thoughts had rendered the food tasteless and bland. Van sat across from her, finishing seconds. She wiped her mouth with her napkin and pushed her plate aside.

Jane appeared at the mess hall door. "All finished?" she asked. "I've been sent to show you to your guest quarters in case you want to rest."

Both Van and Aliesa followed Jane out through the corridor and they took a flight of stairs to the crew's quarters. Jane led them through several bulkhead doors and into a small room at the end of the walkway which contained a couple of bunks, a table and a chair. "It's not the Ritz, but it'll do the job. Both of you have free run of the ship. If you need anything, just ask." Then she turned and pulled the door closed behind her.

Aliesa sat on the chair in the room. "So what are we supposed to do now?"

Van leaned over and caressed her face, tilting her chin upwards. "I can think of a couple of things." Then he kissed her.

His lips were soft and sensual. He lulled her. Then he became more ardent. He lifted her to her feet and without letting his lips leave hers he shuffled her over to the bed.

When he stopped he pressed his forehead to hers and began undoing the buttons of her military uniform. "I'd love to tear these clothes right off your delicious body but it might be a tad embarrassing requisitioning another."

"Mmmm," Aliesa said. "I'm going to have to wear shirts with a lot of buttons in the future. I love watching you undress me."

"You're going to have to be as careful with mine you know," Van said. His eyes had darkened, to the color of the sea and his fingers trembled as he worked the buttons. Finally he got them undone and shoved the shirt over her shoulders and it dropped to the floor. He cupped her breasts with his hands and leaned closer to kiss them. "I love it when you're braless."

"Enjoy it while you can because the only reason I'm not wearing one is because of that damned cocktail dress."

"You have beautiful breasts."

Again, Aliesa cringed.

One breast used to be larger than the other so her serum had corrected yet another flaw. To stop her hands from shaking she reached over and began unfastening the buttons of his shirt. She had them undone in no time. He shucked it while she undid his belt and lowered his zipper. She shoved his pants and boxers over his buttocks. She trailed her hands across the fine dusting of hair on his chest. She nipped at his skin with her teeth and as her hands went lower, she bent her knees and her mouth found him.

She stroked and sucked. She ran her hands from stem to tip, taking him deep into her throat and out, lapping the bead of fluid gathering at the end.

"Shit, it feels too good," he said and in one fluid motion he righted her and kissed her like they'd run out of time.

So distracted, Aliesa only noticed her pants had been removed when he grabbed her bare buttock and slide her beneath the bulkhead on top of the bed.

He began at her toes and worked his way north, stopping at the apex of her thighs to run his tongue across her folds.

She felt the tsunami approach. She braced her hands on the bulkhead above her and held on as he banked the storm. "Van...I...oh, God..." and it flooded her. Waves rippled through her body, flattening everything in its wake, engulfing her. In complete ecstasy she floated on the receding current.

Then Van worked his way higher.

He entered her, driving deep.

He set a brisk rhythm and didn't let up.

She didn't want him to.

She wanted him as out of control as she'd been. Soon she felt another wave building.

Never in her wildest dreams did she ever think she'd ever experience this kind of abandon—a place where nothing mattered except being everything to the person in your arms.

Van drove one final time and she felt his body wrecked by his release.

She closed her eyes to stop her tears from falling. At this very moment she knew she had to tell him everything. When she mustered the courage she opened her eyes and found Van staring at her.

"Are you crying?" Van said. He rolled off her and pulled her onto her side. "Did I hurt you?"

She shook her head. "No. You didn't hurt me."

"What's wrong then?"

"I'm not the same person I used to be," she said. "I used to be a weak and inept Poindexter, I never used to be this able-bodied emotionally strong Wonder Woman."

"I know," he said. "Being with you has changed me for the better, too. As long as we're growing together it's all good."

He had changed, too. He took a chance and worked with her.

He rolled onto his back and yawned. "The next few days are going to be difficult so I think we should try to get as much sleep as we can."

He kissed her head and tucked her beneath his arm.

She should have been more specific. She should have told him about her serum.

Instead she closed her eyes, basked in his warmth. A few more days wouldn't hurt. The news would keep until they returned to Boston.

Chapter 32

The wail of the klaxon woke Aliesa from a dead sleep. Van bolted into a sitting position and smacked his head on the bulkhead. A bump bloomed at the point of impact.

"What the hell was that?" she asked.

Still rubbing his head, Van slid out of the bunk and pulled on his pants. "It's an alarm."

"What for?"

"I'm on my way to find out."

Aliesa tossed the covers aside and reached for her clothes. "You're not going anywhere without me. The last time you left me in bed things spun out of control."

Van passed over her clothes.

They entered the passageway.

Crewmembers scurried from their quarters and hurried to their respective stations. Van momentarily detained a half-running seaman. "What's happening?" he asked.

The young recruit gulped air. "A container ship went down south east of Los Angeles. Due to our proximity, we've been dispatched to search for survivors."

Aliesa guessed the young recruit had regurgitated the CO's words verbatim. Then he turned and hurried on his way.

"What about us?" she asked. Then she shook her head sheepishly. "Don't I sound like the most spoiled person on the planet? That didn't really come out right."

"It sucks because it will put us behind schedule, but this ship has a job to do. We're not the priority. It does create a whole other problem though. We'll miss our ride back to Boston."

She'd been given a reprieve. She had some more time to figure out how to tell Van her secret. He'd bared all to her. How his sister died, finding out about his heritage after his mother passed.

She followed close behind Van as he climbed the stairs to the deck of the *Udesto*.

The crew bustled. The emergency called all hands on-deck. The lifeboats had been readied for deployment. Mid-ship, the commander stood at the rail combing the water with a pair of binoculars.

Van walked over to him. "Can you give me an update, Commander?"

The second in charge dropped the goggles. "Three hours ago we received a mayday from the container ship called the *Wonton Foo*. The recorded transmission occurred in this general vicinity and there's been nothing since."

A seaman ran over to the commander. "I saw something off the starboard bow."

The commander raised his binoculars and searched the surface of the water. "I don't see anything," he said.

Then there was a loud boom. The *Udesto* lurched forward—grinding, twisting metal scraped and groaned.

The klaxon boomed again, but this time it didn't stop.

It blared over and over again. The engines ground to a halt. The commander raised his goggles and surveyed the black water.

"Containers in the water!" he shouted.

He grabbed the intercom on his belt and pushed the button. "No sign of the *Wonton Foo*, Captain, but there are several containers afloat in the water. Permission to lower a tender for a closer inspection."

The captain's voice crackled through the receiver. "Permission granted," he said. "We're all-stop until each department files a damage report."

The commander made a couple of calls on his handheld marine radio and arranged for a dinghy to be lowered into the water. As it dropped over the side of the *Udesto*, Van watched the crew climb the ladder into the smaller boat.

"And here I thought slamming into cargo containers on the high seas was nothing more than an urban legend," Aliesa said.

"It doesn't happen often. The odds of hitting one are pretty slim. "There are between five and six million boxes in transit on the water at any given time. Two thousand are lost overboard every single year."

Aliesa did the calculation in her head. "Less than point zero, zero, zero, 5 percent. You're right. Not very much."

"We hit one, didn't we?" Van said.

"Yes, but the odds increased exponentially when we raced toward its last reported location. And just so you know, a twenty foot container has to weigh over sixteen tons to sink."

"Are they all sealed?" Aliesa asked.

"No. Usually the metal is old and damaged."

Again Aliesa did the mathematical computation. "A twenty foot box has a volume of thirty-eight meters. Based on the density of seawater and volumetric displacement it would take fifty-seven days to sink. Of course, my calculations are for an empty container—the container's cargo would cause fluctuations."

Van raised his eyebrows at the commander who nodded, duly impressed.

"In my experience, containers sink much more quickly—anywhere from a few days to a few weeks."

A crackle came through the handheld. "We've found a survivor. He's in pretty bad shape. We're going to need a basket."

"I'll have one standing by." The commander clicked off the handheld and barked orders at two ensigns. "You," he pointed at the first seaman, "get a Stokes, and you," pointing at the second, "notify sickbay to standby."

Van and Aliesa stood back and watched the tender zigzagging around submerged containers on its way back to the *Udesto*. Once the tender arrived, the Stokes litter dropped onto the lifeboat. The crew lifted the limp survivor into the wire rescue cage and secured him. Then they gave the signal to haul him up.

The basket twisted and turned as it was winched aboard.

Aliesa noticed the ashen face of the man strapped into the cage; dark, straight hair, round face and sunken eyes. Her gaze travelled to the splint cradling his nearly severed arm. The flesh had been mangled and torn. The mulched laceration might have been the work of a shark. Or maybe this man's arm simply got in the way of one of the containers going over the side of the *Wonton Foo*.

A man pushed through the seamen who'd gathering on deck. Tall, thinning hair, a stethoscope slung around his neck. He placed the stethoscope inside the man's shirt and listened carefully, all the while his eyes surveying the damage in the victim's arm. "Get him to sickbay, stat."

Then he turned toward the commander. "I'll do my best to stabilize him, but these injuries are more than I'm equipped to handle. If I can stabilize him, there's a shot his arm can be reattached. But he needs EVAC. He needs a Dolphin, and he needs it now." He turned and hurried after his patient.

The commander buzzed the captain and relayed the doc's recommendation. When he disconnected he took notice of Van and Aliesa standing close.

"Please excuse me, my presence has been requested on the bridge."

"Mind if we tag along?" Van asked.

"It's a free ship," the commander said.

They fell into step behind him. Aliesa tugged on Van's sleeve. "What's a Dolphin?"

"It's a Eurocopter. It's used for air-sea search and rescue. And, if there's enough room, our ride out of here."

The down draft of the Dolphin's main rotor caused ripples to radiate on the surface of the water. Steadily, Aliesa's harness inched closer to the chopper.

The first few feet were exhilarating, seeing the cutter

and crew beneath her, amidst the bobbing containers from the *Wonton Foo*. But all too soon, she could see sharks in the water, too.

They'd likely had a feeding frenzy with the lost crew of the freighter. She held tight to the harness. She could do this. She'd watched as the survivor had been lifted first, then Van, now it was her turn.

She remembered Van's instructions.

Head up not down.

The bright red-orange belly of the chopper wore the same Coast Guard stripe. A rotor, clattered loud and steady. The kick of the wind made the skin on her cheeks flutter against her teeth as she inched closer.

The cable pulled her higher and higher. Her lungs constricted and it hurt to breathe. Inside the chopper, Van clung to the raised clamshell door. He reached out his hand and she grabbed it so he could haul her inside. Once he shut the overhead door, he removed Aliesa's cable.

"You did great," he said.

She tried not to let him see how badly she shook.

The inside of the chopper was as black as a cave. A medic huddled over the Stokes stretcher. He checked his patient's IV and checked the screen of the portable device monitoring the vitals.

Suddenly, alarms sounded.

"Tachycardia," the medic said. "Oxygen saturation is low."

Aliesa squeezed around Van and hurried over to the medic to offer assistance. "I'll use the airbag while you set the pads and charge the defibrillator," she said.

The medic raised the microphone on his headphones

and notified the pilot of his plans.

Pads were placed on the chest of the patient and the portable AED blinked when it was fully charged. The medic shouted, "Clear."

Aliesa removed the airbag from over the patient's nose and mouth and held her arms high.

The body of the patient bounced on the plastic gurney when the paddles released the jolt of electricity.

The monitor returned to beeping normally.

Aliesa put the airbag back to the patient's mouth and continued administering oxygen.

"He's stable," the medic said. "Let's hope he stays this way. We're still a half hour out."

The Dolphin clattered across the open water at a hundred and fifty miles an hour.

Aliesa pumped the air bag.

By the time the Dolphin landed on the roof of LA General Hospital her hand had cramped. She gladly surrendered her job to one of the waiting nurses. The doctor rushed out of sight with the victim, the medic racing alongside, giving him an up to the minute status report. Once the paperwork had been completed and the patient taken to surgery, the crew and passengers piled inside the chopper and flew back to Los Angeles AFB.

"Thanks for the lift," Van said, getting out of the chopper.

The medic thanked Aliesa and shook her hand.

A jeep honked and pulled beside the Dolphin. A lieutenant behind the wheel of the vehicle shouted. "Your name Elliot Vance?"

Van nodded. "Hop in. Your ride to Hanscom is nearly

ready for takeoff."

Aliesa slid into the back seat and Van hopped in beside the lieutenant. The vehicle zipped to the other side of the base and stopped beside a massive airplane, a veritable metal Moby Dick. The loading ramp of the four-engine turbo-prop yawned and two large pallets had be chained and strapped inside the cargo bay.

For the last little while Aliesa had been feeling queasy, likely due to the fact she hadn't eaten all day. Not to mention the adrenaline highs and lows. Van helped her out of the back seat and she wobbled on her feet.

They walked up the rear ramp, squeezed around the payload and noticed six seats, three on each side, welded to the fuselage immediately behind the cockpit.

"The guests of honor have arrived," the lanky pilot said.

"Sorry to hold you up," Van said.

"It's not your fault. Did the man rescued survive?"

"Not sure," Aliesa said. "He's still in surgery."

"I'll keep my fingers crossed." The pilot motioned to the passenger seating. "You can relax, now. We'll be ready to take off in about ten minutes. I'll let you know when to buckle up."

"Thanks," Van said.

Aliesa sat in the aisle seat and Van sat beside her.

He turned toward her. "Are you okay? Are you sick?"

The queasiness in her stomach had turned into full-fledged acid reflux. "There's a lot to be said for being drugged and travelling in a coffin."

"Not feeling very good, huh?" Van put his hand on her forehead.

"How long a flight is this?" Aliesa asked.

"Six hours. Five with a tail-wind."

"I'll never make it."

"Yes, you will." Van lifted and kissed her hand.

Her stomach roiled. Her mouth watered and she kept swallowing the bile creeping into her throat.

All of a sudden she sprang out of the seat, hurried into the small lavatory behind the cockpit and retched.

Chapter 33

———————————————

With the time change, Aliesa and Van arrived at Hanscom in the middle of the night. The clear sky reflected the ambient glow of the full moon like a spotlight. Aliesa had never been so happy to be on land in her life. She stood and brushed herself off. Van and one of the pilots came bounding down the ramp.

"You made it," the pilot said. "I kept it as steady as possible. The tail-wind made a big difference."

"I survived," Aliesa said, feeling her cheeks burn.

"Nice to see a color other than green on your face."

Van reached out and shook the pilot's hand. "Thanks for the lift."

"Anytime," he said, running to catch the other crewmembers who'd already deplaned.

Both Van and Aliesa walked to the car pool on the other side of base. The admiral had indeed gotten Van's motorcycle out of the BU impound and it sat waiting for them.

"I bet the last thing you feel like doing is climbing on the back of my motorcycle."

"Actually, I'm kind of excited about it."

"Yeah?"

"Yeah," she said.

He collected the keys from the office; they put on their helmets, and drove back to Boston. Aliesa wrapped her arms around Van and rested her head against his back. She breathed the cool morning air as they raced though the sleeping city to the downtown core. He drove into the Bayfront Towers underground parking.

They stowed their helmets and Van removed one saddlebag to take upstairs and they got into the elevator.

"I'd like to stop in the lobby," Aliesa said. "My mail box is probably bursting."

She was right. The box had been jammed with mail and flyers. While she pulled and flattened crumpled letters, outside a newspaper delivery truck pulled to the curb and dropped a bundle into the box. The driver of the truck jumped out and carried a stack through the front door of her building and dumped them into the rack.

She sighted the stand of papers through the vestibule's locked glass door. The headline jumped off the page at her.

BU Murder Victim Finally Identified.

The bold sub-header below drew her attention across the page. *The woman believed to be Dr. Aliesa Atworth has now been identified as Evelyne Mathews of Charlestown.*

Her breath caught in her throat.

She opened the door and snatched a paper from the stand. To stop tears from pooling in her eyes she blotted her eyes with the back of her hand. "I guess it's open season."

"I told the admiral to release the information. It was cruel to keep her family waiting any longer." Van nudged

Aliesa toward the elevator. "You need to stop beating yourself up. She'd been targeted. Someone wants to eliminate anyone and everyone who knew about the cocaine and your research."

Aliesa's nausea came rushing back. They got back on the elevator and the doors slid closed. She was more tired than she'd ever been.

Van put his arm around her. "You have to trust me," he said. "I won't let anything happen to you. We need to get to the bottom of this. Until then, you'll never be safe."

He used the word again. Trust.

She needed to trust him—with her life, her love, and her secret. "Do you have any theories about who is behind all of this?"

"Not yet. We need to find the common denominator. Something or someone connects all of these murders."

The elevator shuttled them to the penthouse floor. Van completed a thorough search of the premises before he let Aliesa enter.

She hung her jacket and walked across the hall, stopping when she reached the living room. So much had happened, she'd forgotten what transpired the last time she'd been here. Wide eyed, she noticed the dried puddles of wine dotting the floor like blood splatter. Glass shards glistened.

She'd used broken wine bottles to fend off Axel. Van stepped in front of her. He put his hands on her arms and turned her toward the primary bedroom.

"Go and take a shower. I've got this," he said, giving her a gentle shove.

She closed the bedroom door behind her.

He listened at her door.

When he'd cleared the suite minutes earlier he'd seen both bedrooms had been used by Jorge and Axel so he'd need to strip the bed before she got into the shower.

He went back into to the living room and plugged in his phone. Wine bottles had been placed on the floor. As he restocked the bar fridge he remembered the vial he'd found and Drew had analyzed.

Of course. The vial.

Aliesa had left their cozy bed at the Get-Away Inn and returned here to get her vial of serum.

When they'd first met, she'd called it medicine. Shortly thereafter, she referred to it as serum.

Drew said the vial contained biological material. Stem cells.

He walked into the kitchen and pulled out the olive jar—the vial still neatly concealed. He returned it to the shelf, swept the broken glass, filled a bucket with warm soapy water, and washed the floor.

Then he called ABC Inquiries.

"Hey, Simone, is Drew in?"

The phone clicked over to Drew using the intercom. "Where the hell have you been?"

"I'll fill you in later," Van said. "Have you gotten any leads from the Trojan Horse I installed on Devine's computer?"

"Nada. He's so clean he squeaks," Drew said. "Anything else?"

"A while back I asked you to complete a dossier on Grayson Everet."

"When you dropped off the grid I slid that task onto the back burner. I'll get right on it. What am I trying to find exactly?"

"Any sort of connection. Something linking Hernandez to Grayson Everet."

"I'll see what I can find."

Van pressed end and walked across the hall with his saddlebag. This time when he listened at Aliesa's door he heard water running. He headed into the other room, stripped and made the spare bed, then took his own shower. Less than ten minutes later, clad in a pair of jeans, he stopped at her door. The sound of running water had ceased, so he went into the living room, ordered pizza, and waited for her to emerge.

Half an hour turned into an hour, and still no Aliesa. He went to her door and knocked. No answer.

He barreled inside.

Still swathed in a towel from the shower, Aliesa had fallen asleep on the freshly made bed.

His heart pounded—a crazy out-of-control need to protect this woman threatened to overwhelm him. He would do whatever he had to do to keep her safe. Her dewy skin, sweet scent, and skimpy towel caused a whole bunch of physical reactions, but as much as he wanted to tear off his clothes and make sweet love to her, he knew she needed to sleep.

So did he.

A heap of dirty linens lay on the floor at the base of the bed. She'd neatly folded the duvet and placed it on the chair. He covered her with it and walked into the bathroom to turn off the light. He reached inside the door, but before he could find the switch his gaze settled on the contents of the trashcan—an empty vial, wrapper, and used syringe were among the refuse.

She'd been using the serum on herself. She wanted it so badly she risked her safety to come back here to collect it.

But why? She was no addict. If she had been she would have been suffering the effects of withdrawal. Then again, she had spent a huge portion of their flight vomiting.

He switched off the light and sat in the living room. His cell phone rang.

It was Drew.

"What have you got for me?" Van asked.

"I started with Grayson Everet's phone records. It didn't take very long before I got a hit. Prior to his death, he'd made regular calls to a man named Jules Wolcott."

"Jules Wolcott? Why does his name sound so familiar?"

"Jules Wolcott was the man Saul Devine contacted when you told him Dr. Marcus Hernandez was murdered. He's the CFO of Panacealla."

Van stilled and he started making the mental connections. Panacealla funded Hernandez's anti-leukemic. They were the parent company of both Capill Industries and Medevac.

"Van? Are you still there?" Drew asked.

"I'm here," Van said. "I think it's time Aliesa and I retrieved the digital recording device from Saul Devine's phone."

"Want the name and number of the cleaning company

again?"

"No, thanks. I've got it." Van disconnected and scrolled through his contacts. He found the number under S for *Spit and Polish*.

With a little luck he'd still be awake.

A man answered.

"Frank? It's Van."

"Who?"

"The guy who worked the night shift for you last week at Lucas and Devine. I was hoping we could make the same arrangements once again."

"When?"

"Is tonight too soon?"

Chapter 34

Aliesa came bounding down the hall dressed in a pair of slacks and T-shirt. She stopped and inhaled deeply. "Do I smell pizza?"

"You might want to nuke a slice; it'll be cold by now."

She grabbed a piece and took a bite. "I usually eat it cold." She gazed through the slider and across the city. The sun had dropped below the towering buildings of Boston's downtown core. "How long did I sleep?"

"All day. I didn't wake you because we're pulling the night shift again at Lucas and Devine. Come and sit. I have a few things I want to discuss with you."

The tone of Van's voice told her something happened. She ate one piece in three mouthfuls and grabbed another slice for their conversation. When she sat, he stood and went over to the bar fridge. He reached behind one of the remaining bottles and withdrew a vial. Her vial.

Aliesa swallowed the pizza and reached for it. Happy and resigned. Van deserved the truth. "Where did you find it?" she asked.

Van shook his head. "I'm the one asking the questions," he said. "Is this the reason you came back to your apartment?"

Aliesa nodded.

"Why?" Van said. "I told you it wasn't safe?"

No longer hungry, she dropped the remainder of the slice on top of the pizza box. She closed her eyes. "*It's* all I have left of my research. Thousands of hours of work."

"You can always start over."

"It's not so simple."

"A large part of the process is harvesting donor stem cells. Then there's the problem of getting my hands on the reagent. The reagent was what got me into this mess in the first place. It was the Camu camu fruit Hernandez sent me."

"Whose stem cells are in this vial?"

"They're mine," Aliesa said.

"Would they be of use to anyone other than you?"

She thought for a moment. "Not unless the person had the same blood type. Even then, they might not be as compatible as a sample derived from their own stem cells."

"Then why did you risk it?"

"Everet called it the fountain of youth. But the analogy is fairly accurate."

"Answer the question."

"Because I needed them, all right?"

"But why?"

"To keep you interested in me." She'd finally said it.

"You were going to inject me with those cells?"

"Very funny."

Van started to chuckle. Soon the chuckle turned into an all out belly laugh. In between whoops he managed to spit out a couple of words. "It kinda is."

Aliesa balled her hands into fists and gritted her teeth.

She could have smacked him, but she knew she'd only hurt her hand if she did.

"Hilarious." She crossed her arms and blinked in rapid succession.

"Are you telling me this serum turns you into some kind of Super Woman?"

"In many ways."

"Then these stem cells are like steroids."

"No, they're not drugs. These supercharged cells live longer. They make me healthier and stronger." She took a deep breath. "Okay, smarty pants, why do you think I did it?" She never used Grayson's term because she thought it might jinx the project. But unless she did, people simply didn't get it. She'd really found the freaking fountain of youth.

"You did it because you were feeling insecure about us. We'd just made love and by your own admission you said you'd never had a lasting relationship. You thought you needed a little boost. But honey, I'm here to tell you don't need help in any department."

He scooped her up so she straddled his lap. He smoothed his hands through her hair and she leaned forward to give him a kiss. A firestorm exploded. When he pulled back, his ragged breathing sounded much like hers.

"Don't you realize I want you all the time? And it's not the stem cells. Believe me. If we didn't have to get ready to go out to work tonight, I'd prove it."

Aliesa could feel the evidence of his arousal—her body was so attuned to him, she already moistened in anticipation.

"Now go and get your coveralls for *Spit and Polish*. We

have to stop to get the keys for our shift."

They drove to Little Italy, to Joe Spina's place. Van parked his motorcycle and they climbed the stairs to Joe's apartment.

A chain lock held the door open no more than three inches. "Yeah," Joe said. When he recognized Van he closed the door, unhooked the chain and reopened it. "Hey. And this must be the little lady Mr. Devine can't stop asking about. I'm Joe."

She nodded. "My name's Aliesa. Mr. Devine's been talking about me?"

"He's got a job offer. Think I understand why. You're lovely."

Van stepped forward as she wrinkled her brow.

"Thank you for doing such a thorough cleaning job the last time," Joe said.

"You're welcome."

Van handed Frank an envelope. "It's all there. Count it if you like."

"I trust you. Besides, if it isn't, you'll never pull another shift."

"This is the last anyhow."

"Damn. I was just beginning to enjoy this arrangement."

"Thanks again." Van and Aliesa turned to leave.

"My pleasure," Joe said. "Nice meeting you, doll."

They drove to the offices of Lucas and Devine. Van parked in the alley around back. The spot reserved for Saul Devine.

"What if he returns later tonight?" Aliesa asked.

"Then he has one of two options. He can park elsewhere or send for a truck to have me towed."

They began in Saul's office. While Aliesa dusted, emptied the garbage, and vacuumed, Van removed the bug from the phone.

She had the routine down pat and he simply followed her lead. With both of them working together, they were done in a few hours.

They wheeled the cleaning cart into the janitor's closet. He retrieved the digital recorder from the return air duct on the wall and they headed back to her apartment to listen to several hours of recordings.

The mundane recordings were hypnotic.

Saul's monotone voice almost lulled Aliesa to sleep.

"I can't listen to his wife giving him another shopping list or his friends arranging another golf date. I need to go splash cold water on my face."

She stood, stretched, and was about to leave when the tape clicked to the next phone call.

Saul? This is Jules Wolcott.

Jules. What an unexpected pleasure. What can I do for you?

I'm calling because there's been an oversight. A few weeks ago, my secretary was supposed to mail out some invitations to your firm for our annual awards nights. Somehow she dropped the ball, so I'm going to courier the invitations. Your firm's been on retainer now for a few years and, because you've done such a good job for us, I wanted to show my appreciation.

How very nice of you. When and where is it?

It's this Saturday night, at the Ritz Carlton. Should be a pretty good party.

You certainly know how to do things right. My wife will be thrilled.

I hope so. There'll be a short awards presentation—for employees who've made valuable contributions this past year—an eight-course meal and we'll finish off the evening with a dance. There'll be a full band, of course. I hope you can make it.
I'm certain we can. Thanks for including us.

See you Saturday night.

Van switched off the recording.

Aliesa sat back in the chair. "Do you think Devine and Wolcott are in cahoots?"

"Hell, no. I think Wolcott put Lucas and Devine on retainer and invited them as an afterthought to give Panacealla legitimacy. But there's only one way to find out. We need to go to that party."

"It doesn't get any better than the Ritz Carlton." The sun appeared overtop of the balcony railing and she wobbled on her feet. "Oh, God. I need to do something to turn my internal clock around. Here it is morning again and all I feel like doing is crawling in bed. Got any ideas?"

Van stood and put his arms around her. "I do," he said, dipping his head for a kiss.

He took his time. He nipped at her lips and trailed kisses along her graceful neck.

Breathing heavy, she stepped out of his reach and opened her eyes. His little talk with her must have worked because brazenly she licked her lips at him. In one smooth motion, she grabbed the hem of her shirt, pulled it over her head, and dropped it on the floor. Then she reached to unzip her pants. The striptease got his heart hammering in his chest. She wriggled out of her pants by gyrating and shoving them inch by itty-bitty inch over her hips.

This woman oozed sensuality. He'd grown hot and hard from her striptease. She stood before him in the living room wearing nothing more than a couple of scraps of lace.

He wanted her.

He stood and lifted her. She wound her legs around his waist and pressed her warmth against the hard ridge of his arousal. He strode into the bedroom, placed her on the bed, and leaned toward her.

She was beautiful—her long graceful neck, the swell of her breasts and the gentle curve of her hips. Perhaps his pause made her think she had to do something to further ignite his passion, because she started to roll toward him.

"No," he said. "Don't move. Lay back and relax. This isn't about me, it's about you."

She had no idea what kind of effect she had on him. He couldn't let her touch him and maintain his control. He needed to take things slowly.

He drew a ragged breath. Their eyes locked.

He undid the buttons of his shirt and let the cotton fall to the floor. His belt buckle clinked as it dropped. His pants and boxers followed the same path.

Her pupils dilated and his heart did a crazy flip. He knelt on the edge of the bed and slid her lacey briefs over her long legs. From her pink toenails, he worked his way north. His lips found the inside of her thighs and she gasped.

"I'm going to make love to all of you," he said. "Show you what it'll always be like between us."

Her first orgasm struck the moment his lips found her slick folds. He licked and kissed her through the pull of the undertow and when the last wave washed ashore he barely gave her a moment to breathe before he continued his ascent.

His tongue ran circles around her navel as he inched higher. A flick of his wrist opened the front closure of her lacy bra. Her small, firm breasts were full and rounded and her nipples were as hot and hard as him. He suckled her until her breathing became strained. Then he reached between her legs and brought her to climax yet again.

He straddled her and watched her breathing normalize. When she opened her eyes they were tear-filled. He kissed her forehead, the corner of her eyes, her cheeks and then her lips.

He took his time, making love to her with his mouth. He swirled his tongue around hers, pushed her legs open and held his weight above her. He hovered. One push and he slid into her, matching the glide of his tongue with every stroke.

He knew he wouldn't be able to hold off for very long. He'd made love to her, cherishing all of her. She was his match in every way. His soul mate.

The inner tightening signaled the onset of her third climax. Only this time he knew he'd be joining her. The slow build crested and churned into a raging tsunami. The tidal wave shimmered and frothed and crashed ashore leaving both of them spent and dazed, so much so his ears rang.

Her eyes slowly focused on him, confusion marring her face. "What was that?"

"Did you hear something, too?"

"It sounded like my phone." She swung her legs to the floor. "I plugged it in to charge when we got home." She ran into the kitchen and grabbed it from the counter.

When he joined her she was staring at the call display tears springing to her eyes.

"Something wrong?" he asked. "Who is it?"

"It's Evelyne's mom."

"Are you going to answer it?"

She nodded.

Use the speaker," Van said.

Aliesa did as he asked and pressed the button to answer the call. "Hello," she said. Silence dragged for a few moments. Long enough for Van to think they'd somehow been disconnected.

"Aliesa?" A small voice asked. "Is it really you?"

"Yes, it's me, Beatrice." Aliesa's bottom lip quivered. She bit down on it.

"I had to make sure. We've been told so many different things over the last week I don't know what's real anymore."

"I know. I've been in protective custody. I'm so sorry about Evelyne."

"They told me." Beatrice's breath caught and it sounded like she smothered a cry. "I'm calling to ask if you would say a few words at the service. Evelyne thought so much of you, it would mean a great deal to her father and me."

Aliesa gulped. "I'd be honored."

"Thank you," Evelyne's mother said. "The service is at nine tomorrow morning at the Divine Cross. We've arranged to have her interred in a shady corner of the grounds. I think she'd like that."

"She always preferred the shade to the sun," Aliesa said. "I think she'd like that very much. I'll be there." Aliesa pressed the end button, set the phone on the counter as Van pulled her into his arms.

"How will I ever be able to face them? I'm the one who set this whole thing in motion. If I hadn't contacted Hernandez for the reagent, Evelyne would still be here."

Over the last several days, Aliesa hadn't had a moment to grieve. She was no stranger to the process; she'd said she'd lost her mother to breast cancer and her father to a mugging. Van understood because he still bore the emotional sores of loss from his mother's death not even three short months ago.

He wanted to tell her she shouldn't go to the funeral—she'd be an easy target, but he knew arguing would be useless. She needed to go—for Evelyne, her parents, and for herself. She needed to get past losing her friend in such a violent way.

Van led her into the primary bedroom. "How does a bubble bath sound?"

"Like something completely foreign," she said. "I've never had one before."

"Then stand back and let me get things set up." He leaned over and ran the water. Then he reached for the shampoo, without bubble bath he had to improvise.

As he leaned over to pour the shampoo underneath the stream of water, Aliesa wrapped her arms around him.

"Will you come with me to the funeral?" she asked.

"You betcha."

Chapter 35

V an parked his bike on the street a few blocks from the Charlestown church, which suited Aliesa. The walk would help her focus. She brushed off her black slacks and straightened the collar of her blouse.

"Am I dressed okay?" she asked. "I really wanted to wear the little black skirt and jacket but it would have been too risqué for travelling on the back of your motorcycle."

"You're perfect," Van said, giving her hand a squeeze.

At the end of the street squatted Divine Cross—a quaint hundred and fifty year-old church—a relic and the heart of the east end community.

They walked through the wrought iron gate and along the moss covered cobblestone path to the slate steps.

Vines trailed over the block-like façade. The stained glass cathedral shaped windows depicted Christ at different stages of his life—the swaddled babe, the shepherd, the preacher, and the martyr. The steep slope and spire of slate on the roof reminded her of a rocket pointing heavenward.

The double doors were burled oak. Both were propped open and stopped with an iron weight on the hardwood floor.

A stack of cream-colored booklets was fanned out across the surface of an intricately carved hall table pressed against the wall. Beneath the caption "In Loving Memory," was a black-and-white photo of Evelyne with her crooked smile.

She'd never seen the picture before but she thought it captured the essence of her dear friend—her cockeyed grin, her teasing eyes, her pixie-like nose.

Instantly, her eyes brimmed and her throat constricted. "I'm never going to get through this without crying," she said.

"No one expects you to. You're grieving. Everyone came here today to remember Evelyne."

She wiped the tears from her cheeks and took a deep breath. "You're right."

"Are you ready?" Van asked.

She nodded and stood tall.

Van opened a door to the chapel and Aliesa stepped inside. Soft organ music hummed through the brass pipes towering above the sculpture of Christ on the farthest wall.

The old wooden floorboards creaked under her weight. She and Van walked along the center aisle flanked with wooden shoulder-high box-pews. Each door boasted a family name; only those left open were available for seating.

A smattering of people mingled at the front of the church. People waited in line to give their condolences to the Mathews, who stood vigil in front of their daughter's coffin. On top of the closed casket was a picture of Evelyne surrounded by a lush spray of exotic blooms—birds of paradise, orchids, and protea—amidst a carpet of greenery.

Aliesa and Van took their place in the line and greeted the Mathews in turn.

"Aliesa," Beatrice Mathews said. "We're very happy you could make it."

"I wouldn't have missed saying goodbye. Evelyne was my dearest friend." *My only friend.*

While Ian Mathews greeted another guest, Beatrice came to attention. "Oh," she said. "I have something for you." Then she turned and removed something from her purse in the first pew. An envelope. She rejoined Aliesa in front of the casket and handed her the envelope. "I want you to have this. It was Evelyne's favorite necklace."

Aliesa teared at the memory of the compass charm Evelyne had worn almost every day she'd known her.

"You know the necklace I'm talking about, don't you?"

Aliesa nodded mutely. Evelyne used to joke about Aliesa being one of the most socially lost people she'd ever known. She clasped the envelope tightly to her chest. "Thank you. This means a lot to me."

The friar stood at the pulpit and asked everyone to take their seats. On the wall behind him a two-foot brass cross gleamed.

Van scanned the church on a continual basis. He led Aliesa to one of the vacant box-pews and both climbed the steps and sat inside.

The friar began the service by welcoming everyone, saying a prayer, and directing them to sing a selection of hymns.

Aliesa had never been one to go to church. She'd renounced religion after her mother died. But there was something quiet and calm about the friar. He didn't paint a picture of Evelyne as a devout follower; he spoke of her love of life, her flair, and her willingness to listen. The honesty of his words rang true.

He seemed to know her pretty well. Aliesa remembered one of the many conversations she'd had with Evelyne—one about the existence of God. Ev didn't want to rule out the idea of a higher power, but the scientist in her believed more in evolution than creation, and of course she told her she totally believed in the fabled fountain of youth.

"Dr. Atworth," the friar said. "Would you like to come and say a few words?"

Van squeezed her hand. She shook off her trance, exited the booth and stood at the pulpit just beyond the casket.

She took a moment to appreciate all of the solemn faces of the crowd. These people were Evelyne's family and friends—loved ones searching for answers.

Aliesa had written out some notes on cue cards. In fact, she still clutched them tightly in her hand. But as she stared out over the congregation she decided she didn't want to read notes, so she set the envelope and cue cards on top of the podium, and placed her hand on Evelyne's casket. "The first thing I want to do is set the record straight," Aliesa said. "Evelyne taught me far more than I ever taught her."

It was the truth. Aliesa didn't have the foggiest notion how to be a friend. But Evelyne did. And she took the time to teach her. Aliesa regaled the crowd with Evelyne's birdseed muffin story and the tofu pizza fib. When Aliesa surveyed the crowd she saw smiling faces—people remembering their own stories of Evelyne's antics.

Finally, Aliesa told the crowd Evelyne had changed her life and she'd always be her very best friend. Then she walked back to her booth, stopping briefly to place a comforting hand on Beatrice's shoulder as she passed.

Van nodded and smiled at her as she slid in beside him. "You did great," he whispered.

The friar returned to the pulpit, said a prayer, and led the congregation in another song. He summoned the pallbearers and asked everyone to follow the procession into the garden cemetery.

The crowd gathered around the grave as Evelyne's casket was carefully lowered into the ground.

Ashes to ashes, dust to dust.

The friar made one final announcement. "Beatrice and Ian ask everyone to join them in the rec hall, on the other side of the cemetery, where refreshments will be served."

One by one people began to migrate to the far building. Van and Aliesa were among the last people to leave the grave. "I'll meet you inside," she said. "I just want a moment to say goodbye."

Reluctantly, Van gave her the privacy she requested and followed the crowd.

When she was alone she plucked a bird of paradise from the floral arrangement, kissed the bloom and placed it on the surface of the coffin.

She turned to head into the rec center and suddenly remembered Evelyne's necklace. She patted her pants pockets, but both were empty.

The church. She'd placed the envelope on top of the

pulpit with her abandoned speech.

She hurried back inside the place of worship to the podium where she'd left it.

Empty. Nothing but gleaming wood.

She scoured the ground. She lifted the altar skirt and checked every conceivable nook and cranny.

Just when she thought she'd lost Evelyne's special keepsake, a deep male voice echoed throughout the empty nave.

"Is this what you want?"

Chapter 36

Aliesa breathed a huge sigh of relief. "Oh, thank goodness you found it."

The tall, muscular man stood in the first enclosed pew. Sandy hair, square jaw, and black cotton T-shirt pulled taut across his pecs.

She hurried across the platform in a flurry. She stretched out her hand to grab the dangling necklace but the man pulled it away.

"If I were you I wouldn't take any more chances on losing this sentimental piece."

He must have overheard the conversation when Beatrice gave it to her. But oddly, she didn't remember seeing him.

"Here," he said. "Why don't you let me put it around your neck?"

Hesitantly she turned around.

The man distended the necklace between his hands, reached over her head, and fiddled to close the clasp.

"There," he said.

Aliesa almost managed to thank him before he grabbed her by the neck and pulled her toward him. She stumbled against his solid chest and he tightened the grip around her neck.

"I'm going to have as much fun with you as I did with your friend. People just don't realize how much skill and finesse it takes to bring you the very brink of death, then allow you to resurface, only to start the process over again. I strung your friend along four times before she finally gave up."

Aliesa clawed at his arm but he just continued to tighten his hold even more. She tried to scream, but the raspy whisper dribbling across her lips meant her throat had been painfully constricted.

Her croak wouldn't be heard by a soul. Then again, even if she did manage to belt out a scream the chances of anyone hearing her at the rec center were slim to none.

"Why are you doing this?" She struggled to enunciate each word. Her oxygen supply had nearly been depleted.

"I'd love to cite some noble cause but there really isn't one. I was hired to kill you. My client has kept me very busy recently and since you're the last on my list I thought I'd take my time. Make the most of it."

Arms and legs flailing, she desperately tried to pull much needed air into her lungs, but the man's arm squeezed her airway. Her field of vision began to darken around the edges. Soon she would lose consciousness.

Sounds and light flickered. Fond memories flooded her mind. From above, her mother, father, and Evelyne smiled down upon her. They called to her.

I'm coming.

She mouthed the words but no audible sounds were spoken. She closed her eyes and accepted her fate. It would be quicker and less painful if she did. The jaws of the void opened and swallowed her.

She floated. The band around her neck loosened and she drew air across bruised airways. When her eyes fluttered open the monster who strangled her reached out and grabbed her by the throat once again.

This time the darkness came quicker.

She closed her eyes to obliterate the man's twisted smile and wild eyes.

In the distance she heard a wallop.

The hold on her had broken and oxygen flooded her lungs. Once again, the darkness abated. Still somewhat lightheaded, she blinked to clear her vision and gulped air. Her throat felt as though she'd swallowed broken glass. When she sat up she saw Van squaring off against her attacker.

Van had his hands in the air, ready for his opponent to make the first move. "What's wrong? Not interested in attacking someone your own size?"

Long strands of blond hair had escaped the man's neat ponytail. "No money in it."

"I'm devastated," Van said. "Guess Wolcott's intel isn't as good as it could be. Maybe he should have hired someone who was in more of a hurry to get the job done. How long has it been? Two weeks?"

The smirk on the predator's face turned into a frown. From his belt he plucked and flipped open a stainless Milano Stiletto blade. He lowered his stance and began evasive maneuvers. "There's no rushing a job like this. It takes time to eliminate all the loose ends."

Van knew he'd guessed right. All of the murders were carried out to protect Wolcott and Panacealla's reputation—erase any trail leading back to them. Van grabbed one of the hymnals from the shelf in the pew and rolled it. Not much of a defensive weapon but enough to deflect the blade when his opponent pounced.

Surgical steel flashed.

Van deflected a series of downward strikes with the rolled book before he dropped the wad of paper and shackled his hand around the killer's knife-wielding wrist. Van swung him around in circles dumping the man onto the surface of the communion table. Van repeatedly slammed his closed fist on the wood surface until the blade flicked from the man's fingers and skidded onto the floor.

Wrist still shackled, Van flung him against the railing in front of the choir's seats. Van jabbed once, twice, and then took a hard elbow strike to his neck. The blow blinded him to the roundhouse which sent Van sailing over the rail bowling through the chairs.

He face planted on the floor. Spots dotted his vision and his entire body ached. Van waited for the man to collect his knife and closed in for the kill. Chairs scraped as his opponent moved them out of his path to get to Van. Vibrations from his footfalls shook the floorboards and became stronger against his cheek as the man approached.

Van blinked to clear his vision and envisioned the killer's actions. The man would grab a handful of Van's hair and pull his head back to expose his jugular. The moment Van felt hands in his hair he jerked his head back, square against the man's face.

The killer cried out in pain and landed hard on his haunches. Van rolled and got to his feet. He shifted his weight onto the balls of his feet, and began a countdown. He figured he had about a two second window to hit his mark. A moment too soon and he'd strike air, a moment too late and his shin could be sliced to ribbons.

Blood dripped from the killer's nose. The moment Van saw the fog lift from the man's eyes he set himself into motion. His foot impacted the knife. The toe of Van's shoe swept the blade out of the killer's hand and sent it sailing through the air, stabbing the door of the pew, two rows away from where Aliesa had dragged herself to hide.

Before Van regained his balance, the killer knocked him over by landing hard on top of him. They rolled to the right and then to the left, each man vying for position. Neither succeeded. They sprang apart and while Van got to his feet the killer darted up a small set of stairs at the side of the pulpit.

Van had no choice but to follow him. He took the risers two at a time to the balcony. Second rung from the top he sprang into the air as high as he could and flew hands first into a roll.

The tactic worked. The kick from his opponent, meant to trip him as he crested the top, totally missed his mark, so he immediately turned and disappeared somewhere amidst long waist-high wooden pews.

Van got to his feet and scanned the balcony.

This had to be where the killer had hidden, virtually undetected, during the service. In hindsight, Van should have swept the entire church before relaxing his guard.

He checked left. A bank of vertical brass organ pipes of different lengths climbed the wall. In front of him, five pews tiered downward. From where he stood he couldn't see to the floor between the rows, but he knew his opponent would be laying in wait.

There had to be another approach.

He almost discounted the idea when it surfaced, but soon realized he didn't have any choice. He squeezed between the last pew and the organ pipes, over on the far side of the balcony. He slipped off his shoes and socks and with bare feet balanced himself on the top edge of the pew backs. From here he'd have the best chance at spotting the killer first. As quietly as possible, Van stepped from pew back to pew back, working hard to maintain a light foot and correcting his balance with outstretched arms like a tight-rope walker.

He spotted the killer crouched between the first and second pew. Unaware of his lofty approach, Van launched himself into a perfect swan dive, landing on the man with a thud.

Impact caused the killer's chest to grind into the floor, with luck snapping one or two ribs. Before Van's theory could be put to the test, Van felt teeth sink into the meat of his bicep.

"Now you've gone and done it," Van said through clenched teeth. "I'm going to need a rabies shot." Truer words were never spoken. Like a dog with a bone, the killer locked his jaw, refusing to let go.

Van grabbed a bible from the pew shelf with his other hand and swung it against the man's already tender nose, using the spine as a battering ram. The blows shattered cartilage, which finally caused the man's jaw to release.

Disoriented, blood gushed from the killer's nostrils.

Van pressed his knee hard into the man's back but couldn't seem to grab a hold of his flailing arms. Like a bronco, the man bucked, tossing Van against the front lip of the balcony.

Without pause the man charged, ramming Van. For a moment Van's feet left the floor and he came dangerously close to toppling over the edge. But the killer had already mapped out Van's demise. The man pulled him back from the brink and shackled both hands around Van's neck. "What? No smart remark now?"

Van smelled sweat. The killer's stale breath whispered across his cheeks. "I'm going to kill you first, then I'm going to take my time with your girlfriend, make her beg to die."

Blood rushed to Van's cheeks. Pressure pulsed and throbbed where the man constricted the blood flow around his neck. A sound similar to rushing water filled his ears. "Not bloody likely." Van's voice scraped. It sounded as rough as sandpaper.

The strangler put his weight into his hold by angling down on Van. All of a sudden, Van heard a thunk. The strangler loosened his grip and staggered, widening his stance. Van took advantage of the opportunity and thrust his knee upwards into the man's crotch.

The strangler's hands instantly released Van's neck and, when the man doubled over, he noticed Aliesa standing directly behind, gripping a substantial brass cross like a baseball bat. Van kneed the strangler again. Doubled over, the blow impacted his already broken nose. The man sat in the pew, hitting the seat hard, holding his face with his hands.

Van sucked air in and out of his lungs. He waited for the strangler to surrender. He kept his eyes trained on him and knew the very instant of attack. When the strangler lunged at Van, he ducked low almost head-butting the killer's waist. Then he burst upright, using his quads to launch the man over top of the balcony railing and into mid-air.

Van turned around and watched the killer flapping his arms and bicycling his legs to try to right his body, but there simply wasn't enough time. In the next second, the assassin slammed head first into the boxed pew, his neck snapping on impact.

Draped inside the coffin-like pew, the killer's sightless eyes leered at Van standing on the edge of the balcony.

"Is he dead?" Aliesa asked.

Van turned around and stepped toward Aliesa, who still held the cross in tightly clenched fists. He reached out and took it from her. "Yes. It's over," he said.

She began to shake.

"It's all right. Shaking is normal. Adrenaline," he said. He helped her into the choir bench and sat beside her. He pulled out his cell phone and dialed the admiral.

"Morningside."

"I've got a situation," Van said.

"I'm listening," the admiral said.

"I need a clean up crew."

"How many?"

"One. I don't want the man who hired him to realize his asset is dead."

"And who is this man exactly?"

"The CEO of Panacealla Pharmaceuticals Inc., Jules

Wolcott."

The admiral took a moment to digest the information.
"Sir?"

"Location?"

Van gave the admiral the name and address of the church. Twenty minutes later, a couple of plain-clothes men arrived. They snapped a million pictures, wore rubber gloves, and carted the killer off in a body bag, then disinfected the church on their way out. No flashing lights, no sirens, no fuss, no muss.

When Van and Aliesa finally descended from the balcony, she seemed more like herself.

"Thank you for saving my life," she said.

"Thank you for saving mine."

Van hoisted the cross and placed it back on the hooks on the wall behind the pulpit.

"There. Good as new. Brings a whole new meaning to the words Divine Cross though," Van said. He searched her eyes for any kind of reaction. "It was a joke."

"Guess I don't feel much like smiling." She stilled. "Will I ever be able to relax my guard?"

"Not until we confront Wolcott."

"How do we do that?" Aliesa asked.

"We're going to crash his party.

Chapter 37

Once the church had been cleaned, Aliesa climbed onto Van's bike and they drove across town to the offices of ABC Inquiries.

"What time are they open till on a Friday?" Aliesa asked as they boarded the elevator.

"Till six." Van punched a button and the door closed.

"I'm a little worried about this party at the Ritz Carlton," Aliesa said. "I don't have anything appropriate for such a formal party."

"Neither do I," Van said.

They opened the door and found Simone siting at her desk working on a crossword puzzle.

"I've got a job for you since you're not too busy," Van said.

Simone raised an eyebrow. "Contrary to what you think, you're not my boss."

"Fine," Van said. He poked his head inside the inner office. "Is it okay if I borrow Simone this afternoon?"

Drew shrugged. "It's okay with me."

"Great," Van said, he sat on the edge of her desk. "I need another favor, Simone."

"What kind of a favor?"

"I need you're mad shopping skills. Aliesa needs a

cocktail dress," Van said. "And I need a tux."

Simone dropped the folded newspaper and pen. She rubbed her hands together, then abruptly stopped. The expression on her face made Aliesa smother a giggle.

"Are you shitting me?" Simone asked.

"I'm totally serious," Van said.

Simone raised her eyebrows. "You're taking her out on the town?"

"It's business," Van said. "We're going to a party at the Ritz Carlton tomorrow night."

"The Ritz?" She whistled, then she snagged her phone and dialed. "I'll see if I can get her a hair appointment... Connie?" she said. "Does Armando have any time to do a wash and blow dry for Aliesa?"

Simone sat forward in her seat. She checked her watch. "Perfect. Oh, and what about a manicure and pedicure?"

Aliesa could hear a muffled voice through the receiver. "We'll be there," she said, disconnecting.

Van crossed his arms. "Wait a minute, if Aliesa spends all of her time at the salon, when is she going to find a dress?"

"She doesn't have to," Simone said. "I put a couple of cocktail dresses on hold the last time we went shopping. Aliesa will go to Armando's to be pampered and I will pick them up before I take you shopping."

"Where do you want me to meet you?" Van asked. "I have a couple of things I have to do first."

"Fine," Simone said. She grabbed her purse from the drawer of her desk and dug out a flexible tape measure and cornered him.

Aliesa watched from the door.

"Stand up," Simone said.

Van huffed but complied.

Simone measured his waist, shoulders, arm length, and inseam.

"Is this really necessary?" Van asked.

Simone ogled him. "It is if you're going to pretend to be Aliesa's date and not the hired help."

Her comment shut his mouth.

"I think I've got everything I need," Simone said. She scratched measurements on a piece of paper and wrote the name of the store on a separate sheet. "Meet me here in about an hour, give or take." Then both Aliesa and Simone breezed out the door.

Like the last time, they set off for Newbury Street and Armando's. Simone hailed a cab. "Do you mind if I ask you a personal question?" Aliesa asked.

"Not at all," Simone said.

"What's wrong with you and Van? You guys seem to barely tolerate each other, and yet both of you go out of your way to help the other."

"Is it obvious?"

"Kind of hard to miss."

"Van saved my life seven years ago. He put away my boyfriend for drug trafficking. He cleaned me up and got me this job. He turned my life around. Without Van, I'd be dead and gone."

The cab pulled in front of Armando's. Simone paid the cabbie and they went inside.

Before Aliesa was whisked away for her appointments, Simone gave her two options. "The silver lamé or the slinky black number, your choice," she said. "Personally, I think you should go for the black. It's elegant, it fits you in all the right places and it's ultra sexy."

"The little black dress it is."

Van walked into Drew's office after Simone and Aliesa left for the salon.

His heart squeezed. As much as he knew Aliesa would be safe with Simone, a familiar panic swelled.

The assassin had been eliminated and he'd have the element of surprise tomorrow night with Wolcott.

He dug out the burner cell phone he'd retrieved out of the killer's pocket and handed it to Drew.

"Where did you get this?" Drew asked. He couldn't even flip the broken face open.

"From the man who tried to kill Aliesa at Evelyne's funeral today. He Peter Panned off a balcony. It's a long story. I'll tell you all about it when this thing is over. Can you make it operational?"

Drew pried off the back of the phone. He pulled out the SIM card and put it into an adapter attached to one of his computers and data began filling the screen.

Van slid into a seat beside him.

"The only thing on this card are texts to and from the man who hired him," Drew said.

"Is there any way you can figure out the identity of the man?"

Drew shook his head. "The instructions likely came from a burner phone, too. Kill everyone and only contact him when the contract is completed. The last text says JM eliminated."

"Jackson Mercante."

"He would be my best guess."

"Any way we can put this card into another phone?" Van asked.

Drew wheeled his chair over behind his desk to the filing cabinet. He opened the bottom drawer, rummaged through a dozen or so handsets and pulled one out. He wheeled over to Van, removed the SIM card from the reader and installed it in the new phone. "Here," he said. "Good as new."

Van stood and slid the new phone into his pocket. "Wish me luck," he said.

"Where are you going?" Drew asked.

"I have to get the tickets for the party tomorrow night before I meet Simone."

"Good luck," Drew said. "Not with the tickets, with Simone."

"Thanks. I'm sure I'll need it."

Van hopped on his bike and headed to Beacon Hill Law Office of Lucas and Devine. He parked in the alley beside Saul Devine's shiny black BMW.

He walked inside and right past the receptionist, disregarding her shouts of protest. He attempted to do the same with the secretary sitting at the desk outside of Saul's office.

"May I help you?" she asked.

He ignored her.

"Do you have an appointment?" she asked, standing.

"No," Van said. "But I won't take much of his time."

"I'm afraid that's impossible. He left strict instructions not to be disturbed."

Van nodded. "I see." Without saying another word he barreled through the office door, across the jewel-toned Tabriz rug to one of the leather back chairs in front of the antique desk.

The painfully thin woman charged after him. "He wouldn't listen, Mr. Devine. Would you like me to call the police?"

Saul's gaze shifted from the file on his desk to his intruder. He sat back in his seat and removed his glasses. "It's all right, Ida, I'll handle this."

The anorexic woman backed out of the office and closed the door.

"Maybe you should call the police. Detective Lowry isn't it? He seems to keep you well informed," Van said. He sat in the chair, crossed his legs, and propped his elbows on the armrests to steeple his fingers. "Though I don't think he will be of any real assistance in this instance. He hasn't been privy to all of the sordid details because of his inferior pay grade."

Van seemed to have Saul's complete attention now.

"What's this all about, Mr...?"

"The name's Elliot Vance."

Saul stood and stretched out his hand. "Nice to meet you, Mr. Vance. May I call you Elliot?"

"Not if you expect me to answer." He shook Saul's hand. "I prefer Van."

Saul sat in his tufted leather chair and adjusted his half-moon spectacles. "What can I do for you, Van?"

"I'm here as a courtesy."

"How so?"

"Jules Wolcott, the CEO of Panacealla Pharmaceuticals, has gotten himself into a hell of a mess.

Is the conglomerate your client or Jules?"

"I represent the conglomerate and as such I cannot discuss any company particulars with you."

Van reached into his pocket and dug out a one-dollar bill. "I'd like to retain your services," he said, placing the bill in front of Saul. "If you accept, I'll tell you everything I've discovered since the shooting at Boston U when I took Dr. Aliesa Atworth into my protective custody. If you don't accept, I'll say goodbye and be on my way. You'll be completely and entirely on your own when things go down tomorrow night."

Van watched Saul carefully.

Saul seemed to digest his words. "I assume you're referring to the party at the Ritz."

Van nodded and he folded his arms across his chest. "Your choice."

"Would you mind if I made a phone call to Detective Lowry?"

Van checked his watch. "If you hurry, I've got another appointment." Simone would make him pay if he kept her waiting too long.

Once Saul hung up the phone he scooped the dollar and pocketed it.

Van proceeded to tell Saul everything. Once he'd finished Saul rubbed his hands together. "What do you want me to do?"

"I need two invitations," Van said, not pausing for breath. "This isn't the type of party one can crash. Besides, I want Jules Wolcott to know we're in attendance."

"Whom are you referring to when you say we?"

"Myself and Dr. Atworth."

Saul Devine stroked his chin. Van could almost see his synapses firing inside his brain.

Saul reached into the top drawer of his desk and pulled out two filigreed cards and handed them to Van.

"Thank you."

Saul shook his head. "Now all I have to do is explain to my junior partner why I gave his tickets away."

Chapter 38

With the assassin dead, Van knew he could relax his vigil over Aliesa. But knowing something didn't always make it so. As much as he knew she would be safe with Simone, he didn't stop worrying, until he and Simone went to collect her from Armando's.

Reality had come crashing down on him when he thought he'd almost lost her this morning. When he rushed inside the church and saw the killer squeezing the life out of her, he knew how much she meant to him. He knew he didn't want to live alone any more. He wanted to be with her though the good and the bad.

He called Aliesa a cab to take her and all of his parcels back to the condo. He parked in the underground and met her at the curb to get everything to the penthouse. He went outside and found her bent over, with her head inside the cab, her derrière wriggling in the air.

He paid the cabby and collected as many of the bags as he could manage. She reached in the back and pulled out a zippered hanger bag. "I can hardly wait to see your new suit," she said.

When she faced him he felt like the luckiest man in the world. This beautiful creature chose him. Her hair shone and her skin glowed, her curves had rounded and there seemed to be more meat on her bones. Everything about this woman, everything from her brilliance to her brawn, excited him.

They walked inside the penthouse, dropped the packages and dove into each other's arms. She had his shirt off and his pants around his ankles before he'd even gotten her bra unclasped. She kissed and stroked him into hardened steel.

Perhaps their brush with death this morning spurned both of them to feel alive in the most basic of ways. She wanted and she took, as did he.

His hands were shaking as he fiddled with her pant's clasp and zipper. Success made him strip off her trousers and undies together. He lifted her, braced her back against the wall, and drove into her.

He captured her wanton cry with a searing kiss—a duel of tongues and lips. Fast and without finesse, he took her against the wall. He pounded into her like he couldn't get enough. The rush to climax came upon them mere seconds apart. The moment he felt her inner muscles tighten, he couldn't stop his floodgate from opening. Both of them panting and slick from exertion, he tipped her chin and got lost in her eyes. "I can't seem to get enough of you?"

She swallowed and took a second to catch her breath. She shook her head. "Fine by me."

"Good," he said, already on the move. Still nestled inside of her, he carried her into the primary bedroom. "Because I fully intend to keep you in bed until we need to get ready for the party tomorrow night."

She smiled at him. "Dedication like yours is hard to find, let alone maintain."

"Well, then, I guess I've got my work cut out for me."

She pulled him onto the bed beside her. She straddled him. "I do love a challenge."

At five o'clock the following afternoon, Van let Aliesa use her bathroom and he used the one in the other room.

He showered and shaved. He unzipped his new Italian suit and spread it out on the bed. He pulled out his shirt and cursed Simone. He didn't know how Simone had managed to switch the white shirt he'd selected with her favorite.

He slipped on the pants, the purple shirt, and tied his eggplant tie when he heard his cell phone buzzing. He raced down the hall and into the bedroom, plucked his phone from the nightside table and answered.

"What took you so long?" Simone asked. "On second thought, I don't want to know."

Van chuckled. "Nice job on switching the shirt."

"You're welcome. The purple really pops," Simone said. "I just wanted to call with your itinerary. A corsage will be delivered within the hour. The florist truck will ring when they arrive. And the limo will come to collect you two at six-thirty."

Van smiled. "Thanks, Simone. I owe you."

"I didn't do it for you, blockhead. I did it for Aliesa. If you screw this up, you'll have to answer to me." On that warning, she disconnected.

A moment later, his phone rang again.

The florist. He grabbed his wallet and met the deliveryman at the door. He raced back upstairs, grabbed his jacket and knocked on the primary bedroom door. "Are you almost ready?" he asked. Since she didn't answer him, he knocked again, this time louder.

She opened the door.

The sight of her took his breath. The slip of a dress accentuated her every curve. The shimmering black fabric plunged between her breasts, hugged her waist and hips before plummeting to her ankles. She wore open-toed black patent pumps, her toenails and fingernails were polished with clear lacquer, and Evelyne's compass necklace dangled around her neck.

"You're very handsome," she said.

"I really like the suit." He handed her the corsage—a single exotic orchid. The purple flower matched the color of his tie and the hankie protruding from his breast pocket.

Aliesa removed the corsage from its container. "I feel like a teenager on the way to her first prom."

Van pinned the flower to her dress. "Your chariot awaits."

Van still didn't understand how her serum had altered her. It seemed she only had one thing left to do. When Wolcott was apprehended for his crimes she'd start her research again and make the world a better place.

They exited the condo, took the elevator to street level and walked outside to the curb. Aliesa began scanning the traffic for a cab when a limousine arrived.

Van reached out and opened the door. "After you," he said.

A limousine. She closed her gaping mouth and gently lifted the hem of her dress as she scooted across the seat. Van slid in behind her.

And, just like Cinderella, they were whisked through the evening traffic to the ball.

At the Ritz, the doorman assisted them out of the car and as quickly as the limousine appeared, it sped out of sight.

They walked through the elegant foyer, past the reception desk, following the signs for the PPI Banquet.

A crowd bubbled in and around the ballroom. Couples mingled in their finery, sipping champagne, served to them by the black-tied waiters. "There must be over five hundred people here," she said.

Aliesa glimpsed inside. "Things have really changed since the last time I was here. My dad and I attended a literacy fundraiser way back when. I remember the walls of the ballroom being buttercup-yellow with huge breathtaking crystal chandeliers." She admired the smaller, modern starbursts above.

At least the view outside hadn't changed. The floor-to-ceiling windows showcased a romantic view of Boston Common. Round tables topped with taupe and white linens dotted the room. The head table sat a dozen people separated at the center by a speaker's podium.

"Shall we go inside?" Van asked.

Aliesa's palms began to sweat when she saw invitations being flashed at the door to the ballroom. What had they been thinking trying to crash a party like this? She should have known better. Both she and Van would be escorted to the curb. Instead, Van reached into his breast pocket and presented two embossed invitations to the woman at the door.

"Thank you," she said and consulted her list. "Please be seated at table number thirty-eight."

While Van led her away through the throng of people, she tapped him on the shoulder and whispered. "How did you get those?"

He smiled and winked. "I have my ways."

She drew a deep breath and finally relaxed. At least they weren't going to be discovered and thrown out. They cut through the rounds glancing at the numbers protruding from the flower centerpieces. Based on their number, their table had to be located somewhere in the back. When they came upon the correct one, there were four people already seated. Van led her to one of the open seats where she noticed the man who would be sitting right beside her.

Van pulled out her chair and the man turned toward them. His eyes widened and his mouth gaped.

If she could have crawled into a hole in this particular moment she would have. The last time she'd been confronted by this man she'd been working undercover with Van, wearing a pair of *Spit and Polish* coveralls, pushing a vacuum.

Van stuck out his hand. "I'm Elliot Vance and this is Dr. Aliesa Atworth."

Caught off guard, the man extended his hand. "I'm Saul Devine and this is my wife, Elizabeth."

Aliesa felt Saul's glare boring into her.

She had to do something to get Saul to stop staring at her.

"Excuse me, but are you the same Dr. Atworth from

the paper the other day?" Elizabeth asked. "Something about a murder at BU?"

"Yes. The woman was my assistant," Aliesa said.

"How awful." Elizabeth shook her head and turned to face her husband. "What's wrong, dear?"

"I recognized Dr. Atworth." The way Saul eyeballed her, she hoped he didn't remember her from the other night. He cleared his throat. "Must have been from the newspaper coverage."

"Maybe you recognize me from Bayfront Towers, Mr. Devine," she said. "I'm part of the consortium which owns the building."

"Ah, yes," Saul said, his brow smoothed and he nodded. "Forgive me for being so personal, but do you have a twin sister? There's a woman on my cleaning staff who is the spitting image of you."

Aliesa smiled. "No. I'm sorry; I'm an only child. But you know what they say, everyone has a twin out there somewhere." She turned toward the other couple at the table and exchanged introductions. The gentleman worked for the Department of Agriculture. "If I decide to continue with my research, I'll need to apply for transfer agreement. Whom should I contact?"

"I'm not certain off hand, but if you give me your email address I can get you the name of someone to contact."

"Perfect," she said. Despite the question being a diversionary tactic, she really did need to apply for a transfer agreement. She opened her clutch and rooted through the contents. "I don't have a pen."

"Here." The man dug his business card out of his pocket and handed it to her. "Shoot me an email and I'll get back to you."

A tapping on the microphone at the head table drew everyone's attention. "Good evening, ladies and gentlemen. My name is Jules Wolcott, PPI's CEO. Welcome to our annual awards ceremony."

Applause echoed throughout the room.

Aliesa and Van turned their seats around so they could see the presentations and speeches. There were awards for excellence in research, development, marketing, and sales. The entire program lasted a little over an hour.

Once the business had been seen to, waiters began bringing out the first of several courses: soup, salad, salmon or roast beef. Once the plates were cleared, Jules Wolcott approached the podium. "Coffee, tea, and desserts will be served in the reception hall. The orchestra is going to set up and the tables will be rearranged to allow for dancing. Enjoy."

Chairs scraped. People stood and stretched and filtered out through the three sets of open doors.

Van and Aliesa followed the crowd. People gathered haphazardly through the hall. They sipped coffee, mingled and chose from a selection of sweets on the center table.

Aliesa spotted Saul and Elizabeth Devine talking with Jules Wolcott near the chocolate fountain and she nudged Van. Immediately, he steered her toward them.

The conversation ceased as they approached. Van plowed ahead. "Jules Wolcott," he said, reaching out his hand. "Great party. Thanks for inviting us."

Wolcott angled his head and confusion wrinkled his brow. "I'm sorry, you have me at a disadvantage. You are?"

Aliesa wondered how this man didn't know who they

were.

"Terribly sorry. I'm Elliot Vance and this is Dr. Aliesa Atworth."

The man deserved an Oscar. He didn't even blink when Van introduced her.

"This is a closed party, by invitation only. How did you manage to acquire an invitation?"

Saul Devine shook his head and raised his hand. "He got it from me."

Wolcott's head spun toward Devine.

"Don't be angry with Saul. He had the company's best interests at heart. I represent a consortium considering investing in PPI. I'm here making an assessment." Van smiled and turned toward Saul. "I hope you managed to smooth things over with your junior partner."

"Didn't have to," Saul said. "His wife went into labor this afternoon. No word yet. He's going to text when she gives birth. It's their first child."

"All's well, then," Van said.

Aliesa watched Wolcott. He didn't seem in the best mood.

"I certainly hope you like what you see, Mr. Vance. PPI is a blue-chip investment all the way," Wolcott said. A uniformed attendant from the Ritz approached him and spoke close to his ear. "Excuse me," Wolcott said. "I have an issue to attend to."

Elizabeth leaned close to Aliesa. "Do you know where the powder room is?"

Oddly enough, she'd noticed it on her way into the hotel. "Yes," she said. "Follow me."

As soon as the women trotted off, Saul turned toward Van. "Consortium? You bugged my office. No other way you could know about Detective Lowry."

"You are no longer a suspect and I will vouch for you when this goes down. Honest people have nothing to hide."

"Want to tell me what is going to happen?" Saul asked.

"You'll find out soon enough."

"Doesn't sound like something to look forward to."

The phone in Van's pocket vibrated. Elizabeth and Aliesa were headed this way. They wormed their way through the crowd. After a momentary pause, the phone buzzed again.

Van placed his hand on Aliesa's arm. "How about we go for a stroll in Boston Common and wait for the orchestra to set up?"

She smiled at him and his stomach did a little flip. Her eyes were heavy lidded, almost sultry and he was instantly reminded of their lovemaking this afternoon. He put her hand in his and they walked outside into the opalescent light of the moon. He led her across the street and into the park. With his hand placed on the small of her back, he felt her shiver. "Are you cold?"

"A bit."

He shrugged out of his jacket and slipped it over her shoulders.

The phone in his pocket vibrated again.

Van led her to the closest bench and they sat. He

dug the assassin's phone out of his pocket and pressed buttons to retrieve three text messages. He scanned them. "It seems our host is a little stressed out. Want to hear what he has to say?"

Aliesa pressed closer and checked the handset.

"He's sent three messages in rapid succession. This is the first one. *What the fuck? Atworth and Vance are here.*"

Aliesa hugged Van's jacket close. "I get the impression he doesn't like the fact we're crashing his party."

"It gets better. Here's the next. *Get the job done or you can kiss the final installment, you were supposed to collect tonight, goodbye.*"

"Job? Are you serious? Wolcott talks like he hired someone to work the counter at Dunkin' Donuts. Can't wait to hear the last one."

"It's not much better. *I want proof before I turn over another cent.*"

"What does that mean? He wants a finger? A pound of flesh? What?"

"I'm not sure," Van said. "But based on these texts, I think Wolcott intended to hook up with the killer later tonight to pay his contract outright."

"So what do we do now?" Aliesa asked.

"We wait for Wolcott to take matters into his own hands."

Chapter 39

Van placed Aliesa's hand in his and they strolled along the path around the pond. He figured Wolcott's patience had run thin and it wouldn't take much to get a reaction out of Wolcott.

"And how do we get Wolcott to reach for the gauntlet?" Aliesa asked.

Van pulled out the phone with the assassin's SIM card and replied to Wolcott's text. The killer would say something cocky. Aliesa watched him type. *Invite Atworth and Vance to your room later and you can watch.* He pushed send.

"How do you even know he's staying here?" Aliesa asked.

"I don't, but I'd put money on it." He pocketed the phone. "Now we wait for him to reply. He's not going to like the idea so it shouldn't take him too long."

Van leaned in and kissed Aliesa gently on the lips. "You worry too much."

The phone vibrated in his pocket. "See?"

He dug out the cell and read the message. *"I don't want to be implicated."*

Van texted three words. *You won't be.*

Again, Van dropped the handset in his pocket and

stood. He extended his hand to Aliesa. "Shall we?"

They crossed the street and headed back inside the Ritz to the main ballroom. As Wolcott promised, the tables had been arranged in the shape of a horseshoe around a dance floor. An orchestra sat in place of the head table and the toe tapping sounds of Glenn Miller filled the room.

"Let's dance," Van said.

"What? No," she said, shaking her head. "I don't know how."

"C'mon. I'll show you. Just follow my lead," Van said, not taking no for an answer. He led her out onto the floor and twirled her under his arm and pulled her close. He circled her waist and whispered in her ear. "Have I told you how beautiful you are?"

She faced him and smiled.

They swayed to the music, contented to hold one another.

At nearly eleven o'clock, Aliesa insisted she sit the next song out and asked Van to get her a glass of water. When he returned, Wolcott had cornered Aliesa.

"There you are," Wolcott said. "I was asking Aliesa if she'd like to come to my suite to discuss her work—strictly business of course. I took the liberty of making inquiries and the good doctor's project at BU sounds like something Panacealla might be interested in funding."

Van eyed his watch, then at Aliesa. "I don't know. It's getting kind of late."

"Things are winding down," Wolcott said. "It won't take long. We can go upstairs now if you'd like. I've already signed off with the staff. One nightcap. No pressure."

Van turned to Aliesa. When he saw her face, he knew she really didn't want to go. After her ordeal yesterday, he really didn't blame her.

"There's no harm in listening to your proposal," she said.

Atta girl.

"Follow me," Wolcott said. They walked to the elevator. Wolcott said his goodbyes to several people who were leaving the party. The elevator doors slid open, and they got onboard. Passengers got off on the fifth and seventh floor, but Van, Aliesa, and Wolcott rode the elevator right to the top.

Wolcott led them to the presidential suite. Van wasn't surprised. Wolcott had a high opinion of himself and this confirmed it.

"This suite is one of the perks of having our year-end party at the Ritz," Wolcott said. His brittle smile appeared as if it might crack. He sailed across the room and lifted the phone. "Please send champagne and strawberries."

Van surveyed the room. Soft taupe walls and a sand-colored ultra suede couch stretched in front of the fireplace. A panoramic view of Boston glittered in the moonlight and spanned the length of the living room.

"Is this a real masterpiece?" Aliesa asked. She stood in the alcove in the front hall staring at the art on the wall.

"All of the paintings at the Ritz are original oils. The collection is worth millions," Wolcott said. He pulled a cell phone out of his pocket. "Would you excuse me for a moment? I have to take this call." Wolcott walked into the bedroom and closed the door behind him.

The assassin's phone in Van's pocket vibrated. He checked the screen. *Atworth and Vance are in the penthouse suite.*

Someone rapped on the door behind him. He turned, spied through the peephole, and opened the door.

An attendant wheeled in a bottle of chilled champagne and an enormous silver dish of plump strawberries. Half a dozen crystal flutes tinkled as the cart lumbered across the Berber carpet. Wolcott came bounding out of the bedroom, placed a bill in the attendant's hand and left.

"Please sit and make yourself comfortable." Wolcott gestured to the sofa and he placed the strawberries on the coffee table.

He waited until Aliesa and Van sat. "Dr. Atworth," he began. "Would you mind telling me about your fountain of youth research?"

Van nearly barked a laugh. He nodded and Aliesa turned her attention to Wolcott and began with the basics. "The most laborious task is harvesting the stem cells. The work is painstakingly slow."

"Why not use placental stem cells?" Wolcott asked.

"Largely due to the ethical debate and availability. Besides using stem cells from the donor speeds up the process. These cells have what I refer to as 'residual memory.'"

Van listened to Wolcott and Aliesa engaged in their scientific techno-babble. Then he remembered something Aliesa had told him. Grayson had been the only one who ever referred to her serum as the fountain of youth.

Fuck me.

The answer had been staring him in the face all along.

Panacealla had been funding Aliesa's research so they could keep an eye on her work. When Wolcott discovered she was on the brink of discovering something big, big enough to keep cells younger and healthier longer, he had to do something about it.

He watched Wolcott who fiddled with the foil and wire cage on the bottle of champagne. The cork from the champagne bottle exploded and slapped the ceiling of the suite. Sparkling wine frothed from the neck of the bottle and spilled down the sides.

A strange cold crept over Aliesa again. Similar to the sensations which occurred when she happened across Jackson Mercante. Her arms and legs were so numb her blood could have carried ice crystals. An awareness of this creepy man's thoughts assailed her.

Had her serum altered her genetically at the cellular level? Had her DNA strand sequences made her sensitive to mind reading?

Never before had she had she been receptive to this type of insight. She'd been brilliant—able to process and interpret information at a rapid rate, but she'd never been so adept at precognition. She'd put her experience with Mercante out of her mind, but tonight she knew she could no longer deny the fact she had developed an anomaly—an all-seeing eye.

While Aliesa sat in the presidential suite and explained her research to Wolcott, she sensed waves of hatred emanating from him. Hatred aimed directly at her. This man wanted her dead.

Van frowned at her. "Are you cold?"

She nodded.

He slipped off his jacket and handed it to her. She wrapped it around her shoulders and snuggled into the warmth.

"What did you mean when you said cells have residual memory?" Wolcott asked. He jumped and went over to the bar where he could pour their drinks. He kept eyeing the door of the suite and checking his watch, waiting for his hired assassin to arrive, no doubt.

Vocalization often helped Aliesa put things into perspective. Maybe it would keep her calm. "The human cell is a lot like an automobile. Each and every car on the road has a million different available options. And although some auto parts are interchangeable, when it comes to repairs or upgrades it's best to stick with the same make and model. Often it ensures greater success. Am I making sense?"

Again, Wolcott checked his watch and eyeballed the door.

"Are you expecting someone?" Van asked.

"No." Wolcott shook his head. "Why do you ask?" He filled each crystal flute with champagne. He carried two over to the coffee table and set them in front of Aliesa and Van. Then he collected his and sat in the chair.

"You keep glancing at the door," Van said.

"Sorry," Wolcott said. "It's a nervous habit."

"I'd like you to explain something to me," Van said.

"I'll certainly try."

"Why did you kill Everet, Mercante, and the junkie at

Medevac?"

Wolcott nearly choked on the drink he'd been sipping. "I didn't kill anyone."

"Not directly, no. You contracted the hits but that doesn't make you any less responsible."

Wolcott drank the contents of his glass and stood to refill it.

Then the weirdest thing happened. Aliesa began hearing Wolcott's interior monologue—as if she'd stealthily slipped inside this man's head and could hear his thoughts.

If this fucking bitch of yours hadn't made the discovery of the century, I wouldn't have had to. Come on now, be a good girl and drink your champagne, then there'll be only one person left to eliminate.

She gasped and turned toward him. "Me? What did my discovery have to do with any of this?"

Wolcott's eyes widened and he shook his head.

Van continued. "You and Hernandez had quite the operation going. He took all the risks and you reaped all the rewards. Then, along came Aliesa. Her project was going to cost you millions."

"My investment was nowhere near a million dollars."

"You were one of my backers?" Aliesa asked.

"I'm not talking about the investment capitol for her research," Van said. "I'm talking about the lost revenue to Panacealla if Aliesa's anti-aging serum ever hit the market. Every single drug you manufacture would be impacted—from vitamins to pain-killers to cancer treatments—you'd lose millions."

"How very astute." *It won't do you any good, both of you will be dead before the night's over. Drink darling, and say good night.*

"It's not over yet." Aliesa faced Wolcott. His eyes widened and he tipped his head sideways. She wanted to tell him she could hear his thoughts but it would spoil her fun. "You mean to tell me you killed everyone who had any knowledge of me and my work, no matter how far removed?"

"It seemed like the only course of action to keep everything under wraps. It kept you two running around in circles. When I considered the losses the company would incur from Aliesa's work, I knew I had to sacrifice Hernandez's cocaine operation for the greater good. His anti-leukemic has already been contracted with an associate of his."

Aliesa lifted her crystal glass and brought it to her lips. *That's right. Drink every drop.*

She pulled the flute away from her mouth. "I'm really thirsty, may I have another?" she asked.

"But you haven't finished the first one," Wolcott said.

"I'm going to drink it this very minute." She tipped the contents against tightly closed lips.

Wolcott sprang to his feet and turned to collect the bottle from the cart.

In one fluid motion, Aliesa leaned across the table, placed her full glass beside Wolcott's, snatched his and sat back guzzling the contents. She finished as Wolcott returned to refill it.

Van turned back and forth between Wolcott and Aliesa with an odd expression on his face. She gave him a reassuring smile and nod to let him know she hadn't lost her mind.

Wolcott poured Aliesa a second and set the bottle on

the table. He sat and smiled smugly and drank his. Again, glancing at the door.

"He's not coming," Van said.

It seemed to take a moment for the words to register. Wolcott acted sluggish. "What?" Wolcott sat back in his chair.

"The man you hired to kill Aliesa and me. He's not coming because he's dead. I killed him."

Aliesa felt his panic rise, but it quickly subsided. *Even better. I'll poison you, too, and save myself a ton of money.*

"Sorry to disappoint you," Aliesa said. "I switched glasses. Yours contained the poison, not mine."

Wolcott already appeared beyond help. He reclined in the chair, frothed at the mouth, his eyes remained fixed on Aliesa, and he labored to breathe.

You...you...fucking...bitch.

Air wheezed in and out of his lungs and he sagged. His eyes were wild.

Suddenly, he stilled and his life abruptly ended.

Van pulled out his cell phone and punched numbers.

"It's all over, Admiral," Van said, upon connection. "I need another crew. The Ritz Carlton. The presidential suite."

Van dropped his cell in his pocket, sat and put his arms around her. "A team's on its way," he said. Then he pressed his hand to her forehead. "You're freezing."

He stood and disappeared into what she guessed was the bedroom. A moment later, he returned carrying a blanket, which he swathed her in. He rubbed her arms and tucked her head under his chin.

"It's all over," he said. "Lean against me and try to

relax. I'll get you home as soon as I can. It shouldn't be too long."

She shivered against him. They waited for about twenty minutes while he crooned assuring words, and the tension in her began to abate.

Finally, justice had finally been served for Evelyne.

There was a knock at the door.

Van rose, spied through the peephole and let a team of five men inside. All of them nodded at Aliesa, but spoke only to Van. She listened as Van ran through the sequence of events leading to Wolcott's demise. They were the same crew which cleaned the crime scene after Evelyne Mathews's funeral. This one wasn't half as bad as the other. Poison left less mess than doing a swan dive off a balcony.

Aliesa's mind drifted.

It was over.

What was she going to do now?

She didn't know whether or not she even wanted to resume her research. This project of hers had caused the death and destruction of so many people. The exact opposite of what she'd ever intended.

She caught bits and pieces of the discussion on the proposed story to tell the press. Richardson, a man she surmised to be Van's boss, suggested a cover story where Wolcott died of a massive coronary. Nothing more. What was the point in exposing all of the rest? Everyone involved was dead—everyone except Aliesa.

"It's your call," Van said to the team. "I'm going to take Aliesa home and let you guys finish here. I'll file a full, detailed report in the morning."

They left the hotel and hailed a cab. In no time, they

were riding the elevator to her penthouse.

The debilitating cold she'd experienced earlier had dissipated, but she still felt weak, almost drained.

Inside, she shucked Van's jacket and handed it back to him.

Then he twirled on her.

"Want to tell me what the hell happened at the Ritz?"

Chapter 40

Van had only seen Aliesa like this on one prior occasion—the night she slipped and fell into the pool of Mercante's blood. Last time he had to place her in the shower fully clothed. He'd assumed then she'd been suffering from shock, but right now he didn't know what to think. He'd been watching her very carefully when they were still at the Ritz and he saw her switch her drink for Wolcott's. Somehow she'd known Wolcott had spiked her drink with poison.

But how?

He'd kept his questions to himself all the way back to her penthouse. As soon as they were alone he wanted answers. "I'm waiting," he said.

She skirted around him in the hall and walked into the living room straight to the wine fridge. She opened the door, reached inside and pulled out the vial of stem cell serum. At least she thought it was her stem cell serum. Little did she know it was the dummy vial Drew had supplied in case Van needed a bargaining chip.

"It's all because of this," she said. She turned around with the vial squeezed between her forefinger and thumb.

"I know. I was there when Wolcott admitted all

of the murders came about because of your serum. Remember?"

"I'm not sure I'll ever be able to forget," Aliesa said. "But that's not what I mean. This little vial of stem cells has turned me into a different person. I was nothing. Nondescript."

Van snorted. She couldn't be serious. A laugh bubbled from the pit of his stomach. "You're talking in riddles. This is the proverbial chicken and egg scenario. Nothing? If you're nothing, how did you invent a formula like this in the first place?"

She huffed, stomped into the kitchen, grabbed her purse and dumped the contents on the coffee table. She scattered items and grabbed a packaged syringe. She peeled open the sleeve, shoved the needle into the vial and evacuated the serum. "There's really only one way to illustrate my point. I have to show you."

Before Van could open his mouth and say a word, she located a vein, jammed the needle into her forearm, and pressed the plunger.

Aliesa tossed the empty syringe on the kitchen table and rubbed the injection site.

The rush of fluid heated her arm.

It tingled.

She closed her eyes and let her blood stream carry her supercharged stem cells to specific target areas. This was the "residual memory" she'd spoken to Wolcott about—a very difficult concept to explain when she barely understood it herself. Not to mention the other perks. The ones she'd only begun to recognize.

The physical changes were obvious, but these other developments were subtler and easily missed.

"What's happening?" Van asked. "If I didn't know any better, I'd say you recently swallowed a shot of the rarest whiskey."

"Oh, please," she said. "I've never drank whiskey in my entire life."

"Huh," he muttered. "You don't know what you're missing."

Aliesa rolled her head, stretched, pressed her shoulders together and thrust out her chest. She took a deep breath. She ran her hands through her hair and mussed it. Then she skimmed her fingers over her breasts and trailed even lower. She didn't know how to explain the explosion of feelings inside her. She felt hot and cold at the same time and horny as hell.

She licked her lips

Van gulped. "Suddenly I feel like I'm a chocolate dipped cone."

Aliesa grabbed his hand and dragged him into the living room where his restraint snapped because he reached out to pull her against him.

"No," she said, shoving his hands away. "This is my show and I don't want you to interfere." She loosened his tie and pulled him forward working the tails of his shirt free of his pants. Buttons ricocheted as she jerked open the flaps. Her lips plundered his chest. She licked and kissed her way to his belt buckle.

He groaned. He pressed hard and hot against her—she could feel and see the confining fabric of his pants. His breath caught when she placed her hands on his buckle and unzipped him. She shoved his pants over his buttocks and as she dipped she landed on bended knees.

"Oh, baby," he said. "You're taking me to Fantasy Island here."

Once she removed his briefs she moaned. "What do we have here?" she asked.

"You're killing me." Van grabbed his head and let his head fall backwards at the very moment she closed her mouth around him.

She didn't stop. She continued to lick and suck.

"Baby," he said between clenched teeth. "If you don't stop I'm going to cum."

She didn't stop.

He jettisoned his release.

His knees buckled and she nudged him into a sitting position on the sofa. Still on her knees she moved between his knees. She used her tongue and worked her way north.

She didn't stop.

She circled his navel with her tongue and kissed every band and ripple of his six pack. She momentarily pulled back and grabbed the hem of her dress and flung it over her head. Then she shucked her bra and straddled his lap.

To her surprise she felt him already hardening between her legs. She moved back and forth, rubbing against him, letting the pressure within her build.

Then she kissed him.

Her tongue swirled in his mouth. She loved the taste of him. All of him.

Suddenly he tugged her head back by pulling gently on her hair. He used his other hand to move the scrap of lace between her legs to gain entry and he pushed inside her.

She groaned, filling her so completely she bit her lip.

"Open your eyes and hear me," he said. "Do you really think your serum has anything to do with the chemistry plaguing us?"

She did as he asked. Then she rode him. "This isn't me. I'm the dowdy professor who is inept."

"Dowdy and inept? Have you checked the mirror recently? Inept? I'm almost ready to blow another wad."

"Me, too," she said. "Stop talking."

A few more gyrations and she reached the end of her resolve. Her womb contracted, the spasms milking and draining him for the second time—after several moments, when her breathing normalized she continued their discussion. "You watched me take the injection and change. You can't tell me you haven't seen a change in me since we first met."

"I've seen some physical changes in you. And you saw some changes in me. Simone caused those differences not your stem cells. You've become more confident and self-assured with me but familiarity is to be expected as we grow together as a couple. We need to take our time and learn everything we can about each other. Do you think it was easy bearing my soul to you about my mother and father? I'm ex-DEA and I'm related to the kingpin of the Alarcon cartel. You're the only one in the world who knows my secret." Van put his hand on her cheek. "There is one thing though."

"What's that?"

"I want to know how you knew Wolcott had poisoned your champagne."

"I know this is going to sound crazy, but I sense things—things I never did before. It has to be the result of taking the serum." Aliesa waited to see his reaction. "I knew Wolcott had spiked my champagne because I could hear his interior monologue inside my head."

He nodded. "Something similar happened with Mercante."

"You believe me?"

He kissed her forehead. "There's one thing I've learned about you—you don't know how to lie."

She wrapped her arms around him. Tears sprang to her eyes. Tears of happiness. "I guess it's all over then—as far as my work goes. I'm not sure I can continue after all the death and destruction I've caused. What about you?"

"We need to talk about us, not our damned work," he said, giving her a shake. "This isn't over. Not by a long shot." He stood. Her legs still banded around his waist and carried her into the primary bedroom and they got in bed. This time he made love to her like it was their first time all over again.

Sated and resting in each other's arms, Aliesa fidgeted and twirled his chest hair.

Van stilled her hand. "Out with it. What's bothering you?"

"What will happen if I decide not to continue with my research? Will you still want me if I go back to the way I was before taking the serum?"

"You haven't been listening to me," Van said. "The way we are together has nothing to do with your serum."

He jumped out of bed and ran into the kitchen. He opened the fridge, grabbed the jar of olives and a fork, and returned to the bedroom.

"Hungry?" she asked. "Maybe you'd like to order a pizza to go with those olives."

He twisted the jar's metal lid and sifted through the contents. Metal tines tinkled against the glass. He withdrew the fork and dropped the small glistening vial into the jar's cap.

She sat. "What the hell?"

"The injection you gave yourself a little while ago was saline. This is your last remaining dose of stem-cell serum." Van watched her eyes. "I found the vial last week and Drew had a dummy made with sterile saline."

"Why?"

"I didn't know if all of this was about your serum and I figured a decoy vial might come in handy."

"I'm confused. Do you or do you not believe my stem cell serum works?"

"Remember when you told Wolcott cells were like automobiles?"

"What does my car conversation have to do with anything?"

"Humor me."

"Okay, yes, I remember."

"I believe you're the same car you were before you began your stem-cell treatments, only better. Now you've got a few more bells and whistles."

She threw her head back, pressed her lips together, and smothered a giggle. "So what's my make and model?"

"Baby," he said. "You're a Lamborghini Countach all

the way."

She wrapped her arms around him and they fell back onto the bed laughing. She snuggled against him and his heart swelled.

"I'm curious," he said. "Can you read my thoughts?"

"Believe me, I've tried. It doesn't seem to work that way. On both occasions I connected with individuals who were experiencing an extreme emotional turmoil. Mercante had taken his last breath and Wolcott wanted me dead. Maybe I'm only sensitive to extremes. There has to be a trigger, only I'm not certain what it is."

Chapter 41

V an woke early the next morning.

He'd been duking it out with bad guys his entire life. He'd never been without a job.

Until now.

Aliesa, too.

Neither of them knew what they wanted to do with the rest of their lives. He only knew he didn't want to do it alone. Without her, nothing would make sense ever again.

They needed to take some time off to rest and reflect. Figure things out.

And he had the perfect place in mind.

He sat on the edge of the bed and slowly she woke. In her dream-like state she sprang into a sitting position. "What's wrong?" she asked, her voice thread-bare.

"Nothing's wrong," he said, placing his hand on hers. "I didn't mean to frighten you. Want to hear my idea?"

She rubbed her eyes. "What is it?"

"Why don't we go away for a little bit? Take some time to put everything in perspective to figure out our next steps."

"Sounds perfect," she said. "Any place in particular?"

"I'd like to take you home," he said. "I haven't been

there since my mom died."

"Is it far?"

"It's about a two hour drive on some of the prettiest roads you've ever seen."

"Sounds wonderful," she said. She tossed the covers and stood. "I'll jump in the shower and throw a few things into a bag."

It was almost noon before they climbed onto his motorcycle and left Boston behind, heading north along the coast. They catapulted along the winding coastal roads like a couple of dolphins racing the ocean's waves. The fiery sun burned and the surf crashed upon the shore's granite boulders shooting waterspouts into the air. They stopped a couple of times—once to grab something to eat at a diner and once to walk across kelp-covered boulders and the muck of low tide to the water's edge. A man toting a wire bucket of clams, stooped and thrusted his hand into the sand to pull another.

"It's breathtaking," Aliesa said. "How did you ever leave this place?"

Van found a smooth stone and skipped it across the water. "The only way you can truly appreciate any place is to leave it behind. It makes the homecoming all the sweeter."

"How much father is it?"

"Not much," he said. They walked back to the motorcycle and continued on their way. At the crossroad, Van geared down and turned right onto Pelican Point Lane—the road leading to the rustic house his grandfather built—a stone edifice which had withstood the Atlantic's wrath for nearly a hundred years.

Home.

The only one Van had ever known.

He'd lived in some holes during his thirty-two years, but never for very long. This house drew him like a lodestone. His childhood memories were buried here.

He swerved onto the private lane. Broken oyster shells crackled as he braked. Aliesa got off and he tipped the bike on its stand. He opened the weathered door of his father's woodworking shop. Van stood perfectly still and let his eyes adjust to the shadowed interior. The scents of cedar and motor oil reminded him of his dad. His eyes skimmed the old workbench. Metal tools dangled from pegs hammered into the wall.

"Van? Are you okay?"

An odd feeling slithered down his spine—like he'd been caught in someone's crosshairs. He scanned the shed's dark recesses. Half a dozen lobster traps floated in the rafters. A variety of wooden oars and an outboard motor clamped to a sawhorse stood in the far corner.

"Hello?" Aliesa called.

Aliesa's voice broke through his thoughts. "Sorry," he said. "Deep in thought. This was my dad's workshop. He'd putter all day long in here. He was in the Special Forces—killed in the line of duty."

"I'm sorry," Aliesa said.

"Thanks. It was over ten years ago."

"At least your dad died doing something righteous. Mine was killed for his pocket change."

Again, he visually swept the interior of the shed—everything seemed in order—nothing amiss. Saddlebags in hand he spied the lane and the surrounding scrub. Nothing. He shook off his unease, closed the shed, and they climbed the stone stairs to the house.

Lightning bugs glittered and fizzled in the shadows of the bushes some twenty feet away. A huge chestnut tree reached across the flagstone patio. Nut casings crunched as they padded to the solid oak door.

Inside the coach light, he snagged the hidden key. He twisted it in the lock and pushed open the solid panel. The corrosive sea air made the old iron hinges creak. Beyond the threshold of the gleaming maple floor, he froze when he heard scuffling sounds. He herded Aliesa behind him and crouched. The saddlebags were dropped and he put a finger to his lips.

With his back to the wall, he slithered across the front hall toward the kitchen. When he pounced he scared the crap out of a squirrel cracking nuts on the kitchen counter. The scruffy little rodent launched nearly five feet into the air and tore beneath the living room sofa.

Aliesa had trailed Van and saw the whole thing unfold. She giggled. Laughter bubbled to the surface like freshly poured soda. Soon she had tears in her eyes.

And it was contagious. Van's chuckle became an all out belly laugh. "Can't be right all the time," he said. "It's so good to hear you laugh."

"Now what do we do?" Aliesa said. "I think he's been a guest here for a while. I don't think he's going to go quietly."

Ashes dusted the floor in front of the room's massive stone fireplace. "I'm thinking the hearth might have been the squirrel's point of entry."

"It would seem so. I installed a chimney cap a few

years ago but it doesn't appear to be doing the job. Remind me to inspect it later." He walked over to the pantry and grabbed a jar of nuts. From the sofa, he Hanseled and Greteled a trail of peanuts, each one a couple of inches apart, all the way to the front door, which he left slightly ajar.

"I don't think the little fella will come out with us watching," Aliesa said.

"Let's watch from the primary bedroom." He reached for her hand.

"Let me grab the saddlebags and I'll unpack while you watch."

Aliesa collected the bags at the door and they walked across the oak tongue and groove floor into the bedroom. Van swung the door, leaving it open barely a crack to keep checking on the squirrel's progress.

She loved the cabin. She loved everything about it. From the secluded location, the worn floor boards beneath her feet and the timber walls.

A large king-sized bed practically filled the entire room. Opposite was a long dresser. She placed the saddlebags on top of the bed and opened them. She'd brought all the clothes Simone helped her pick out, a sweater, warm pants and her mom's and dad's keepsakes. It took her all of a few minutes put things away in drawers. The task completed, she went over and stood beside Van behind the nearly closed door.

"This feels a lot like déjà vu. You know, the both of us

standing behind a door, peeking out to see if the coast is clear."

He turned toward her. "If you went to take a shower, I could haul you in the closet."

"Sounds like fun," she said, winking. She stood on tip-toes and kissed him.

"On second thought, let's skip the shower. No point wasting well water if we don't have to." He dipped his head and kissed her. He lifted her and carried her over to the bed.

They were a frenzy of arms, flinging shirts, and pitching pants in a rush to get naked. They fell into a rapid rhythm to reach completion.

It seemed the squirrel had found the nut trail and vamoosed.

Over the next few days they got to know each other's idiosyncrasies, likes and dislikes. Aliesa, a city girl since birth, she'd been introduced to fishing, canoeing, and, most recently, cooking eggs.

Van went to take a shower and Aliesa cracked a couple of eggs into a pan as soon as she heard the water stop. She loaded the toaster with bread and poured orange juice when she heard something ringing.

Her phone.

The last phone call she had was from Evelyne's mom, asking her to speak at the funeral. She'd darted into the primary bedroom and answered it.

"Dr. Atworth?" said a timorous male voice. "I was about to leave a message."

"Who is this?" Aliesa asked.

"It's David Boyle," he said.

The President of Boston U. Aliesa had met him on

several occasions when she'd been fundraising.

"I wanted to take a moment to assure you security here at the university has been increased. We've taken many steps to assure there will be no more vandalism. Evelyne Mathews's death was a tragedy and a terrible waste—murdered by someone searching for narcotics. We've created a bursary in her memory. I'm so sorry for your loss. Mrs. Mathews told me you two were very close."

Aliesa thought about the cover story which had been fabricated to keep her stem-cell serum out of the spotlight. "We were like sisters," she said.

"I hope I'm not intruding, but I really do need to know what your plans are for the upcoming term."

"I've decided not to return to the university. I'm sorry, but I'm not able to come back right now."

"You've had a terrible shock. I understand your reluctance, but maybe you'll feel differently in a few months. I'd be happy to arrange a sabbatical leave."

Aliesa could smell something burning. Then the smoke alarm wailed.

"That's fine," she said. "Sorry to cut you off but I've got to go."

She ran back to the kitchen where she saw Van fanning smoke toward the open front door. Two blackened squares smoldered in the toaster, as did the eggs in the pan.

"Ooooops," she said.

He turned and saw the cell phone in her hand. "Everything all right?"

She placed the phone on the kitchen counter. "The university called. I told the president I wouldn't be back.

He suggested I go on sabbatical."

"Do you think you'll be able to walk away from your work cold turkey?" Van asked. He pulled out the garbage and dumped the charred remnants.

"I could ask you the same question," Aliesa said. "Right now, all I care about is being with you."

Van circled the counter. He wrapped his arms around her and gave her a hug. "Grab your coat. Lets go out for a motorcycle ride. See some of the sights around here. Maybe visit the town hall."

Chapter 42

V an had been giving the idea of marrying Aliesa a lot of thought. He wasn't getting any younger and the time had come for him to sprout some roots.

If she'd have him.

He pulled in front of the town's municipal buildings and they got off the motorcycle in the quaint little town of Cuttlefish Cove.

She pulled off her helmet. "What do you need at the municipal offices?"

"I need a license."

"Oh," she said.

He turned toward her. "Will you marry me?"

"What? Seriously?"

He nodded. "Once we get the license you'll have ninety days to change your mind."

"But I didn't bring any identification," she said.

Van hung his helmet on the handlebars. He dug her wallet out of his saddlebag. "I had to do some checking to make sure the clerk would be in today. I brought your wallet along on the chance you said yes."

"Yes," Aliesa said. "I'll marry you."

Van picked her up and spun her around.

"Not today, though. I'd like to get a new dress, if it's all right with you. Maybe we could ask Simone and Drew to join us. Is there anyone you'd like to ask?"

"One person. The admiral. I saved his ass a few years ago and he's had my back ever since."

They went inside the office, paid the clerk forty dollars and got their marriage license. They photocopied the clerk's upcoming work schedule so they could make sure they planned the wedding on an appropriate day. Then they went to Delilah's, a small restaurant on the outskirts of town and ate brunch, to replace the one Aliesa had burned. It was mid-afternoon by the time they headed back to the home on Pelican Point.

Van pulled the bike into the shed. They climbed the stairs holding hands to the door and stopped when they saw it standing ajar.

"Guess we can't blame it on the squirrel," Aliesa whispered.

Van dragged her behind him and they pressed against the side of the side of the house. "You stay here."

"Not a chance. We do this together or not at all."

He gritted his teeth realizing it would be futile arguing with her. When he pushed open the door he saw a trail of nuts. What the hell? He could hear the crunch of cracking shells. They followed the trail down the hall and when he stepped into the kitchen the squirrel on the counter jettisoned off the counter and dove toward the couch, only to change directions when he landed, he took a wide berth around Van and Aliesa, streaking out through the open door.

"Well done," a deep voice boomed.

Van strode over to the couch where a large man with

a tangle of thick white hair stood. They shook hands.

Van smiled. "How the hell did you get here?"

"By boat," he said, his lips curling into a smile. He leaned around Van. "You must be Aliesa. I'm Admiral Morningside."

Van walked over to the picture window and spotted a cabin cruiser tied to the dock.

Aliesa walked over and shook the man's hand. "Nice to finally meet you."

"Likewise," the admiral said.

"Is there some squirrel removal book I should read?" Aliesa asked. "Both of you laid a trail of nuts."

"I taught him everything he knows," the admiral said.

"Don't believe a word he says," Van said. "I told him about our furry friend. He needed to hear our side of what happened." Van walked over to the shelf in the dining room which held a selection of a half dozen bottles of liquor. He grabbed the bourbon and three glasses and returned to the great room. He splashed an inch or so in each glass and passed them around.

"I came to discuss it in person," the admiral said.

"Thanks for giving us some time to put everything into perspective." Van put his arm around Aliesa and he pulled her close.

"Have you?" the admiral asked.

"As much as possible," Van said. Aliesa nodded.

"Have you figured out what you want to do next?" the admiral prodded.

Van knew the admiral well enough to know he came here for a reason.

Aliesa cleared her throat. "I've taken a leave of absence from the university."

"I proposed to Aliesa this morning and she said yes."

"Congratulations," the admiral said. "Wonderful news."

Van reached out and squeezed Aliesa's hand. "We'd like you to come to the ceremony as soon as we nail down all of the details."

"It won't be anything elaborate," Aliesa said. "There will only be a handful of people."

"It would be my pleasure," the admiral said. He sat back on the sofa and crossed his arms. "I have a proposition for the two of you if you're interested."

"I knew it," Van said. "You rarely make personal appearances unless you want something. What kind of proposition?"

"It's much easier to argue a case in person than over the phone or by text."

Aliesa went to stand. "Would you like some privacy?"

Van kept her beside him. "No. We're a team. You have as much right to listen and offer your opinions as I do." He kissed her hand. He faced the admiral. "Go on."

The highs and lows of this day made her head spin—BU, the marriage license, and now Van's job offer. She held her breath.

She loved Van with all her heart, but she wondered if she would be able to deal with him putting his life in danger on a daily basis. But her motives were selfish. And she knew Van would never be happy working a nine-to-five job.

"I've got clearance to begin working on a brand new Department of Defense Program, one which is top secret and way above most security clearances."

"In D.C.?" Van asked.

"No. As a matter of fact, the facility is here in Maine. Not far from here. In Kittery."

"Kittery?" Van said. "I've been there a couple of times. The Portsmouth Naval Base is located just across the Piscataqua River."

"How far away is it?" Aliesa asked.

"About forty minutes," Van said. "Would I be required to live on the base?"

"Not if you didn't want to."

"I'm still listening," Van said. "How about a breakdown of my responsibilities?"

The admiral drained his glass of whiskey and placed it on the coffee table.

Van added another inch of amber liquid to his glass.

"You'd enlist candidates. All of them will have to undergo a series of physical and emotional tests to see if they will actually be suited for the program. Then there will be the practical applications. There will be rigorous training, all under your strict supervision."

Aliesa had been holding her breath. She couldn't tell if he was interested or not.

The admiral turned to her. "What do you think, Aliesa?"

"I'm not the one you have to convince," she said.

"Not true," the admiral said. "You are as involved in this thing, as I am."

"I'm sorry?" Aliesa narrowed her eyes. "I'm not following."

"The moment Van's investigation drew to a close, I had to perform due diligence and write a comprehensive report detailing the particulars of this case, which includes seven deaths, to my superiors. Grayson Everet shared a ton of correspondence from you with Jules Wolcott." The admiral swirled his glass of whiskey. "Wolcott didn't want your research to ever see the light of day, but the President of the United States and I have a different idea."

The president? She faced Van. "Did you know anything about this?"

The admiral raised his hand. "No. No one does. No one will ever know, even if you accept my proposal."

"Two proposals in one day. Aren't I the lucky one?" Aliesa held the glass of bourbon between both hands. "I'm not sure I want to continue my work. Seven people lost their lives because of me."

"You didn't kill those people," Van said. "Wolcott was a greedy bastard. It was all about profit and loss."

Aliesa took a sip of bourbon. The liquid burned clean to her stomach. "He put money ahead of people's lives. My goal has always been to improve the human condition—not destroy it."

"Then you'd be on the same page as the Department of Defense. Based on what I've read, your stem cell serum would create an elite fighting force to boost national security. Give certain men and woman highly specialized skill sets—superior strength, intelligence, advanced sight or hearing."

"You're asking me to create a bunch of six-million-dollar men and women?" Aliesa set her glass on the table. "I won't do it. It's unethical. There could be catastrophic side effects." The little voice inside her head laughed because she'd already used herself as a lab rat.

"That's where Van comes in. All of the candidates must meet a certain criteria. They need to have nothing to lose and everything to gain. Most will have suffered an injury in the field and have some sort of impairment. All will have to sign a waiver. Most importantly, I'm not talking hundreds of people here. It will be a select few. And you will have complete and utter control. No one will tell you what to do or how to proceed. You will have the ultimate say."

"I don't know," Aliesa said.

"I didn't come here today for an answer. I want you to take your time. Discuss it with Van. You've got a wedding to organize. But I'd really appreciate it if you toured the research facility in Kittery. See if it meets your standards."

Chapter 43

Wedding arrangements ate the next two weeks.

Aliesa called Simone and they made plans to meet in Boston to go shopping.

While she spent the day with Simone, Van went to her condo and met with a realtor highly recommended by Saul Devine. Aliesa decided to lease the condo for a year or so until she and Van figured things out.

The admiral, Drew, and Simone agreed to be present when they tied the knot in the municipal offices of Cuttlefish Cove, and Aliesa found a caterer willing to put on a sit-down meal at the house on Pelican Point.

Everything went as planned on their wedding day. Everyone met at the house and a limousine arrived to take all of them to the municipal office.

The admiral stood up for Van, and Simone was Aliea's maid of honor while Drew recorded the nuptials with his latest surveillance camera. On route back to the house the admiral got everyone's attention and made an announcement. "I've asked the driver to take a slight detour."

"But the caterer is expecting us back within the hour," Aliesa said.

"This won't take long. We'll be back in plenty of time.

It's my wedding present to you and Van."

In no time they pulled into the parking lot of a brick building with a gold embossed sign on the front; TFOY Research.

"Is this Kittery?" Van asked.

"Yes," the admiral said. "This is The Fountain of Youth Research facility I told you about."

The fountain of youth. Grayson had coined the phrase. And he'd obviously passed it along to Wolcott. She chuckled. "I never once called it that."

"You didn't?" the admiral asked.

"Nope."

"Would you like to see inside?"

Aliesa watched Van who returned the gesture. "Don't ask me."

"No harm in checking it out."

All of them climbed from the limo and went inside. A man named Percy French gave them the grand tour.

They walked the halls of the building. Floors gleamed. There were two air locked doors to gain access into the lab area.

All of her equipment, equipment she requested of Grayson and never received funding for, gleamed on the counters. It was a scientist's Eldorado. She couldn't keep the smile from her face. She walked from station to station beaming like the sun.

"I think she likes it," Van said to the admiral.

True to his word, they arrived back at the house on Pelican Point right on time.

As much as possible, Aliesa put the research facility out of her head and enjoyed the rest of their day. They sipped champagne cocktails and ate a delicious meal.

With the day drawing to a close, Simone and Drew left to return to Boston. When the admiral rose to leave, Aliesa stood, too. "I need a transfer agreement to procure the most effective cytokine."

"Does this mean you accept my proposal?" The admiral asked.

She turned to face Van. "What do you say?"

"When do we start?" Van asked.

"Aren't you going on a honeymoon?" The admiral asked.

"We've been on one for the past three weeks," Van said, winking.

Aliesa blushed.

"Both of you need to go and fill out some forms at the navy base and report for a medical examination. Once it's completed you can get started whenever you like."

A couple weeks after they were married, Aliesa and Van stopped and collected some groceries on their way home from TFOY Research facility. They'd fallen into a routine outfitting their offices and laboratory. The admiral had greased the wheels of her transfer agreement and her first shipment of fruit would be delivered in a week. She'd begun harvesting and freezing stem cells from their very first member of what she referred to lovingly as her Bio-Ergonomic Enhancement family—The BEE Team. While Van got into the shower, her phone rang as she put away the groceries.

"Hello," she said.

"Dr. Atworth?" a female voice said.

"That's me," she said.

"This is Dr. Oronto's receptionist from the naval base." She remembered the friendly redhead who sat behind the desk in the doctor's office. Both her and Van had a complete physical exam and the standard blood panels—standard operating procedure when accepting a position with the US government.

"What can I do for you?"

"Dr. Oronto would like you to return to the office to have some follow up tests."

The small hairs on the back of Aliesa's neck bristled. She put her hand across the handset and listened to make sure she could still hear the water running in the shower. "Is there a problem?"

"During your last visit you signed some paperwork allowing your previous records to be sent from your GP in Boston. Dr. Oronto has questions about a few things. Are you free tomorrow afternoon, say around two o'clock?"

Mentally, Aliesa went through her calendar for the following day. She'd set some time aside to do some paperwork in the afternoon. "I'll see you then."

Aliesa disconnected. Her mind clicked into overdrive. The admiral wanted to speed up the work and the scientist in her want to take it slower. Conducting human trials when her serum hadn't been thoroughly tested went against everything she tried for years to uphold. She'd taken personal risks and she still hadn't had a chance to thoroughly document the results of her own treatment. She really needed to record everything before she injected any serum into these new candidates. Candidates materialized without really knowing the inherent risks.

Suddenly two strong arms encircled her waist.

She leaned back.

"Mmmm. Miss me?" she said.

Van pulled her against him and nuzzled her neck. She could feel him pressing hard against her. In the recesses of her mind she could hear his voice telling her exactly what he wanted to do to her without him even uttering a word.

"Let me finish putting these groceries away," she said.

"All right." He released her and flung off his towel. He stood before her gloriously naked. "First one into the bedroom gets to be on top." He darted into the bathroom.

She grabbed the remainder of the groceries, whipped them into the fridge, and ran for the bedroom, dropping items of clothing along the way.

She never expected to be so happy—living the dream with the man who'd been instrumental in helping her reach her goals. She loved her work, had a husband who loved her, and more mind-blowing sex than any woman deserved. Every once in a while she thought about the lives who had been sacrificed, but thankfully those reservations were few and far between.

She couldn't wait to wake every morning and get home at night. Most nights, they began their evening by making love. They lounged in bed, deciding what to make for dinner, and then they'd talk or read. They'd discuss and hone their dreams. When the moon took residence in the sky they'd fall asleep nestled in each other's arms.

At around two in the morning, she tossed and turned, apprehension over her appointment with the doctor the following day had taken root. Careful not to disturb Van, she padded out into the great room.

A bad case of *what ifs* assailed her. *What if* she'd miscalculated with the amount of cytokine and cell mutation resulted? Cell mutation could present with an acute inflammatory response or, the worst-case scenario, cancer. Her mother and her mother's mother had died from breast cancer so the likelihood of her having the predisposition were high. She started with her right breast and palpitated around the areola and the surrounding tissue for anomalies. Then she did the very same with her left breast. Nothing. All felt normal.

What if the cellular improvements had caused tissue to die prematurely? Maybe the cells enhanced due to her injections had literally sped through their life cycle and although they had affected an enhancement, the body couldn't support or sustain these supercharged cells. If the body's cells had a faster life cycle, her tissues might already be in a geriatric state. She could be prematurely aging. She rushed into the bathroom and stood in front of the mirror. She had a few more wrinkles around her eyes, but nothing jumped out at her. Her gums and teeth were pink and healthy. She switched off the light and resumed her post at the window again.

What if her serum didn't effect a permanent change in the body? *What if* things returned to their pre-serum state? She'd digress into a mousy, socially inept woman who didn't know how to interact with friends, let alone strangers.

Her sudden scream cut through the silence like a

machete.

She'd been so engrossed in thought she nearly jumped out of her skin when he placed his hands on her shoulders.

"I thought you heard me," Van said. " I didn't mean to frighten you."

"I didn't hear you," Aliesa said shaking her head. She took a deep cleansing breath to calm her racing heart.

"What's wrong sweetheart? Couldn't you sleep? Or did you have to use the bathroom and got waylaid by this amazing view of the glistening Atlantic?" Van wrapped his arms around her waist.

"I've been standing here thinking about all the risks we took over the last few months," she said.

"I know." He rested his chin on the top of her head. "They were necessary risks. We did what we had to do to make you safe. You're not having second thoughts about us, are you?"

"No, never," she said. "Though I am wondering if I'm doing the right thing with my work. There really hasn't been enough time to determine what kind of damage the serum did to my body."

He spun her around and searched her eyes. "Are you okay?" He ran his hand up and down her arms. "You'd tell me if something was wrong wouldn't you?"

Sheesh, he freaked out easily. "I'm fine. Sometimes I can't help myself. It's a scientist thing. I worry. Okay?"

"There's been something I've been meaning to ask you," Van said. "Have you had any further instances where you can read people's thoughts?"

"No, nothing. Not a single one since Wolcott."

He pulled her into his arms and after a few moments

they went back to bed.

In the morning, they went to work, as usual. He went to screen applicants and she went to the lab. She asked Percy French for two favors: to give Van something to keep him busy for a few hours and to drive her to the naval base for her appointment.

Aliesa waited for Dr. Oronto in the examination room.

The solitude gave her more time for reflection. She'd never been particularly lucky. She'd been brilliant when it came to her work, but she'd never been happy. She'd lost both of her parents and she'd resigned herself to being a geeky professor who didn't have any friends or social skills. Along came Evelyne. Again she'd been robbed. Then, Van arrived in her life. Was her blissful happiness going to end with the doctor telling her she had one of the three *what ifs?* Cancer, premature aging, or degeneration—conditions, no doubt, brought on by her foolish decision to inject herself with an experimental serum.

It would serve her right.

Dr. Oronto knocked on the door and walked into the room, a thick folder tucked under his arm. "Good to see you again, Dr. Atworth." He pulled the file and opened it. He flipped pages and found what he wanted. He placed the folder on the counter and approached Aliesa who sat on the examination table. He swung his stethoscope, placed the buds in his ears, and the metal cup on her chest. He listened intently. Then he repeated the process on her back.

"Huh." He grunted. He pulled off the scope and swung it around his neck.

"What's the problem?" she asked.

"Your old records described a pronounced heart murmur. I thought maybe I missed it when I examined you the first time."

"Oh, that," she said. So much had happened recently she'd forgotten all about it. "I've always had it."

"Not any more you don't."

For the first time in an hour, Aliesa relaxed. Her shoulders dropped and she took a deep breath. "I'm okay then?"

"You're fine," he said. He went back to the file. "There's more."

"Oh?" she said, her anxiousness returned with a flourish.

"It says here you were diagnosed with severe endometriosis."

"Correct. My mother had it. She conceived me in vitro. The doctors said I'd never conceive."

Dr. Oronto helped Aliesa off the table. "Would you mind following me? I'd like to show you something."

Aliesa trailed the doctor to a room on the other side of his office with a large ultrasound machine. "Has my condition worsened?"

"Please," he said, patting the table. She jumped up and lowered the waistband of her pants to her pelvis. The doctor squirted cold, clear gel on her belly and moved the transmitter handset around until he spotted something on his screen. Then he froze the image and pushed the screen closer, so Aliesa could see.

Amidst the snowy screen, she saw two small throbbing masses. She narrowed her eyes and zoomed in closer. "Is that what I think it is?"

Thoughts, other than Aliesa's, bombarded her. The

panic and worry cut deeper than any serrated knife. Her breath caught and the terror forced her to lie back on the examination table. She closed her eyes and tried to make sense of the tumult of emotions. Only then, did she realize Van was transmitting them. He'd caught wind of her appointment and had driven over to the base like a madman. He slid into the parking lot and slammed on the brakes. He contemplated killing Percy, who sat out in the waiting room, and had every intention of bursting into each examination room until he found her.

Raised voices and shouting across the hall signaled his close proximity. Doors slammed.

She turned to Dr. Oronto. "It's my husband. He thinks you called me here because I'm not well. He's under the impression I've been hiding things from him. If you don't want him to upset all of your other patients you might want to ask him to come in here."

The doctor seemed confused but did as she asked. When he came back, Van stood beside him—his complexion whiter than the sheet draped over her abdomen.

"I'll give you a few moments," Dr. Oronto said.

"I needed a coffee break so I grabbed a couple cups and went to your lab at the TFOY. One of your lab techs said you had an appointment here this afternoon. Why didn't you tell me? This is why you were awake last night. You were worried." Van strode inside. "No matter what's wrong, we'll face it together. You and I, as a couple." He came over to her, lifted her hand and kissed it.

"I'm sorry I didn't tell you about my appointment. In hindsight, I know I should have," she said. "Especially since I couldn't stop thinking my stem-cell serum might have done some damage to my body."

Sweat shone on his brow. "Is it cancer?"

"No. I don't have cancer."

He let out the breath he'd been holding and sighed. "Oh, thank goodness."

"I was wrong."

"You? Wrong?" Van said. "I don't believe it."

"It's true."

"If there's nothing wrong with you, why are you here?"

"I allowed all of my old medical files to be transferred from Boston and Dr. Oronto wanted to check out a couple of inconsistencies."

"What kind of inconsistencies?" Van asked.

"I used to have a heart murmur and severe endometriosis, but both have completely disappeared."

"You had a heart murmur and what?"

"A condition which in the worst cases, prohibits pregnancy."

"Oh," he said. "And both are gone?"

She nodded.

"It's good news then."

"Yes," she said. "There's more." She sat and turned the ultrasound screen toward him. Dr. Oronto froze the picture on the screen for me so I could see.

Van's attention turned to the screen.

Aliesa placed her hands low on her belly and she rubbed the area.

"Is that a heart beat?"

She nodded waiting for the rush of his reaction to hit her. They'd never spoken about children. She never even thought about getting pregnant because she'd been told she never would.

Instantly her fears were pulverized. Van's smile lit the entire room. He placed his hands over top of hers. His pride and joy flooded her.

"It's two. We're having twins," Aliesa said, smiling at him.

He leaned toward her and kissed her. He opened his mouth to say something but she cut him off.

"I know," she said, beating him to it. "I love you, too."

In that moment she knew they'd handle this and every other adventure to come their way.

Together.

About the author

Diane L. Kowalyshyn writes heart-hammering, high-voltage thrillers—adventures that run on action, intrigue and romance. Before its publication, her first novel, CROSSOVER, earned a Master of FineArts degree. She's an avid sailor who has survived her fair share of squalls, and relied on the pulse of a lighthouse beacon to find safe harbor. When she's not near water or writing, she's exploring exciting new locales. Her books are available worldwide in trade paperback and ebook.

Also by

Crossover
Double Cross
Crossbones
Catch .22
Scadegamutc: Monster in the Mirror
Stage Fright